PASSING
And O

Marie Joseph was born in
Blackburn High School for Girls. Before her marriage
she was in the Civil Service. She now lives in Middlesex
with her husband, a retired chartered engineer, and
they have two married daughters and eight grandchildren.

Marie Joseph began her writing career as a short
story writer and she now uses her Northern background to enrich her bestselling novels. Down to earth
characters bring a vivid authenticity to her stories,
which are written with both humour and poignancy.
Her novel *A Better World Than This* won the Romantic
Novelists' Award in 1987.

Passing Strangers

And Other Stories

MARIE JOSEPH

ARROW BOOKS

Arrow Books Limited
62–65 Chandos Place, London WC2N 4NW

An imprint of Century Hutchinson Limited

London Melbourne Sydney Auckland
Johannesburg and agencies throughout
the world

This collection first published in Great Britain by Century 1988
Arrow edition 1989
This collection copyright © Marie Joseph 1987

Printed and bound in Great Britain by
Courier International Ltd, Tiptree, Essex

ISBN 0 09 963300 0

For Jennifer, David,
Helen and Lucy

CONTENTS

NOT A DANCING MAN

TO fully understand the bewilderment of Bill Hornby, JP, the day he looked through his kitchen window – his arms full of the tomato plants his wife Margaret had asked him to pick up – and saw her doing a passionate tango with her sweeping brush, you would have to know him personally.

To begin with, he wasn't the type to peer through windows, even his own. As managing director of Cartmels Slippers and Handbags Ltd, and a local magistrate, his respectability and integrity were without question. And as enrolment secretary for the Mother's Union and committee member of the horticultural society, his wife's were equally so.

And yet there she was, with the radio going full pelt, dipping and swaying round their big kitchen, with its fitted units and wipe-clean surfaces, her eyes tight closed – an almost indecent expression of rapture on her face – cradling the sweeping brush in her arms like a lover.

Bill's own expression was one of incredulous amazement. He couldn't have been more embarrassed if he'd caught her kissing the milkman, or kneeling down on the floor saying her prayers in the middle of the afternoon. So, quickly dumping the tomato plants in the garden shed, he made his way back round the front of the house.

By the time he had put the car away in the garage, making more noise than was strictly necessary, and let himself in by the front door, his wife was her usual serene self. She greeted him with a proffered cheek, obviously totally unaware that he had been a witness to her abandonment, and flatteringly seemed very glad that he'd come home a whole hour early.

Still with the feeling of embarrassment, Bill told her that as his duties on the Bench had finished earlier than anticipated, he hadn't thought it worth while going back to the works. The radio had been switched off, and now the house was filled with its own special kind of peace – a peace that, since his children had left home, Bill had found to be wholly satisfying.

'Fewer cases than usual,' he said.

Margaret nodded. 'Would you like your sherry now, dear, or will you change first?'

Bill said he'd have the sherry first, and thoughtfully followed his wife's straight back into the sitting room. As she busied herself with the decanter and glasses, he studied her, looking at her properly for perhaps the first time in years.

In her late forties, Margaret had weathered well, no doubt about that. Still slim, her brown hair was only lightly touched with grey, and in her pale blue cashmere twin-set and matching skirt, she was the very epitome of ladylike decorum. Yes, ladylike was the word that fitted. Quiet, unassuming, gentle, with a dry sense of humour as befitted her northern ancestry, but *ladylike*. No doubt about that.

'Anything out of the ordinary today, dear?' she was asking him, sitting down on the sofa with her glass of sherry, ankles neatly crossed, showing no more than was necessary of her slim legs. Then Bill sipped his drink and told her that there had been the usual petty thefts, and no fewer than three shop-lifting cases.

'First offences,' he said, 'and let off with a caution, but we're going to have to clamp down a lot more. The incidence is rising, and always seems to follow the same pattern. Middle-aged women, with apparently no reason for pilfering. One woman had twenty-five pounds in her purse, yet she stole a brooch worth less than a pound. Mitigating circumstances, of course, that's what they always come up with.'

'Poor thing. Perhaps the brooch was a sparkly one,' Margaret said dreamily. 'Perhaps it was just the thing to make an old blue dress look really lovely.'

Bill opened his mouth to explain that sympathy in such cases was entirely misplaced, then closed it again as he remembered the words read aloud by the Clerk of the Court.

It had been pointed out that the woman had brought up three sons – two of whom had recently married and gone to live abroad, while the third had gone to University – and feeling unwanted, she had stolen the brooch, because she had claimed that was the only way she could make her husband take notice of her, even though she was deeply ashamed and regretted the whole episode.

He had studied her downcast eyes and trembling lips, while the phrase 'of a certain age' had washed over him, leaving him totally unmoved.

'Heard from either of the children today?' he surprised himself by asking, and Margaret's blue eyes widened with astonishment.

'We had Jane's weekly letter yesterday,' she reminded him, 'and Tim only writes if he wants anything. Remember how he was when he was a little boy? He had to be forcibly held down before we could get him to write his thank-you letters. A leopard never changes its spots.'

Bill had finished his sherry, but he still sat there, feeling a strange and inexplicable unwillingness to go upstairs and leave his wife alone. And that was ridiculous, because wasn't she alone every day in the big house – and most weekends too, he reminded himself uncomfortably, while he played his usual golf and drank with his friends in the club house.

'What have *you* done today, dear?' he asked. 'Been to one of your meetings?'

Again the start of surprise, and that irritated. Dammit, she asked him how his day had gone every time he came in.

'Thursdays are my meeting days,' she told him in her gentle voice, then she took his sherry glass from him and went through into the kitchen, leaving him there, his big hands clasped between his knees, issues too ephemeral for him clouding his mind.

He was too busy, far too busy to be bothered with problems he couldn't begin to understand. Women's problems at that. . . . But that glimpse of his wife had shown him a woman he didn't suspect existed . . . and Margaret was, well, she was 'of a certain age', wasn't she?

Could it be that, like the women in Court that day, she was lonely? Lonely and feeling unwanted? He reached for his pipe, placed where she always left it, at the ready – on the small table by his chair. He never smoked until after dinner – had made it one of his rules – but he felt in need of some kind of comfort, and that in itself was ridiculous because he wasn't to blame for her extraordinary behaviour, was he?

Pressing down the tobacco with more force than was necessary, he struck the first match, then puffed away until a miniature bonfire glowed in the bowl of his beloved pipe.

He'd been quite within his rights to put a damper on Margaret's vague ideas of finding a job. How would it have looked, a man in his position, with a wife who went out to work? His whole being, his very ancestry, had rebelled at the idea. There was plenty for her to do around the house and the garden; and besides, he'd pointed out quite rightly, she wasn't trained for anything. School, the Women's Land Army during the war, then marriage to him the minute it ended.

As the tobacco smoke rose above his head and hovered there like ectoplasm, he relaxed, sliding down in his chair so that his stomach protruded and his double chin settled pouch-like over his white collar. Oh, no, *his* wife had nothing in common with the pathetic trio in Court that afternoon. Menopausal imaginings were far beyond his wife's intelligence.

The last of the afternoon sun streamed through the window, making him feel pleasantly drowsy, and he tapped his pipe out in the ash-tray, folded his hands over his stomach and closed his eyes. . . .

Margaret had liked to dance when he first met her; light as a feather in his arms, on the rare occasions she could persuade him on to a dance floor. He recalled how she used to tease him, saying that dancing with him was like taking a walk backwards. Not that he'd minded other men dancing with her, but when it came to him having to dance with their wives . . . well, he just wasn't a dancing man, that was all.

Margaret had understood. Of course she had.

It was no good, he couldn't drop off to sleep, not even for the five or ten minutes he always indulged in before dinner. Funny the way that glimpse of her face as she danced round the kitchen floor had disturbed him.

And he didn't like being disturbed, he told himself as he got heavily out of his chair and went through into the kitchen.

'All right, dear?' he said and she swung round from the cooker, her eyes wide with that irritating surprise again.

Dammit, why was it such an extraordinary thing for a man to ask his wife if she was all right, for goodness' sake?

'Why haven't you got the radio on?' he said suddenly, and going back to stirring things in pans, she told him that she'd thought he was asleep and didn't want to disturb him.

But you have disturbed me, he told her silently; and almost without volition, angrily almost, he stretched out his hand and switched on the radio.

Into the streamlined kitchen poured the sound of soaring violins in the strains of an old-fashioned waltz.

He didn't know what to do. There was really nothing he *could* do. But in his bumbling way, he tried. Holding out his short arms, he walked towards his wife:

'Would you care to dance with me, love?' he said.

WHAT DID KEATS KNOW
ABOUT IT?

I DIDN'T often walk the park way back from the shops now
that the children had both started school. It isn't much of a
park as parks go – a square of asphalt, used as a car-park; a
stretch of well-trodden grass; and a round bed, drooping
daffoldils in spring and sparse faded roses in summer.

But it was a really beautiful day. One of those vivid blue
days, with a sky the colour you only expect to see on travel
brochures, and a sun so warm that I wore my one decent sun-
dress, shortened and resurrected.

I walked slowly, dragging a laden shopping-trolley behind
me, daydreaming vaguely about finding a job, or having
another baby, or (getting down to more mundane reality)
taking down the living-room curtains for a much-needed
wash.

I saw Melissa Eton before she saw me. She was sitting on
one of the two benches facing the rose-bed and I reckoned it
must have been all of two years since I'd seen her last.

We'd gone to the same school, been at university together,
both read English there, been married within a few months of
each other – and there the parallel of our lives ended.

Melissa had married 'into money', as my Lancashire
grandmother would have said, and moved into one of the new
detached houses set well back from the main road. Gavin and
I had driven the car out that way when they were being built
and toured the show house, exclaiming at the open staircase,
the grey stone fireplace, and pretending that the selling price
of twenty thousand pounds was just a little beyond our reach.

There was a car, a long cream convertible, parked on the

square of asphalt; I knew that it belonged to Melissa, and I wondered what she was doing, sitting there all alone at eleven o'clock on an ordinary summer Tuesday morning, staring at the round rose-bed. She turned round and saw me and I went to sit beside her, and we said the usual things about how long it was since we'd last met, and wasn't it a beautiful day? At least, I said them. Melissa just sat there, quite still, and I couldn't see the expression in her eyes because of her dark glasses.

'How's Gerry?' I asked her, and she said, 'I'm leaving him. My cases are in the car over there. I've left him a note on the mantelpiece, just like in a television play, and when he comes home this evening and reads it, that will be that.'

With a sudden jerk I seemed to see the grey stone fireplace in that lovely room, the staircase rising in a wide curve, and Gerry as I'd seen him last, already inclining to fatness, a director of his father's firm, prosperous and self-opinionated, a pillar of the community.

There was a giant-size packet of detergent powder sticking out of the top of my trolley – half a pound extra it said on the side – and I leaned over and wedged it down out of sight among the other groceries to hide my embarrassment.

'Your little boy?' I said, because that was the first thing that came into my mind. 'He'll be the same age as my eldest. Seven?'

'Eight,' she said, 'and away at boarding school. Gerry went away to school at that age so of course Robert had to go too.'

It was a plain statement of fact, but it conveyed a lot more; and I remembered Robert, almost a head smaller than my Peter – dark, like his mother; fragile, with stick-thin legs and a mature sensitivity too great for his age.

'Where will you go?' I asked her. 'Have you got somewhere to go, Melissa?'

She took off her dark glasses and rubbed her eyes, and I saw the tired pouches beneath them and the web of worry lines that made her look a lot more than her thirty-two years.

'I'm waiting for someone,' she said then. 'I met him at a party almost a year ago, and I've been seeing him ever since.'

I started to get up and she smiled. 'No need to run away, Jane. I'm too early, but once I'd written the letter and propped it on the mantelpiece, I couldn't stay in the house. You understand?'

I tried to. I honestly did. I told myself that it was happening all the time. People got married, then fell in love with someone else. It was as simple as that.

But Gavin and I had been guests at Melissa's wedding – she and I were quite close friends then – and giggled together afterwards at the contrast to our own. We'd been married in the local registrar's office, with only a handful of friends there. I had worn my going away dress and jacket. But Melissa had been married in a fashionable church, with the organ playing, and walked down the aisle on her father's arm, the long train of her dress trailing behind her, attended by four child bridesmaids in Mabel Lucie Atwell frocks carrying baskets of flowers.

Almost I had envied her. Then I'd glanced sideways at Gavin sitting beside me, handsome in his borrowed morning suit, and I'd known that the trappings, as he'd called them afterwards, didn't mean a thing. What mattered was knowing that we loved each other and would go on loving each other, with the for-ever-amen kind of love. . .

Oh, hell, who am I to be so smug? Who am I to condemn? 'What went wrong, Melissa?' I asked gently, and she answered: 'Nothing went wrong. Gerry gave me everything. But they were all the things *he* thought I ought to want. All our friends were *his* friends, business acquaintances mostly.' She sighed deeply. 'We did a lot of entertaining – it went with his job, of course. That's partly why he insisted on Robert going away to school, I think, and why he wouldn't listen to my idea of finding a job. What have you done with your degree, Jane?'

'Nothing,' I said. 'And it worries me sometimes, especially

when I read the papers and see what's going on in the world. I feel guilty when I remember how we used to talk at university, and how we were going to help to change things – how we were going to revolutionize the whole order – and I know now that my horizon is set no farther than my own front gate.'

'That's because you're happy,' she said, and a terrible sadness crossed her face. 'If you're happy, then you're safe. No one can touch you. No one can look at you and will you to fall in love with them. And oh, Jane, I love him so much! His name is Joe and he's six years younger than me, and I love him so much it's like a pain that hurts when I think about him.'

She still wore her hair the same way that she had worn it all the time I'd known her – jaw-length, parted in the middle, dead straight; and she had the same childish gesture of tucking a strand behind her ear as she talked.

'Maybe I was wanting it to happen. Maybe I was so bored that subconsciously I willed it to reality. Maybe every woman dreams, if she's honest, of being swept off her feet by someone who understands her as only she understands herself.'

As she said that, she was all at once touchingly vulnerable, and the feeling I had of being God and judge and jury all rolled into one left me and I asked her reasonably, 'Couldn't you have stopped it, Melissa? Couldn't you have found the strength to send him away?'

She stared straight at me. 'That's what you would have done, isn't it? You always did have everything cut and dried. On the one side is happiness, but if you step over the line to reach it, you break the rules and then you have to take the consequences. So you don't step over. But is it as simple as that?'

I knew what I was going to say would hurt, but I had to say it. 'And Robert? What about Robert? Gerry won't let you have him, will he?'

I was thinking about my Peter, sitting at his desk in school, and Valerie, thoroughly enjoying her first year in kindergarten. Prim little Valerie, with her good-little-girl expression. Already she knew that black was black and white was white.

'No, Gerry won't let me have him,' Melissa said, and suddenly she was angry with me. Just as she had been angry when we'd been students together, and we'd talked and argued. Even then we'd never been able to see the same side of the coin.

'Do you think I haven't thought about that?' she said, clenching her fists on her yellow linen skirt. 'Thought about it until I've almost gone mad? You can't understand a woman taking a step that will separate her from her children, can you Jane?'

There was no need for me to hesitate. 'No,' I said, 'I can't.'

Then I took my handbag from the top of my laden trolley and passed her a cigarette. While I lit it I was groping for the right words. It seemed important that I should find them. If she hated me for them, never mind. Perhaps it had even been meant that I should walk the long way home that day just so that I should meet her and say them.

'Look, Melissa. We're not old, not by a long way. But we're not children. In another ten years we'll both be middle-aged, and then the things that will really matter will be friendship and, let's face it, the money to buy the things that will make us comfortable. Passion, and sleeping with someone – well, I suppose they'll still matter, but they won't be all-important. Aren't we too intelligent to believe that the world is well lost for love?'

She actually laughed, but I was determined to have my say. 'Has he any money, this Joe?'

'No, he has no money,' Melissa told me gravely, but there was a proud ring to her voice. 'He's a freelance writer, and you know what that means. Remember the novel I wrote in my last year, when I should have been swotting for my exams? Remember how many publishers I sent it to?'

'Eight?'

'Eleven. Well, Joe has that same obstinate belief in himself;
one day he'll have a book published, and in the meantime he
has what he calls his bread-and-butter jobs. At the moment
he's packing parcels in the basement of Harrods. You'd be
surprised how many undiscovered geniuses are doing
that. . .'

And I thought about Gerry in his well-cut suits, and I
thought about the house set back from the road with its
curved staircase rising from that spacious room.

'And you're prepared to give up all you've got . . . for
something as hazardous as that?' I said.

She drew deeply on her cigarette. 'But I've got nothing,'
she said simply. 'Can't you see that?'

No, I couldn't see, and I knew I never would. It was as
though we were talking different languages, each unable to
understand the other's point of view.

'I'm certain of one thing,' I said firmly. 'That you're
making the biggest mistake of your life.'

At first I thought she hadn't heard me, but suddenly she
said, 'Do you remember the poetry readings we had in
college?' I nodded.

She threw her cigarette on to the ground and stamped on it
with her heel.

'*I am certain of nothing but the holiness of the heart's affection,
and the truth of the imagination. . .*'

'Keats,' I said promptly, and she laughed.

'Good old Jane! What I'm trying to tell you is that, in all
these months of doubts and fears, that has remained. The
one thing I'm certain of – the holiness of my heart's affection.
Surely you can see *that*?'

I tried to see. I tried very hard to see, but it was hopeless. I
found myself groping again for the right words, the sensible
two-and-two-make-four words that might bring her to her
senses, that might reveal a glimpse of the future. I put my
hand on her arm. . . .

But it was too late. She had seen him coming, the shadows

left her face and all at once she was young again and
incredibly beautiful.

'He's here!' she said, and I jumped up and said something
about good-bye then, and good luck, but she wasn't listening.
Already she had forgotten me.

I saw her wave and start to walk towards him, and then she
was running, her dark straight hair bobbing on her shoulders,
and he was holding out his arms wide, as a man does to a
child he loves.

Quickly I pulled my trolley over the grass and, when I
reached the path, I turned and they were there, oblivious to
everything, and I saw him, I saw the way his hands went up to
cup her face, holding her still for his kiss.

Oh, God, I thought. How young he was, how thin and
shabby, and what a fool was Melissa. Give it two years, I
thought angrily, and as I turned into my own avenue the
trolley thumped off the pavement, nearly scattering the
shopping in the road.

Silly, stupid Melissa, behaving like a bemused adolescent,
giving up everything, and for what?

This is what life is all about, I told myself furiously as I
unhooked the long sitting-room curtains. This is what life
really is. Coming home from the shops and feeding the
curtains into the washing-machine and pouring in the soap
powder, and feeling a small triumph at the half-pound you've
got for nothing.

And Melissa. Clever, beautiful Melissa, quoting Keats to
me at eleven o'clock on an ordinary Tuesday summer
morning. What had Keats known about it all, if it came to
that?

I switched on the washing-machine and, arms folded
across my chest, listened to its rhythmic thumping. And then
I remembered how I had seen him hold her, and the gentle
heart-stopping way his hands had held her face steady for his
kiss.

'Oh damn you!' I shouted aloud, and my words sounded

strange and frightening in the emptiness of my neat little blue-and-white kitchen.

'Damn you, Melissa! Damn you! Why did I choose to take the long way home from the shops?'

PASS ME A SLICE OF GRASS

WE DRIVE OUT to the health farm, my friend Beth and I, one bright summer's morning. Beth is going because she says every nerve in her body is alive and twitching after yet another disastrous love affair, and me because I am recently forty, and fat with it too.

It is the first time in all the twenty years of our marriage that I have been away without Don, but he has gone to Scotland with his friend, old Jim from across the road, and the girls have gone to stay with their grandmother down in Dorset. I am feeling rather hurt because it was all arranged so easily.

The whole thing really started off as a joke, with Beth telling me one day that she'd heard about this marvellous place where in two weeks flat they turn you into a mere shadow of your former self, sending you home looking sleek and streamlined and vitaminized to the eyeballs.

I honestly thought I was indispensable to my family, but Don told me the graveyards are full of them – indispensable people – and the last time he slapped my behind he told me it was like tickling an elephant with a drinking straw for all the effect it had on me. Then he went on to say that in India when wives were fat and forty their husbands threw them away and started again. He laughed as if he'd said something funny. . .

Beth divorced her husband ten years ago, and I think she still loves him. He's married again – with two children and a wife who mothers him and even washes his socks with reverence – so Beth says. She, I might add, is *not* the sock-washing kind.

She is looking marvellous, but then she always does. Her

hair, a tasteful shade of pale mink, is arranged in a style I have
tried over the years to persuade my hairdresser in the High
Street to emulate. 'Smooth,' I tell him, 'and flicked up at the
ends,' and he smiles at me through the mirror and goes on
rolling me up, sending me home with a hair-do like the one
Claudette Colbert used to wear in her heyday. He must have
a one-track mind, because I notice that all his clients leave the
salon with curly fringes. Perhaps his mother liked Claudette
Colbert too. . .

Beth is always being fallen in love with, or so she says.
Sometimes I think she exaggerates but then I tell myself not
to think such ignoble thoughts about my best friend, and she
is my best friend and has been ever since we were prefects
together in the sixth form of the local grammar school.

Once I asked her why she thought it was that men were
always getting me in a corner and telling me how worried they
were about the possibility of being made redundant, or how
mean their wives were to them, without ever making a single
pass at me. And Beth explained.

'It's because you are the motherly type,' she said kindly,
'whereas I,' and she sighed with satisfaction, 'I somehow
bring out that combination of lion, tiger and wolf in men – the
animal instincts.'

'You mean that you're sexy and I'm not,' I suggested, and
readily – too readily – she agreed.

We turn into the grounds of the health farm, driving down
miles of twisting road flanked on either side by magnificent
parkland. I catch sight of a deer and Beth brakes sharply as a
squirrel runs straight across our path, and I sit by her side and
want to be sexy, and to have the opportunity to say no to a
man when he makes a pass at me.

Beth must have read my thoughts. . .

'Hope the men at this place aren't all the fat and bloated
executive type, coming to be dehydrated after a year of
business lunches and whisky swilling,' she says. 'If we're
lucky there may be a writer or two, or maybe a television

producer coming to unwind from the stress of modern living. You know, all hollow-cheeked and twitching cheek nerves, with something absolutely beastly having happened to him in the woodshed in his childhood.'

'If there is, he'll tell me all about it and turn to you for consolation,' I say.

And then Beth laughs, and I laugh with her. Because of course she knows, and I know, that for me there is only one man – Don – and my wanting to have the opportunity to say no is nothing more than feminine perversity.

The health farm is there before us, and it is magnificent: Georgian-pillared, opulent, with a flight of steps leading up from a circular drive. A fountain plays in the forecourt, with four naked cherubs peeing gracefully into a little pond, and it is like the film set from a gothic novel. I am all for heaving our cases from the boot, but Beth says we must arrive with Presence, so we climb the flight of steps and inside find ourselves treading a carpet so thick it almost tickles our knee-caps.

At the reception desk, we are bade welcome by a pretty girl who looks and sounds as if she left Roedean only last week, and a dear little man in a grey alpaca jacket is dispatched to fetch our cases.

Beth winks at me, a wink that says, 'This is the life,' as we are ushered up a winding staircase, flanked by oil paintings in the original, to our respective bedrooms. They are adjoining – Beth's is a symphony in white and brown, whilst mine is a poem in lilac and cream.

We are told that our Consultant awaits us down in the treatment rooms and, wrapped around in the towelling dressing-gowns provided, we descend the staircase again. I note without surprise that Beth has managed to tie her gown so that it looks like a sari; mine looks like what it is – a towelling bathrobe. A middle-aged man, unquestionably a tired millionaire, passes us in the corridor, and he smiles at me in a friendly way, and then smiles at Beth, but more suggestively.

I sigh. In the consulting room I tell a youngish, white-coated man with a face that looks as if it hasn't been used much that I am only here to lose weight, and that almost everything else about me is revoltingly normal.

He makes me drop the robe and stand on a weighing machine, and is disappointed with me.

'I'm afraid, as you're only here for the week, we'll have to put you on the starvation diet,' he tells me sternly, like a father, and then continues, 'to get rid of the slight flab.'

So . . . chastened and slightly deflated, I collect my treatment sheet and wait outside in the corridor for Beth to come out and tell me how she's fared.

She is inside for a good ten minutes longer and emerges flushed and happy to tell me that as she doesn't need to slim but is only in search of spiritual solace, she will be on the normal diet and eat in the dining room.

We dress for dinner, at least Beth dresses for dinner . . . I dress for a small glass of apple juice and a slice of melon, which I eat in a room with a high-domed ceiling, along with a trio of women who make me think of the Fat Women from Antibes.

I have not yet got used to making my meals last a long time and, feeling ravenous, I go back to my room and put through a call to Don at his hotel in Scotland. They eat early up there, he tells me, and describes in detail the plate-sized steak embellished with mushrooms, and the sherry trifle with whipped cream. When he comes to the Gaelic coffee I tell him to stop and ask him if he's missing me; and he says the noise in the background is old Jim come to tell him he's got their drinks already lined up in the bar.

I ring my mother-in-law down in Dorset, and she tells me that the girls are fine and how rewarding it is to cook for children with such 'nice' appetites, and that they have eaten two helpings of everything, including her apple pie and cream. She asks me if I'm feeling better and I remind her that I am not ill, just fat.

Down in the blue lounge dripping with chandeliers and furnished with genuine Chippendale, Beth is in earnest conversation with the millionaire, who looks not half so tired. She beckons me over to join them and introduces him as Giles and tells us that she has just eaten her way through the most fabulous tomato salad, followed by chicken fricassee and cheese and biscuits. Anxious not to play gooseberry, I wander over and work on a jigsaw, half completed.

A gaunt young man comes and tells me that if I start with the sky I'll find it easier, and in between passing me bits and telling me where they should go, confides in me that his marriage is on the rocks and that he is a believer in mind over matter, and vitamins, and that we are what we eat.

'Then in that case, there isn't much help for me,' I say, 'because all I amount to at the moment is a slice of melon,' but he doesn't smile. I don't think he has smiled for a long time. He starts to tell me all about his wife, who of course has never understood him, and I listen and feel sorry for him, and he tells me I am kind – that he knew I was kind the minute he set eyes on me.

Out of the corner of one of my kind eyes I see Beth disappearing through the french windows with her millionaire, and I know she's done it again. My new friend draws up a chair the better to see the jigsaw, and passes me a slice of grass. . .

I go to bed early that night with my tummy rumbling so loudly it wakens me up far too early. When my breakfast is brought to me – a glass of hot water with a slice of lemon floating on it – I drink it to the last dregs and even chew the slice of lemon.

My Consultant comes in with my list of treatments for the day, and I meet Beth in the corridor. A radiant Beth who tells me she has had a pot of tea and a peach and a slice of wholemeal toast, plus an exquisite little jar of honey. When

we compare notes, we see that for our first hour we are
sharing a sauna together. And a few minutes later her hair is
pinned up underneath a chiffon scarf, and just before we go
into the sauna she coats her face with cream.

'Might as well have a beauty treatment at the same time,'
she smugly tells me, while I sit there on my slab, my own hair
straggling wetly round my face as I perspire. My friend Beth,
I think, must be the only woman in existence who can manage
to sweat profusely and still look elegant at one and the same
time.

After the excruciating heat and plunging cold of the sauna
finally comes the nicest part. Lying down on lounging chairs
with heads down and feet suspended heavenwards, with little
squares of damp cotton-wool on our closed eyelids. I want to
go to sleep, but Beth wants to tell me about her new friend
and I listen, knowing that I have heard it all before.

'He owns a chain of stores,' she says. 'In South Africa, but
he's in London for three months.' She gives her throaty
chuckle. 'Long enough for us to get acquainted. . . He's
already asked me to have dinner with him the day after we get
out of here.'

'I'm not surprised,' I say, the iron entering my soul again,
and I lift one pad of cotton-wool and catch her smiling to
herself, like a cat that's just finished off a double ration of
double dairy cream.

'How was *your* friend?' she asks me kindly.

'Sad,' I say, and fold my hands over my chest and go to
sleep.

For the rest of the morning we go our separate ways – Beth
for a hand-massage and me for a blanket bath. My nurse is
pert, blonde and pretty, dressed all in white with shoes to
tone, like a nurse in an American TV hospital drama.

There is no such thing as modesty, I have discovered, and I
drop my towel at her request and, trying not to look too
flabby, climb on to the high bed to be wrapped up in a sheet,
covered by two blankets and topped with a billowing

eiderdown. As she wraps me around and tucks all the corners in, I tell her I know now what it must feel like to be embalmed, but she says the worst is yet to come.

'If you get too hot, just yell out,' she says as she plugs me in, switches me on and leaves me with my head sticking out, and I think about Don and the girls, and how they would laugh if they could see me now, but soon I am too hot to think about anything.

I suffer quietly because I have always been the type to suffer quietly – something to do with having been brought up by an aunt who was so stoical she would have made even the Spartans seem like a bunch of hypochondriacs. The pretty nurse comes in and lays a cold wet cloth on my feverish brow.

'Only ten minutes more,' she says and smiles at me, while I concentrate on imagining all that flab round my waist dissolving and melting away, and I visualize myself at Don's next annual dinner and dance wearing a size ten dress, while all his colleagues faint away at the very sight of me.

Unwrapped once more, I am shown the sheet on which I have been lying, saturated with perspiration, and I feel proud and after a cooling shower, very, very clean.

I am first into the light-diet room, and fall on my slice of pineapple and juicy pear with almost hysterical relish. We are supposed to rest on our beds until three, and I look through my window and see Beth walking across the lawn towards the swimming pool, her towelling robe swinging open to show her bright green bikini and her long brown legs, the tired tycoon in tow.

I am not in the least bit surprised that Beth is not sticking to the rules. At school she was just the same – as allergic to discipline as I am to strawberries. I lie down dutifully and close my eyes, and dream about chips, golden and crisp, sticky buns oozing cream, and boxes of chocolates at least a yard square.

It is a beautiful day, and I make for the pool dead on the stroke of three, and am joined by a plump dark lady wearing a swim-suit with an unfortunate frill round her thighs. She tells me that her husband, her children and even the dog are all mean to her, and she can't think why, as she has always been the possessor of a most unselfish disposition.

Over a cup of china tea, Beth tells me that she is going out with her friend after dinner, for champagne in the pub in the nearby village. She says I can go with them if I wish, and I think about little cellophane bags of nuts and packets of cheese and onion crisps, and decline with thanks.

'It's not worth coming if we don't stick to the rules,' I tell her as she lights a cigarette and blows the smoke straight at the NO SMOKING notice.

For dinner I am allowed a thimbleful of soup and a minute cube of cheese, and a young girl in a silver trouser suit comes and sits by me and tells me that she is there to recover from a broken engagement, and that her doctor has told her that her nerves are as taut as violin strings.

I make my call to Don and he asks me how is the shredded carrot, and old Jim comes on the phone and says he doesn't know why I'm bothering, that he's always liked his women with meat on their bones anyway – and there seems to be a lot of laughing and clinking of glasses in the background, and I know for certain I am feeling sorry for myself.

I wander through into the billiards room, and there is a tiny man whose face seems familiar playing billiards all by himself, and my sad friend from the night before tells me that he is one of the Queen's jockeys in for a couple of days' toning up.

'Would you like a game of draughts?' my sad friend asks me and I refuse politely, saying there are letters I must write, and go to my room and watch a play where all the action seems to be taking place round a dining table.

The next day I feel marvellous, and stop thinking about food and conclude that my stomach must indeed have shrunk obligingly. I have a hand massage and an invigorating rub down with salt, and another sauna, and in the evening when my sad friend invites me to take a turn with him around the grounds, I accept.

I have seen Beth disappearing into the rhododendron bushes with her rich friend and I walk along the twisting paths, waiting with pleasurable anticipation to be made a pass at – already rehearsing in my mind my gently phrased refusals. But it appears that something quite dreadful *did* happen to my companion when he was young. Not in the woodshed, but in the gentlemen's lavatory at Euston Station, before it was rebuilt. And he tells me about it, though not of course in detail, and I say that he must forget all about it and look forward, not back.

'You must think positive thoughts and let your own willpower take over,' I say, feeling like Patience Strong and Pollyanna rolled into one, and he says he has tried and it doesn't *work*. I remind him of his mother, he says, the best girlfriend he ever had.

There are little white statues dotted here and there in the grounds, each one illuminated by a cunningly concealed spotlight, and I stop and admire them and hope that he will stop and admire me also. But he is wondering aloud whether it is worth carrying on, and I say that yes, but he explains that what he is wondering about carrying on with is LIFE. And so I give up.

That night Beth comes into my room and sits on my bed and smokes and tells me that her new friend is just over the moon about her. He wants her to fly back with him to South Africa, because his wife is in Sydney, Australia, which sounds a bit complicated to me until I remember that all Beth's affairs have been as complicated as Fair Isle knitting patterns.

Suddenly I notice how Beth's neck is getting stringy, and that seems to upset me more than the fact that once again she is going to embark on a hopeless love affair. Before she leaves me she tells me that my bed-jacket is the wrong colour, and that she can't think why I don't have my eyebrows professionally shaped because the left one is at least a quarter of an inch longer than the right. When she's gone I snuggle down in bed and think about Don and the girls and how lovely it will be to see them again, and wonder how on earth I could ever have imagined that I wanted to be made a pass at. . .

Before I go to sleep, I get up and study my eyebrows in the mirror. They look all right to me. . .

The week flies by, and the morning we are due to leave I have my hair set in the beauty salon. 'Smooth,' I tell the girl, 'with the ends flicked up,' and she smiles at me through the mirror and combs me out into a curly fringe, just like the one Claudette Colbert used to wear in her heyday.

I have my last appointment with the Consultant, and I tell him honestly that I feel marvellous, and with a touching faith I step on to the scales. . .

Expecting to have lost at least a stone, I find that I have lost exactly *two* pounds. He tells me that it does happen sometimes, but that the diet will have cleared out my whole system, ridding it of acids, and for that small mercy I suppose I must be grateful.

Beth, of course, has lost nine pounds without even trying, and she looks marvellous, but then she always does. My sad friend takes my photograph standing beside the peeing cherubs, and thanks me for lending him what he calls a sympathetic ear.

I am not expecting to see Don until the following day, but as we turn into our avenue, there he is standing by the gate, and he tells me that he's left old Jim living it up in St Andrews with a merry little widow and has travelled down by sleeper to surprise me.

He looks tanned and tired and, I'm glad to say, rather neglected, and I feel his arms around me and think that I've never loved him so much.

The next day we will drive down to Dorset to collect the

girls, but that evening he tells me he is going to take me out and buy me the biggest steak we can find.

'Smothered in onions and mushrooms,' I say, 'and followed by sherry trifle and Gaelic coffee,' and he kisses me and – free of acids, and two whole pounds lighter, and so happy it's just plain ridiculous – I kiss him back.

DO YOU DO THIS OFTEN?

WE ARE ON OUR WAY by taxi, my friend Beth and I, driving through the early Sunday morning on our way to the Hyde Park starting control of the London to Brighton Run of veteran cars.

Beth is going because she is in the throes of yet another madly passionate love affair with a man who owns a vintage Wolseley which in 1902, I've been told, was one of the best-selling cars on the market.

I am going because Beth says it is time I made a stand and showed my husband Don that it isn't always *convenient* for him to play golf every single Sunday with old Jim from across the road; that wives have their rights as well.

Beth is a positive minefield of information on how to treat men, and since her divorce eleven years ago has had plenty of experience to back up her forceful theories. She has got through two near-millionaires, a tiny man who was nevertheless something big in films, and another she swears went to prison just to be able to write a book about it.

All her lovers – and I use the term in its old-fashioned literal sense – have one thing in common. They are wealthy and suave, the two things which my husband, bless his heart, is not. Beth is looking marvellous, but then she always does. She is wearing a long dress and jacket, which makes her look like a cross between Dinah Sheridan in *Genevieve* and Richard Bellamy's wife in *Upstairs Downstairs* – the one who went down with the *Titanic*. Her hair this year is the exact colour of a copper warming-pan, and over it she has tied a large-brimmed floppy hat with a green bow nestling underneath her chin.

The weather is cold but bright, and when I mention, rather

peeved, that I had no idea we were expected to dress up, adding that I'm sure she must be frozen stiff, her smile is smug.

'But I'm wearing a fantastic pair of insulated combs, darling, the like of which the men who climbed Everest wore. I'm simply *glowing*, I promise you, love.'

I sit beside her in my mother's beaver lamb with little round hat to match, plus two of everything underneath, and wonder not for the first time why Beth has *me* for her best friend. Ever since we were sixth-form prefects together she has managed to make me feel too fat, too maternal, utterly devoid of any taste in clothes and sexless to boot. But I *am* her best friend, and I suppose we are living proof of the saying that opposites attract. I know that my two daughters adore her. Last Christmas she gave the twelve-year-old a pair of see-through black pyjamas and the ten-year-old a set of heated rollers, making them her devoted slaves for life.

Don, who once refused to take me to his annual dinner and dance until I'd changed out of the dress which he said was showing too much cleavage, turns into a leering Casanova when Beth is around.

'Get a load of that tan!' he said last summer when she came to call, wearing half a dress. I reminded him, when she'd gone, of his theory that women who sunbathe end up with skin that's only fit to be made into handbags.

'Could it be you're jealous because you merely freckle?' he asked, and I'd have thrown something at him had I been the throwing kind.

Following Beth's shouted instructions, the taxi driver turns into the Serpentine Road, Hyde Park. There are the veteran cars and there is her friend Hugo with his Wolseley, and *his* friend who is introduced to me as Boozer Bates for a reason which is to become apparent.

As he helps me aboard, he gives my hand a little squeeze and I smile at him and wish there'd been time, in the early morning rush, to apply my turquoise eye-shadow.

In spite of the hour there is quite a goodly crowd cheering us on. Sitting up in front of Boozer Bates and me, Hugo clings to the wheel – his droopy moustache actually curving upwards, I swear, with the excitement of it all.

I wish I could forget that I quarrelled with Don. . .

Mean and selfish I said he was when he announced that he was going to pay golf today no matter what, and selfish and mean he said I was when I vowed I was going to Brighton, no matter what either.

My victory is to be a hollow one if I don't enjoy myself, so I turn to Boozer Bates and say, 'Do you do this often? The Brighton Run, I mean?'

'What d'you say?' he shouts back, lifting the ear-flap of his deerstalker to expose a less than shell-like ear.

'Do you do this often?' I say and he beams at me, nods, replaces the ear-flap, then squeezes my knee underneath the tartan rug Hugo has thoughtfully provided. I hope he can't tell that I am wearing two pairs of thirty-denier tights, and wonder just what Beth will have told him about me.

Always she is telling me that I do not know how to *live* – that I do not, in fact, know what *life* is all about, in spite of my approaching middle age. Just then her boy-friend shouts over his shoulder that he reckons at the speed we're going, we should breast Brixton Hill around half-past eight.

Spectator cars are stretched bumper to bumper on our left, and obliging policemen wave the veteran cars through on the right. A car which Boozer tells me is a De Dion Bouton, 1901, a voiturette, is pulled up by the side of the road, with its owner doing frantic adjustments to its engine which for some reason seems to be at the back.

Boozer, most unkindly in my opinion, gives the driver what I take to be Mr Churchill's victory sign.

As we chug through Croydon, Boozer produces a flask from his pocket and takes a swig, then wiping it carefully, hands it to me. I am going to refuse, then catching Beth's eye as she turns round, take a sip, wipe my mouth with the back of my hand the way cowboys do, then pass the flask over to the front seat.

'That's the spirit!' Boozer says, then roars with laughter at the terrible pun before giving my knee another squeeze. A Lanchester passes us and I sense that Hugo's moustache is bristling with indignation. Boozer explains to me that the Lanchester utilizes an epicyclic gear-box, controlled by a pre-selector mechanism. I trust that my smile conveys unbounded admiration at the fact.

Beth is entering into the spirit of the Run by waving a mauve-kid-gloved hand at the small crowds we are passing en route. She has exactly the same fluency of movement in her wrist as the Queen Mother, and I suspect that she has been practising before her mirror.

We are restricted by law to a speed of twenty miles an hour, and by the time we reach the Bolney Cross Roads I feel I have been sitting there, in my mother's beaver lamb and Don's old school scarf, for the better part of my life. It is still only half-past ten and, keeping to the rules which state that the veterans are expected to pass the places listed at roughly the times given, all is going well. Boozer refreshes himself every other mile or so, and I note with alarm that his big face is turning a rather fiery shade of purple.

'Are you married?' I ask him, hoping to distract his attention from the leather-covered flask, and he reacts as if what I've just said is the joke of the year. He throws back his head and laughs until I fear he will fall out of the car.

'Maggie wants to know am I married?' he bellows to the pair in the front, and Hugo doubles up over the wheel in a paroxysm of mirth.

Beth gives me a glance over her shoulder which says that is just the damn fool kind of thing she would expect *me* to ask, and I snuggle down into my mother's beaver lamb and wonder why such an innocuous remark should cause such hilarity. Could it be that I have just made a terrible gaffe, could it be possible that Boozer Bates is GAY?

But he squeezes my knee a bit harder and says, 'Not at the moment, dear,' which makes him laugh harder than ever.

A Humberette, 1904, is close on our tail, and Hugo lowers a pair of goggles which have been reposing on top of his tweed cap and urges his horseless carriage forward.

'Left your old man at home?' Boozer asks me as we approach Patcham. 'That's the spirit!' he yells before I can reply, then at the utterance of the magic word remembers the flask and raises it to his lips. This seems to subdue him for the next few miles as, leaving my knee alone, he stares straight ahead – fishy-eyed, purple-nosed and rather endearingly revolting.

Perhaps Beth is right about me. Perhaps I have become so bogged down with domesticity that I am in danger of losing my girlish laughter. Am I like that dear little Mum on television who watches her children rush out to play in the mud in whiter-than-white shirts, anticipating the joyful moment when they rush back filthy and she can wash them clean again?

Ought I, at this very moment, to be leaping on to the leather-bound seats, urging Hugo on with cries of enthusiasm, waving my little round fur hat about, arriving at Brighton to have champagne drunk out of my boots by Boozer Bates – who seems, incidentally, to have given me up as a bad job?

Now we are chugging into the outskirts of Brighton. At the finishing point our arrival time is checked by a Marshal who looks as important as he obviously feels. Then we are shown where to park according to the number fixed to the rear of the car.

'Now we can have a drink,' says Boozer, coming to life again, and off we go to the signing-on caravan where Hugo hands over the card given to him in Hyde Park, and is presented with his Commemoration Medal.

Off we go again, this time to a plush hotel for lunch. In the Ladies, Beth tells me that Boozer Bates has been married no fewer than four times, hence the near-hysteria with which my harmless question had been greeted. 'Do you mean to tell me there have been *four* women foolish enough to marry *him*?' I say rather nastily, before secluding myself into a cubicle to wrestle with the two pairs of everything.

I ask Beth if she is feeling hot. She is busy at the mirror removing the jacket, untying her hat, and when she catches sight of my mauve jersey two-piece her expression is one of kindly pity.

'No, I'm not hot, darling,' she says gaily. 'These comb things keep one hot when it's cold, and cool when it's warm.' Then she notices the beads of sweat on my brow and tells me about this marvellous make-up which makes it impossible for one to shine. 'They use it on television, love,' she assures me, leaning closer to the mirror to tuck a stray eyebrow into place. 'Haven't you noticed how completely unsweaty that marvellous Richard Baker is? He never ever mops his brow even after telling us the most ghastly news, now does he?'

Ignoring her, I wash my hands and pat away the perspiration with the pressed powder in my compact. She says isn't it too dreary that this year we're having to miss the cocktail party given by the Mayor of Brighton in the Royal Pavilion. Not to mention the annual dinner to follow.

'Hugo has to be at Heathrow to pick up his wife. They're flying to New York. She's meeting him there with his case. It's all arranged,' she says, and I see the unguarded desolation in her eyes.

'But I thought he was getting a divorce?' I say, and my heart aches with an all-too-familiar sympathy for her as she explains in a voice that quivers that she thought so too, but it seems that for the sake of the grandchildren Hugo and his wife are staying together.

I say that surely she means the *children*, but Beth shakes her head.

'Grandchildren, darling. His wife dotes on them, you see. That's why they're flying to New York to see the latest one, born to the youngest daughter who married a doctor out there.'

I can't look at her, so I find my lipstick and lean to the mirror again. Beth is so upset that she doesn't even tell me that it's the wrong shade, and I hope she isn't going to cry.

Only once have I seen Beth cry, and that was when her own divorce came through eleven years ago. I suspect that she is still in love with her ex-husband who married, she says, a girl who wore pink blouses and never shaved her legs.

I have an almost uncontrollable urge to put my arms round her and pat her head, the way I do with the girls when they're upset. I want to say 'There, there' and promise her that it will be all right.

But I know it won't be all right.

My friend Beth, I see quite clearly, is the kind of woman who is doomed to go from one unsatisfactory love affair to another, changing her boy-friends as often as she changes the colour of her hair – a middle-aged swinger.

I am appalled at my thoughts, but she turns to me with eyes sparkling, skin glowing with its November tan, and I know that the tiny chink in her defences has closed once more. *She* is Beth, vibrantly attractive, determinedly gay, ready for the next round, and *I* am Maggie, her best friend from the suburbs, being take out of herself for the day.

We join the men in the lounge, sink into the depths of a red plush sofa and listen as they go over every uneventful mile of the run down together. Another driver, a little man with a thick-knit sweater and a 1904 Oldsmobile, joins us and we move into the bar where the drinks flow free.

Boozer's pale eyes bulge as he talks, and Beth laughs gaily at his every utterance, but Hugo, sipping a lime-juice on account of the drive back, is subdued. I see the way his eyes watch Beth's animated face, then slide away again, and I suspect that his feelings are a mixture of relief at having found a way of escape and shame because he realizes he has hurt her badly.

Before we go in to lunch Beth tells me that on our return to town, she and Boozer are having dinner together.

'Why don't you ring Don and tell him that you're joining us?' she asks, and I tell her that I would rather go home, if she doesn't mind.

'Oh, Maggie!' she says, and that is all, but I notice her eyes are full of anguish.

All through the *Crème Argenteuil* she is uncharacteristically silent, but as the two men are once again covering the winding road from Hyde Park to Brighton, her silence isn't commented upon. I am trying hard not to sweat, watching Boozer drink his wine as if it were water, and – as we start on the *Truite Aux Crevettes* – hoping that Don has remembered to switch the oven on in time to heat the casserole of braising steak right through.

'Maggie, and I went to school together,' Beth says as the *Poulet Rôti à L'Ancienne* is placed before us. I am amazed, as normally she manages to make it quite clear that she is years younger than me.

'Do you remember the time we hung side by side on the rib-stalls during PE, and fell on our heads with laughing so much?' she asks. 'And the time we played truant to sunbathe behind the pavilion on the playing field?'

I push an unwanted *pomme rissole* to the side of my plate and see, in my mind's eye, Beth looking sexy in her school uniform. With the two top buttons of her blouse undone and darts sewn in where no darts were ever meant to be, she had our headmistress, Miss Bleasdale, very worried at times.

At the table next to ours is a family out for Sunday lunch. Father neat in his dark suit, Mother in blue sweater and skirt, and two small boys – one with a pudding-basin hair-cut, scowling into his roast beef, and the other as roundly beautiful as an angel on a Christmas card, clasping fat hands round a large glass of orange juice as he drinks.

I see the way Beth watches them, then almost visibly shrugs her thoughts away. She refuses to even glance at the sweets trolley and smiles radiantly at Hugo.

'I used to fly to New York regularly when I was doing that

fashion thing. Did I ever tell you, darling? I always used to think that the sight of Windsor Castle two minutes after take-off was the most *marvellous* thing. It made me wish I had a Union Jack on me; then at the end of the flight, when the Captain welcomed us to the States, I was immediately thinking in terms of Stars and Stripes.' The brilliance of her smile never wavers. 'I do so *envy* you, darling, I really do.'

Hugo looks as miserable as I feel he should, and after coffee and a sticky liqueur we go to collect the Wolseley. It does not surprise me in the least to find that Beth has decided to ride in the back with Boozer Bates, and I tell her that I don't mind, honestly.

Ahead of us is nearly fifty miles of chugging along at roughly fifteen miles an hour, sitting next to a pensive Hugo who is trying not to look as if he cares what is going on in the seat behind.

The first few miles are punctuated by shouts of mirth, then when I give a quick glance over my shoulder I see that Boozer has fallen fast asleep with his head in Beth's lap. Hugo has seen too, and his nice kind face is set into grim lines. I don't think I should be feeling sorry for him, but I am. I am sorry for both him and Beth, even though feeling sorry always, I fear, has a touch of the self-righteousness about it. I wave to a little boy standing at a bus-stop with his father, who bends to explain us as if we are something out of a museum.

I ask to be put down near Marble Arch, where I know I'll be able to pick up a taxi. Hugo is in a hurry to garage his horseless carriage before going off to the airport and Beth, I guess, will be taking Boozer Bates back to her flat to dry him out before he takes her out to dinner.

'I'll ring you, darling!' she calls, and I say thank you for a simply marvellous day, and off they go into the stream of London traffic, with people stopping and staring from the pavements and a couple of foreign tourists pointing a camera in their direction. Beth, I see, is smiling her wide toothpaste smile for their benefit, turning her best side to the camera, unable to face the prospect of not looking her best even in the album of some unknown tourist from the other side of the world.

The London taxi seems to be travelling at an incredible speed and the driver, who is matey, pushes back his little glass panel and tells me about his son who has gone to work on a sheep farm in Australia and married a girl out there who emigrated from Warrington.

Don and the girls are in the sitting-room staring glassy-eyed at the television, and I tell them all about the Brighton Run and they marvel in a not very concentrated way. I see that I haven't been missed all that much and go upstairs and take off my two of everything, then have a long and luxurious bath.

It is only when the girls are both in bed and we are alone together, that I tell Don about Beth and the end of yet another of her abortive love affairs.

He listens, but not very intently, and then he tells me that the very next Sunday he and old Jim from across the road are going to play golf for the entire day, having lunch at the Club and coming home, I guess, only when it is too dark to see the little white balls.

I feel myself getting mad again, then suddenly I can see Beth's face and hear her voice saying, 'Oh, Maggie!' there in the red plush hotel in Brighton.

'Oh, Don!' I say, but my meaning is quite different and I start to laugh. He grins at me, settles back in his chair and lights his pipe.

'WAS ANYONE WITH YOU WHEN YOU BOUGHT THAT SKIRT?'

WE are sitting drinking coffee, my friend Beth and I, and I tell her about this couple we met on holiday in Majorca last year.

'He's coming down from Lancashire on business,' I say, 'and I'm having a small dinner party for them next Tuesday. Don and I thought it would be nice if you could come and bring a friend. We didn't get to know them all that well, but they've got in touch so we feel more or less obligated.'

Automatically I use words like obligated when I'm with Beth because she puts me on my not-often-used mettle. She's made me feel that way ever since we were sixth-form prefects together, and I suppose you could say she is my best friend, as best friends go.

Beth – in speech, mannerisms and appearance – is a perfectionist and at the moment, with one divorce and three meaningful relationships behind her, she has time at last to spend reconditioning me.

She has been trying to recondition me for years, and to her credit hasn't yet given me up as a bad job, although in the process she has managed on occasions to make me feel like a dowdy, sexless, fat frump; a domesticated moron who lives her life, and here I quote, 'in the shadow of her husband and the lesser shadows of her two children.'

'No more than six,' she is saying now. 'Over that number and intimate intelligent conversation is impossible. Less than six and one tends to find the two men talking together, and the women swapping anecdotes about their children and their hairdressers.'

*

The Entwistles haven't any children, and from what I can remember of Enid Entwistle, she has the kind of hair that can go uncapped underneath the shower each morning and come out looking just the same but wet. But I don't interrupt. Beth is well into her stride, and I know I am listening to a professional.

Don and I have been to what she calls her little intimate dinners, and each time we've come away feeling we've taken part in a television commercial, with after-dinner mints, scintillating conversation, the lot.

I watch her go into action, taking a pad and pencil from her leather handbag – a handbag which exactly matches her narrow-heeled shoes, her Italian leather gloves and her hair – which, at the moment is the colour of an extremely dry sherry.

I reach for the coffee pot and refill our cups; black, of course, for Beth, who if she lives to be ninety will still have a teenage figure, and with a dash of cream for me because I never had a figure like hers even when I was a teenager.

'First things come first,' she says, clicking a gold ballpoint pen into action. 'What are you going to wear, Maggie? The way you look will affect the way the whole evening turns out. You want to make an impression, don't you?'

'Well . . . I hadn't thought too much about that side . . .' I begin to say, but am ignored.

'And to look the part is to play the part,' says Beth firmly.

'I thought my long tartan skirt with my green shirt,' I say, despising myself already for the apologetic tone which has crept into my voice.

Beth closes her eyes as if I've deeply wounded her. '*Darling*, don't mind me asking you this question, but was anyone *with* you when you bought that skirt?'

I shake my head, seeing myself in my mind's eye in the cubicle of the dress shop in the High Street, struggling to fasten the button on the waistband and wanting to believe the assistant when she tells me the skirt might have been made with me in mind.

'No, no one was with me,' I tell Beth, and she nods.

'I thought not,' she says with triumph and then starts planning.

'A long-sleeved hostess gown,' she is saying now. 'A plain dark colour, but not black.' She narrows her eyes and holds the pen out in front of her as if she's about to draw me. 'Something warm in tone. Your face needs colour, but the *right* colour. Cinnamon brown, or a very dark rust.'

'I can't afford a new dress,' I say promptly and explain about the girls needing new winter coats, but I am no match for Beth and should have known it.

She lights one of her small cigars. 'What about the forty Premium Bonds you were telling me about last week? Far better on your back than in Ernie's clutches. Money should always work for you, Maggie. You're not getting any interest on them, darling.'

'But suppose they come up the very week after I've taken them out?' I say, but she merely makes a flourish of a tick on her pad and moves on to the next item.

'Food,' she says. 'Something rather different. Something far removed from hot-pot and black puddings, but not too heavy. With a claret or a burgundy.' She taps her teeth with her pen. 'Then we must take them on somewhere.' She studies a rust-tipped nail with a frown, realizes she is frowning and strokes away the offending vertical line between her brows. 'I know the very place. Sophisticated, with just the right amount of atmosphere. That's what Northerners want when they come down to London: a touch of glamour.'

I feel I must make a stand. 'Ben Entwistle,' I tell her, 'is a well-heeled business man, used to expense account meals; they live in a ranch house with four acres of land, so please, Beth, stop imagining him wandering round Soho in a flat cap, staring open-mouthed at the nude photographs. It's not like that at all.'

But I know I am wasting breath. Beth, who thinks that civilized living stops north of the Watford Gap, is well into her organizing stride.

'Salmon steaks with cream,' she is saying, 'followed by one of your out-of-this-*world* lemon mousses, Maggie. Let them see that fish doesn't have to be cased in batter, flanked by chips and blobbed by tomato sauce. Yes, that should do the trick.'

'Beth has taken me over again,' I tell Don that evening, describing her detailed plans. And not entirely to my surprise – Don has a grudging admiration for Beth's undisputed rôle as the hostess with the mostest – he says it all sounds perfect.

'The only snag as I see it,' he goes on, 'is who will she be bringing along? Not, I hope, that little chappie who was nevertheless something big in films, or the one who said he'd been to prison just so he could write a book about it. I can't see Ben Entwistle getting on with either of those.'

'She's bringing Adrian,' I tell him. 'You know, the one with the purple velvet jacket and the daisy-patterned shirt. The one who always makes the same joke about lying on the sofa with Jilly Cooper every Sunday afternoon.' Then, at Don's blank stare, 'You *know*. The columnist in *The Sunday Times*. He means he's reading the newspaper.'

'Good God!' says Don. 'I don't expect they grow them like him where Ben Entwistle comes from.'

'Now you're talking like Beth,' I say rather nastily, but as Don can never tell when I'm being nasty it is all a waste of time.

So I bow to the inevitable. Don tells me to write a cheque for a new dress, as the money from my Premium Bonds wouldn't have come through anyway, and on the appointed day there we are. The girls are nicely fixed up at a friend's house, my own house smells clean up to the picture rails of salmon poached in cream, and the mousse is sitting in the fridge.

I am wearing the new dress, chosen for me by Beth: it's a dark blue jersey silk with a cleavage that has me rather worried. It is cut so wide there is no way of wearing a bra, and there are two pieces of sticking plaster flattening down my nipples on instructions from Beth.

'What on *earth* are you doing?' Don has asked, catching me at it, and when I tell him he falls about laughing. 'But Maggie, love, we all know you've got them!' Then he laughs some more and I tell him peevishly that one of his sideboards is at least half an inch longer than the other, and exit quickly leaving him measuring them with a pencil in front of the mirror.

Beth and Adrian arrive first: Beth in a champagne silk trouser suit with a neckline that makes my dress look as if I'm wearing a modesty vest, and Adrian in blue denim, accessorized with a black and pink paisley shirt and a gold ring in one earlobe.

Ben and Enid Entwistle are only a few minutes behind them, and I hardly recognize them without their Majorca tans. Ben is wearing a suit which could grace the chair at any top management conference, and Enid wears a tartan skirt which causes Beth to give me a glance which says: 'There but for the grace of me, go *you*.'

Don makes the introductions and over the pre-dinner drinks I see a thought-bubble coming out of Ben Entwistle's balding head. It says, as Don has said it would say: 'My God, we don't grow them like that where we come from,' and I see him trying not to look at Adrian's gold earring.

Enid sits on the sofa and tells Beth all about her little hobby of flower-arranging.

'A wonderful therapy,' murmurs Beth.

'Make free with the wine,' I whisper to Don as we usher them into the dining-room, and it works, because long before we reach the coffee stage Enid is dimpling away at Adrian and Ben is demonstrating his latest chip-shot with one of the berries off my floral arrangement and the cucumber fork.

Out of the corner of my eye I see Beth whispering to Don, and like a well-trained poodle he trots off into the hall and telephones for a taxi.

Everyone piles in and we are driven to this place down a side street in Mayfair. A dimly-lit interior leads down a sharply winding wrought-iron staircase to an even darker cellar.

Beth has a word with a tall man wearing black sunglasses – not for the glare, that's certain – and we weave our way through a tightly jammed crowd of people who seem to be standing around peering with myopic intensity into each other's faces. The tall man leads us to a small table lit by one spluttering candle, and we are cheek by jowl to the disc jockey and his electrified paraphernalia. The noise is so terrific we can only communicate by using sign language, or by shouting at the tops of our respective voices.

A girl in black slacks, with 'not available' printed across the front of her white T-shirt, places four bottles of wine on our table. Adrian does the honours and there we sit, sipping away, trying to give the Entwistles the impression that this is what we Londoners do with our spare time.

Don, using his cupped hands as a makeshift megaphone, asks Enid to dance and off they go, stepping on to a floor which would make our hall at home look as vast as the Sahara Desert. There are so many couples entwined on it, packed so closely together, I tell myself that to end up with the same partner you started off with must rank as something of an achievement.

Ben Entwistle bellows an invitation into my left ear and off we go, clamped tightly together, shuffling from one foot to the other because that is the only way we can move at all. I see he is trying not to sweat, and smile at him kindly to show I don't mind at all if he does.

Adrian doesn't dance. I remember, and I see that Beth's face in one of her unguarded moments is bleak with the special kind of despair I know she suffers from when she is between men. Don and Enid have given it up as a lost cause, and I see to my shame that Don has taken out his beloved pipe and is puffing away, looking as out of place as a curate at a love-in.

I am just going to suggest to Ben Entwistle that we too go back to our table, when I feel his hand sliding suggestively down the small of my back to rest on my bottom and, turning my head in surprise, stare straight into his eyes which are no more than an inch away from my own.

'Hello, Pansy-face,' he says. 'Do you mind me saying that you are the most beautiful woman I have seen in twelve months of Sundays?' Then, before I can think of a suitable reply, he pulls me even closer and, to my horror, I feel him nibbling passionately at my ear.

Rather stunned, I glance over to our table to see if Enid is watching, but she is talking with animation to Adrian, and by the look on his face I surmise that she is telling him how she won three gold stars at the last horticultural show.

Over Ben's plump shoulder I give frantic signals to Don, silently pleading with him to come and excuse me, then I realize that as far as this crowd goes excuse-me dances went out with the dinosaurs.

Then, unwittingly, the young disc jockey comes to my rescue, changing records with the speed of light, changing the tempo to a sultry samba.

'I can't do this,' I say, peeling myself away from Ben, and back at the table I hide my blushes in a glass of wine. Ben, after giving me a reproachful burning glance, asks Beth to dance and Adrian, the only one who has seen it all, winks at me before giving rapt attention to Enid. I lip-read and see that she is telling him now how she made a Christmas decoration out of milk-bottle tops and a stick of forced rhubarb.

Don has disappeared behind a cloud of tobacco smoke and I sit there in the deafening gloom. Me, Maggie, mother of two; no longer very young, but a long way from being old, and wonder could my face *really* be pansy-shaped?

Ben Entwistle has had too much to drink. Ben Entwistle is a sweating near-middle-aged man with a nice little wife. A man who should know better, but just for a moment, with the music pounding in my brain, I am a young girl again – a beautiful girl with a face the shape of a dear little pansy. I look down at my glass and smile at my foolishness.

Then Beth comes back, and Ben holds out his plump arms to his wife and off they go. Don and Adrian clear a space on the table and recreate the final try of last Saturday's match at Twickenham, and Beth says she is going to the loo and I get up and go with her.

And gone is the look of quiet desperation; Beth is herself again, vivacious, animated, the confident Beth I have known since we were at school together.

We lean together towards the too-small mirror, and as she re-highlights her cheekbones she asks me why I wear pink lipstick when it went out last year, and suggests kindly that if only I would have my hair blow-dried instead of set, it would take years off my age.

'Would you say my face is pansy-shaped?' she asks, and in the mirror I see that my eyebrows have raised themselves clean up into my out-of-date hair-line.

'Your friend Ben told me that I am the most beautiful woman he has seen in twelve months of Sundays,' she says, and I open my mouth to say 'snap', but something stops me just in time.

Tomorrow, Ben Entwistle and his nice little wife will be going back to Lancashire, and it is more than likely we will never see them again.

I have Ben Entwistle's measure, and I would stake my life on the fact that he is a harmless, decent, hard-working man who drinks too much, sweats too much and, just once in a while, imagines himself as a Northern Casanova.

But there on the tiny dance floor, he has given Beth what she needed – the masculine flattery, the boost to her ego which means so much to her.

I will be going home with Don who, even if he lives to be a hundred, will never, bless his heart, tell me that my face is pansy-shaped, nor that I am the most beautiful woman he has ever seen. Beth will be going back to her flat, empty until the next man comes along. I give her the answer I know she is waiting for: 'Now that you mention it, I really do think your face is pansy-shaped,' I say, and I sigh. 'No one ever says things like that to me.'

Beth smiles at me through the mirror, widening her eyes.

'Never mind, Maggie,' she tells me kindly. 'I think you look really nice tonight. Honestly.'

'Thank you,' I murmur, and humbly follow her glowing figure to our candle-lit table.

A FRESH BEGINNING

LITTLE Miss Jones was a worrier. Now, at the age of seventy-one, she couldn't remember a time when her inside hadn't been churned up about something.

She came from a long line of worriers.

Her father, Hugh David Jones, had fretted himself into his grave in case the grocery business he ran stopped flourishing. Her mother, Gwyneth Betsey Jones, had followed him sadly a few years later, because due to her inexpert management it did just that. . . .

Enough was salvaged to settle Miss Jones into a small cottage. Her one proposal she turned down, convinced that the bewildered young man, who quite genuinely loved her, might be after her money.

She spent the next two years worrying in case she had made a mistake, and the following ten, when he settled down with her best friend, knowing that she had!

Passing plumply into middle age, Miss Jones took to fretting about her health. The natural high colour in her cheeks she interpreted as a sign of dangerously high blood pressure, and the slight stiffness of her little finger as the onset of a rapidly progressive arthritic condition.

She brooded over symptoms in the out-of-date medical book on the bottom shelf of the bookcase in the sitting-room. She brooded until even the most obscure of tropical diseases seemed symbolic of her own condition. Studying the newspaper headlines in a cold sweat of apprehension, she was convinced that extermination was only a heartbeat away.

Over the years, worrying became as natural to her as breathing. The skin on her broad shining forehead wrinkled itself into permanent tramlines of anxiety. Always on the small side, she seemed to shrink into a frail, pathetic shadow of a little woman, as grey and delicate as a dusty cobweb.

That summer, the summer that never was, when even the people who went abroad got rained on, her only excuse for inquietude was the greenfly on her roses. Then, towards the end of a wet, weeping August, she heard that the small village was being thoroughly and systematically burgled.

'And all by the same man! No doubt about that!' Miss Williams at the confectioner's confided to her over a cottage loaf. 'He must be a thug. A brutal, desperate thug. They say he put a gag in old Mr Davis's mouth and broke his top dentures; and he locked that nice Mrs Evans from the flats by the station in the lavatory, and she had a funny turn on account of being claustrophobic. Goodness knows whose turn'll be next. It's dreadful it is when we can't sleep peaceful in our own beds.'

The till drawer clanged open with an ominous rattle.

'That'll be ninepence-halfpenny,' Mrs Williams said, in the satisfied voice of one who has just imparted bad news.

Miss Jones's round eyes shone like wet marbles. She had to be called back twice to collect her change. And it was the same in the fishmonger's.

Mr Owen passed her usual small packet of frozen fish over with a warning about locking all her doors and windows.

'Not that it really makes much difference, I don't suppose,' he soothed in his booming voice – the same dramatic voice that he used for reading the lesson in Chapel on Sundays. 'Because all he does is simply remove the putty from a pane of glass, lift out the window and climb through. . . .'

Miss Jones forgot all about the small packet of frozen peas she had decided to buy. She walked home in a daze and opened her front door with trembling fingers. Then, with the ease of long practice, she enlarged and exaggerated what she had heard until it grew out of all proportion to reality.

A thug! A brutal thug! Climbing in through her window, in the dead of night. Groping his way past the kitchen dresser, skirting the red-topped table, padding in rubber-soled shoes down the hall; starting to climb the stairs, stopping for a moment on the fourth because it creaked, then on, on, until he reached her bedroom door.

Gripping the door-handle with his big hand – a thug would be bound to have a big hand – Miss Jones was sure of that. Approaching her bed, leaning over her, his hot breath on her cheek. . . .

The evening paper slid through the letter-box and plopped on to the mat below.

Miss Jones jumped as though she'd been unexpectedly shot in the back. She went through the house, locking and bolting with such thoroughness that only a surrounding moat could have added to its impenetrability.

That night she lay rigid in the middle of her big, lonely bed, her brown-spotted old lady's hands crossed neatly on her one-piece bosom. Her short-sighted eyes pierced the darkness and her one good ear strained into the silence.

Around four o'clock in the early light of a cold dawn, she fell into an uneasy sleep, dreaming that her battered body had been found, oozing blood on to the bedroom carpet.

'Old lady puts up a plucky fight!' the newspaper headlines said, and they traced the brutal thug by the scrapings of his jacket fibres found in her fingernails.

Jerking awake, still sleepily unable to distinguish dream from reality, Miss Jones made a fervent vow never to read another 'whodunnit'. From now on her three library books, chosen with care every Thursday, would be from the section harmlessly labelled 'Light Romantic'.

The milkman's on-the-doorstep account of how the Chapel Fund box had been broken into, and the Reverend threatened with what was either a gun or a flick knife – the milkman couldn't quite remember – made her old heart beat wildly in her throat.

'Only a black-hearted wretch would sink so low,' the milkman said over his shoulder as he went back down the path.

Little Miss Jones stood stone-still, her small teeth nervously chewing on nothing as she watched him go.

And then the burglaries stopped, and for a week or so Miss Jones almost relaxed. Apart from a discoloured big toe, which she had persuaded herself *could* have been the forerunner of gangrene, little Miss Jones was in the best of spirits.

She walked home from the shops one grey afternoon with no thought in her mind but the cup of tea she would have the very minute she got in. . . .

She was actually humming the first line of her favourite hymn 'All things bright and beautiful', as she fumbled in the cavernous depths of her tartan hold-all for the front-door key. . . .

The humming stopped dead in her throat as she stared down the hall, through the open kitchen door, straight into the startled eyes of the young man just removing his bleeding right hand from the debris of her kitchen window.

They stared at each other. . .

Miss Jones's grey hair prickled away from her scalp and stood on end like electrified fuse wire.

This then was it. . . .

The materialization of one of her worst nightmares, the culmination of the worst of her fears.

And yet, something was wrong somewhere. In all her nightmare imaginings of being confronted by a thug, Miss Jones had either slid to the floor unconscious or better still died a swift, painless death from sudden heart failure.

But now, face to face with reality, her hair flattened itself back on to her prawn-pink scalp and she felt a strange and unfamiliar calmness possess her.

Sternly she addressed the young man through the jagged hole in her window: 'Come along inside, you silly boy, and I'll look at that hand for you before you bleed to death.'

She unbolted the kitchen door and held it wide.

Obediently and surprisingly he shuffled past her, carefully avoiding her eye. . . . His trousers tapered to a terrible tightness and his black hair folded itself in greasy fronds over the back of his narrow head. His eyes, set close together over his nose, watched her ministrations with suspicion.

Miss Jones found a bandage in her first-aid box, tied it with a double reef knot and offered him a cup of tea.

'Strong, and with plenty of sugar. For the shock to your system – to both our systems,' she told him firmly.

'I'm ever so sorry about the window, missus,' he said, and his small eyes seemed to plead forgiveness over the rim of his cup.

Miss Jones's crumpled cheeks wobbled compassionately as she refilled the teapot.

'Well then, being sorry shows that you're not all bad. That's a good beginning.'

He unzipped the front of his leather jacket and for an uncomfortable moment Miss Jones thought that he was going to pull out a gun – or a flick knife. . .

She sighed with relief as he produced a half-empty packet of cigarettes. He shook one out into his bandaged fist.

Offering him a light, she noticed with pride that the flame was as steady as a rock.

'What made you take up this life?' she reproved him gently. 'You aren't cut out for it really, are you? I can see that most clearly, young man.'

He looked down at the bandage and grinned.

'Looks like you could be right, missus. But I'm giving it up anyway. Yours was one of the last houses on my list. Next week I'm off to join the Army.'

'Oh dear! How splendid that is,' said Miss Jones. 'How glad I am for your sake. It will be a new start, a fresh beginning.'

Daringly, she patted him on the shoulder.

'We'll say no more about today, then. I won't tell the police. I won't tell *anyone*. Off you go into the Army. They'll make a man out of you yet. No one is all bad; I've always believed that and today you've proved me right.'

With an air of baffled bewilderment he backed towards the door, stammered his thanks for the tea and disappeared.

Left alone, Miss Jones brooded happily into her cup of tea.

She had faced a brutal thug, a black-hearted wretch. She had faced him with cool courage and sent him repentant away.

The knowledge was like a bud bursting into flower in her old heart. She had stared fear straight in the eye with resourcefulness and calm deliberation and banished it for ever.

For her, nothing would ever be quite the same again. . .

Miss Jones poured herself another cup of tea and took an immensely satisfying sip.

The young man had left his cigarettes on the table and she nonchalantly shook out one. Lighting it, she blew an amateurish stream of smoke straight through the jagged hole in her kitchen window.

And outside, the young man zipped up his jacket.

Police? Fresh start? What was the old dame on about? Proper glad he'd been to get out of her kitchen. Those beady eyes of hers had fair given him the shivers. . . . He'd be glad to hand back the window-cleaning business to his brother-in-law when he came out of hospital the day after tomorrow. Not that he'd objected or grumbled at doing him a good turn, but cleaning windows wasn't exactly his cup of tea.

Still, the old dame had been pretty decent about the broken window. . .

Whistling tunelessly, he balanced the ladder on the saddle of his bike and wheeled it away, the bucket jangling noisily from the last rung. . .

TWO OF A KIND

'SO IF YOU don't mind,' Emma heard her mother's voice saying on the telephone, 'I'll drive them over this afternoon, just for an hour. It will be Father's first outing since he had his stroke. It isn't doing him any good sitting about in the house doing nothing. He *broods*.'

'Of course I don't mind. I think it's a marvellous idea,' Emma said, one ear glued to the telephone and the other cocked in the direction of the kitchen, where an ominous clatter of dishes warned her that two-year-old Robert had dragged a chair up to the sink and was carrying on with the breakfast washing-up.

Thoughtfully Emma replaced the receiver. Outside the sun, struggling through the haze of cloud, promised the first warm day of spring . . . now she would have to explain to Robert that they wouldn't be going to the park after all. That they wouldn't be taking a paper bag full of crusts to feed the ducks, because Grandma was coming to see them, bringing Great-Grandma and Great-Grandpa, who had been ill. So Robert must be on his very best behaviour.

Not that the child would reply – not in words – but he would *understand* every syllable. For at two, Robert had an uncanny perception; an intuition that went, she comforted herself, far beyond his age. Indeed the clinic doctor confirmed this at his last check-up just a week ago, though how she'd come to that conclusion Emma could only guess, as Robert had thrown the bricks he was supposed to build into an intelligent tower with calculated venom at the nearest window, and scowled, narrowing his blue eyes into furious slits, refusing to answer the simplest of her patient questions.

'He isn't even beginning to put words together,' Emma had

apologized, not trying to disguise her anxiety. 'Doesn't even say Mummy or Daddy, but he understands every word we say to him I'm sure – every single word.'

The doctor, bright and efficient in her white coat, had smiled reassurance.

'There's no need to worry, Mrs James. We've ruled out deafness, and the noise he was making out there before you came in shows there's nothing wrong with his vocal cords. He'll start to talk all at once, and when he does you'll wonder why on earth you were so anxious. Boys are notoriously slow at talking, anyway.'

She had patted Robert's straw-coloured thatch of hair and been rewarded with a jumbled spate of uncomplimentary sounds. The interview, she indicated, had run its allotted span, but before Emma could prise a building block from Robert's tightly clenched fist and lead him off she'd had the final embarrassment of seeing him throw himself on the floor, drumming his heels with passionate abandon.

'Frustration,' the doctor mouthed amid the din. 'Quite normal in a child who can't understand why *you* can't understand what he's trying to say. You must talk to him more. Point things out to him, and say the names clearly and slowly. Make quacking noises for a duck, and barking noises for a dog – you know the kind of thing.'

Oh, yes, Emma thought wearily, she knew the kind of thing all right.

She'd tried all that. Quacking, barking and miaowing, pointing to pictures in highly-coloured books, intoning duck and dog and cat, only to be rewarded by a blank stare from a totally uninterested child who still refused to say even the simplest words.

'He makes me feel, in a strange way, a kind of fool,' she'd told Kim, her husband, and reached just once more for her baby-care manual.

'After lunch,' she told a well-scrubbed Robert, firmly removing a kitchen knife from his clenched little fist,

'Grandma is coming to see us, and she's bringing Great-Gran and Great-Grandpa with her. Won't that be nice?'

Robert beamed his approval, emitting sounds that Emma felt closely resembled her imagined concept of the Russian alphabet. She gave him an exasperated hug, and he in return planted a loving but sloppy kiss on her chin.

'And now we'll find you a dry sweater and we'll go to the shops,' she said with careful clarity, 'and we'll buy you a gingerbread man with currants for his eyes.' She pointed to Robert's eyes.

'Eyes,' she said. 'Say eyes for Mummy.'

But Robert was away, running down the hall and climbing the stairs with his usual disregard for life and limb, returning immediately with a sweater from the drawer in his room, demonstrating once again that he was capable of interpreting everything that was said to him.

And all the way to the shops, Emma persevered.

'Cars,' she said, pointing to the passing traffic. 'Baby,' she said, indicating a tiny girl in a pram, staring wide-eyed from a cocoon of multi-coloured blankets.

'Dog,' she said, stopping by a yapping corgi straining at its leash outside the greengrocer's.

And Robert, his round face haloed by the quilted hood of his anorak, listened serenely but silently.

All through lunch she carried on the non-stop but ever one-sided conversation, while Robert demolished four fish fingers, a mound of peas and a dish of banana custard.

Defeated, she pushed him, protesting on every step with a vehement shake of his head and a phrase that could optimistically have been decoded as 'Me not now', upstairs to rest. Ten minutes later, exhausted, every nerve alive and quivering, she closed his bedroom door, having at last discovered that she hadn't understood which toy he had wanted to take up with him. The process of elimination by which she eventually realized it was his toy telephone had exasperated the child till he was almost beside himself with rage at her non-comprehension.

Emma had hoped to enjoy, before the afternoon visitors arrived, a blissful half-hour with a magazine, feet up on the sofa, but she had just finished tidying the kitchen when the sound of a car drawing up outside sent her hurrying to the door.

Motherly and grandmotherly kisses were exchanged and then Emma turned to her grandfather, standing in the hall, muffled to the ears against the still cool wind and wearing the bewildered expression of the newly convalescent.

Never a big man, he seemed to have shrunk, to have diminished, but Emma was gladdened to see the familiar in-built twinkle in his blue eyes and the same air of vital interest in the world around him.

'Only his speech has been affected, that's all,' she'd been told by Grannie who, having weathered two world wars and the bringing up of five children, was obviously prepared to take a little thing like that in her stride.

'Lovely to see you again, Grandpa,' Emma said. 'Let me take your coat, and we'll have a cup of tea before Robert comes down. He was so excited when he knew you were coming.'

The old man smiled but said nothing and, when they were settled in the sitting-room with the fire switched on in spite of the sunshine now flooding the room, Emma went through into the kitchen and put the kettle on.

'It's difficult,' Grannie said, following her in and laying a bag of home-made buns on the table. 'It's the frustration of it all. He tries so hard to talk, but the words won't come out, not so you'd understand him, anyway. And he gets irritated with himself, yet *he* knows what he's trying to say.'

Emma, busy with cups and saucers and the setting out of the big tray, felt she knew only too well.

But Grannie was obviously enjoying getting it all off her chest. 'I try,' she said. 'I point to things and ask him to repeat them, the way the speech therapist told me to at the hospital, and he manages it sometimes, but most of the time it sounds. . .'

'Like the Russian alphabet,' said Emma, and the old lady nodded and smiled.

Over tea the three generations of women talked about the price of meat, the new shade of Emma's mother's hair and the last speaker at the Women's Institute, and over by the window the old man and the small boy, now rested and awake, eyed each other . . . silently.

When Robert reached for his third bun, Emma suggested that he took Great-Grandpa into the garden to show him the new swing and the daffodils in the border; and, after Grannie had wound her husband carefully into his muffler, the french windows were opened and the two stepped outside.

Teacups were replenished and Grannie, settling back in the easy chair, admitted what a nice break it was to come out, and that it was rather a strain, and that there were times when she suspected that her husband didn't try to co-operate.

'Out of sheer perversity,' she said and Emma, with dismay, saw the old eyes behind the whirlpool spectacle lenses fill with tears.

'Sometimes I wonder if he'll ever talk,' she confided, 'and you know what a great talker he was.'

'Give him time,' Emma's mother said, and wondered if there might be a draught, so Emma got up and walked across the room but, as she started to close the window, her hand suddenly stilled. . . .

Out there on the patio, sitting side by side on the low stone wall, Robert and her grandfather were deep in conversation. Totally engrossed in each other, they failed to see Emma standing there and, with her face a study in sheer amazement, she heard her little son say, in accents loud and clear, 'Quack, quack?'

'Duck', said the old man, stumbling only slightly over the word.

Robert nodded, well satisfied, pointing to the next picture

in the book open on his knee.

'Bow-wow,' he encouraged, staring up into the wrinkled face intently.

'D . . . dog,' said Emma's grandfather, and she saw the way her little son nodded, full of importance.

Then it was the old man's turn.

Pointing to Robert's well-loved and battle-scarred kiddicar, he grasped an imaginary wheel and made the noise of an engine reverberating into life.

'Car,' said Robert, bursting into peals of laughter. 'Car. Car. Car.'

Then he snuggled closer to the old man, laid his head for a brief moment on his knee and, as a gnarled hand rested in a kind of blessing on the unruly head of thick fair hair, Emma – her heart filled with gladness – turned away and closed the window.

FREE FROM THE FAMILY

'ALL I NEED,' I murmured into the stripes of my husband's pyjama jacket, 'is a clear fortnight to get the first draft done.'

It was the midnight hour and usually we were asleep, but that early summer evening the wind howled, the window-frames rattled, the boyfriend of the girl next door had trouble starting his car and from the box-room came the rhythmical drone of Katy's snores. I must have her tonsils seen to, I thought, then. . .

'Two weeks alone,' I went on, 'with the house to myself. After all, I did win the literary prize at school. You can still see my name on a board in the hall, in gilt letters.'

Bill, dithering on the edge of sleep, made appropriate grunting noises to convince me he was listening. I snuggled my chin deeper into his chest.

'It's a wonderful idea for a novel, and it's all written down in my mind.'

'Turn over, lovey, and go to sleep.' Bill was slewing his eyes over to the electric clock on the bedside table. 'It's a quarter past twelve, and I have to be off early in the morning, Liz. . .'

But I twined my cold feet round his legs and began, 'It's a kitchen-sink kind of thing. You know – realistic – nothing left to the imagination.'

I felt Bill grin into my hair.

'Nothing?' he asked sleepily.

'Nothing!' I said firmly. 'Every page full of unbridled passion, and an earthy acceptance of life as it really is. A sort of domesticated *Lady Chatterley*, except of course that I'm not D. H. Lawrence,' I conceded modestly.

Bill jerked awake.

'And what will the chaps at the office and Miss Mingle in the typing pool think when my wife's name appears on a book like that? And what about the girls, when their mother is pointed out as "the woman who wrote that book"?' His voice shook with suppressed laughter and I shushed him into silence.

'What you don't realize is that people today want to read slices of real life, full of the problems and temptations they meet every day and must either resist or succumb to. . .'

'No one's ever tempted me,' Bill said sadly. 'Unless you could count that girl at the library who never charges me on books I keep too long.' He ruffled my hair. 'Has anyone ever tempted you, Liz? I'll bet that baker's roundsman, the one who's the spitting image of Robert Redford, has made many a pass at you over a sliced loaf.'

'Bill, please. Be serious and listen,' I hissed into his ear. 'This is it, briefly. This girl – Elvira, I think I'll call her – lives alone in a dingy basement flat. No one's ever loved her; she never knew her real parents; she is plain, dumpy and. . .' Bill's breath caught on a slight snore, but I didn't need an audience now . . . 'she gave herself to a married man to prove to herself that sex was mere motivation – a mere animal instinct. . . She has her baby, along and untended. . .'

That bit worried me not a little when I thought about the births of Caroline and Katy. Midnight dashes to hospital in taxis, starchy nurses preparing me with efficiency and Dr Williams urging me on. Still I was adamant.

'She feels no emotion of any kind for her child. No mother-love. So she takes it to the wife of her lover – it is doomed, of course – and gives it to her. . .'

'Saying, "Your husband left this behind," said Bill unexpectedly, and we giggled ourselves to sleep.

Next morning at breakfast, Bill chose to discuss summer

holidays. Outside, a grey and folded sky hung low over the house.

Katy shuffled into the kitchen, slid into her seat and eyed her bacon and egg with suspicion.

'I would really have liked a poached egg this morning,' she told me, and I wished I could look at her without wondering if she'd passed her eleven-plus. I'd told myself that I despised women who put so much emphasis on the results; women who took their child's failure as a personal insult.

Caroline had passed, but Katy was a border-line. Miss Anderson had told me, with a note of regret in her plum-in-the-throat voice, that Katy was destined it would seem for the large comprehensive school on the outskirts of the town.

I prodded a slice of bacon angrily round the frying-pan. It was all wrong to segregate children into passes, failures and border-lines.

But, oh God, let her pass, I prayed, then was ashamed of myself for praying.

Upstairs Caroline could be heard taking gleeful possession of the bathroom and running away all the hot water I'd earmarked for washing the sitting-room chair-covers.

'I could always go on a golfing holiday with old Ted,' said Bill, apropos of absolutely nothing.

That was just like Bill. He would carry on a conversation hours, sometimes days, after it was first started, and expect me to know exactly what he was referring to.

He speared his fried egg thoughtfully. 'And if I chose the fortnight when Caroline goes to visit her French pen-friend, that would be two of us out of the way.'

Pushing his chair back, he got up from the table and folded his newspaper into the only folds acceptable on the eight-fifteen.

'And surely someone could take this one off your hands for two weeks.' He ruffled Katy's soft brown hair.

Only then did I realize what was ticking over in his unpredictable mind. Dear Bill, he'd taken me seriously. He really thought I could write a book, given a free fortnight. His faith in me was, I decided, pathetically touching – the eyes of love, still seeing the nine-stone-three-pound me as the sleek-as-a-whippet, dark-haired girl he'd married years ago.

On the doorstep I passed him his briefcase and, silhouetted against a back-cloth of rain-drenched laburnum, he tried again. 'I'm sure we could fix something up, lovey. You think about it, anyway.' And he kissed me lightly on the cheek and was gone.

I did think about it. I thought about it all the time I chased frantically round the house, searching for Katy's other shoe.

'It was in the dining room. I know it. You've moved it,' she wailed and accused.

'Shoes shouldn't be kept in the dining room,' I said, retrieving it from underneath the sideboard and seeing simultaneously my name on the cover of a book. The newsagent in the High Street would have a special display window for it and I would sit at a table in the tiled entrance, graciously autographing copies for a long impatient queue of housewives with shopping baskets on their arms and flattering respect in their eyes.

Dizzy with daydreams, I waved Katy off at the door. She turned at the gate, then bent her head against the rain and trailed her scuffed casuals slowly down the avenue.

Perhaps her tonsils were poisoning her whole system, I worried as I closed the door. Or perhaps she sensed my anxiety about the eleven-plus results. They say that a mother transmits her worries to her innocent children. Neurotic mothers, that is. Not the kind of mother I saw myself as. Sane, sensible, a provider of balanced meals, a dispenser of vitamins, a friend, a confidante, a tiller to cling to in life's storms. . .

But, oh, I hoped that she'd passed, I prayed again as I lit a cigarette and poured myself a third cup of tea.

I blew a stream of smoke towards the boiler, heard Caroline's step on the stairs, looked at the cigarette and hesitated. The day I'd found two cigarette stubs behind the books in Caroline's bookcase, I'd decided not to smoke when she was in the house. But now the evidence wreathed the kitchen like smoky ectoplasm, so I took another guilty puff.

I broke Caroline's egg into the poacher and she came over and stared at it with a resigned expression.

'I'd really have preferred bacon and egg,' she told me sadly.

I sighed, but said nothing. What would have been the use?

Caroline, during the last few months, had developed one or two tiny red spots underneath the skin of her rounded chin. She'd reacted as though she had advanced chronic running eczema. She'd sent to a magazine for a free sample of complexion cream, coated every inch of her face and neck lavishly and threatened to live the life of a recluse until the spots cleared up.

No fried food had been a part of the campaign, so now I could only conclude that her life of seclusion and self-denial was over. I poured myself a fourth cup of tea and sat down opposite her.

'Daddy and I have almost decided that you can go to stay with Odile in Paris for a fortnight at the end of August,' I said.

I waited for incredulous joy to light up her grey eyes, for the sudden hug, the whoop of delight. Instead, Caroline looked straight at me with the expression of a third-rate movie star who has just seen her lover shot dead.

'I never doubted for a minute that I was going. I'd have died if you and Daddy had let me down,' she told me simply. She speared her poached egg with her fork and looked at me reproachfully. 'You know very well that I don't like the yolk hard,' she said.

Still in my housecoat, I let the third member of my family out of the house and went slowly back into the kitchen, a prey to second thoughts. What kind of parents were we, I asked myself, worriedly swishing soapy water round the bowl, to let a young girl of fifteen travel alone to Paris, stay with people we'd never met – people who might let her stay out until all hours, drink, smoke . . . I had a sudden vision of Caroline, wearing the spike-heeled shoes she had bullied me quite against my better judgment into buying for her, walking down a dark alley by the Seine and being suddenly accosted by a thin-faced, unshaven man wearing a black beret.

The telephone rang and it was Enid, my best friend, who lives on the other side of the Heath in a house apparently held together by trailing ivy.

She has an *au pair* girl, an artist husband who works in a bedroom all day in a dusty dressing-gown, a son at Cambridge and a daughter who, at seventeen, went to the Polytechnic and took a bed-sitter in Balham.

Almost from birth Enid's children have been independent. If they could have washed their own nappies, she'd have sat back and let them. They've hitch-hiked their way round this country, cycled all over the Continent, stayed up until they decided it was time to go to bed, smoked from the age of twelve, gone to all-night parties, called their parents by their Christian names from the time they could talk . . . all without any apparent ill effects.

Compared with Enid I am decadent, a square living in a morass of my own anxieties. Compared with Enid, I am positively archaic. We are totally different, yet she *is* my best friend.

Now her Ban-the-Bomb voice shrieked into my ear. 'Liz! Could you meet me for coffee? I've got something screamingly funny to tell you about Royston. He went pot-holing over the weekend and got stuck down a hole. It took four of them three hours to get him out. His letter is simply hilarious!'

I shuddered and promised to be in the Blue Lagoon espresso bar at eleven.

Then I dusted, finished the washing-up, vacuumed, made beds, prepared the evening meal vegetables, bathed, dressed and made up my face, and reached the Blue Lagoon with two minutes to spare.

At first I thought she wasn't there. Then I saw the familiar Audrey Hepburn silhouette wearing the usual too-tight pants and black polo-necked sweater, and the untidy head made more pinlike by a Roman centurion haircut. Vivacity and sheer *joie de vivre* flashed from her eyes. Somehow, Enid's bounding energy always leaves me feeling that I could do with a nice lie-down. Even the way she drinks her coffee, throwing her head back and taking great masculine gulps, leaves me breathless.

I listened to her account of Royston's sojourn down the pot-hole, then just to impress her I told her about my book. 'I know I could do it if I had the house entirely to myself,' I finished.

'But how perfectly splendid, darling!' she said, lighting a cigarette and inhaling deeply. 'Even if nothing comes of it, you will at least have given full rein to your creative urge. I know how you feel. I'd be absolutely stagnant without my pots.'

In her spare time Enid is a potter, turning out what to me are appalling monstrosities and selling them for sums of money which would keep us all in food for a month.

I gave her a brief outline of my plot.

'Real Tennessee Williams stuff,' she enthused, and stared at me for the first time with something approaching awe.

I walked home feeling inspired, uplifted, full of ideas and determination. I lingered outside the book-shop.

'Elizabeth Galway.' It would look good on a book-cover and with some of the royalties I'd re-furnish the sitting-room.

I stopped outside the new glass and chromium-plated furniture shop and stared at a giant purple and black settee, arranged tastefully on a yellow and green rubber-backed carpet. A pale and pin-striped young man came forward and asked if there were any way in which he could help me. I assured him there was no way at all and moved on.

The rain had almost stopped. Perhaps I ought to wash those chair-covers after all. . .

Having let myself into the house, I went through into the kitchen and stared thoughtfully at my new washing-machine. It had cost so much that, when Bill signed the cheque, I felt I ought to wash everything in the house at least every other day just to justify its existence!

I peeled off the covers, fed them into the machine's drum-like interior and was listening malevolently to its thump, thump, when the telephone rang. It was Enid again. Her exuberance came over the wire with the crackle of electricity.

'I've been telling Oliver about what you were telling me in the Blue Lagoon. . . He's absolutely fascinated, Liz. He says you just never can tell about people. I mean, of all our friends you seemed the one least likely to take up writing seriously.'

I raised my offended eyebrows at myself in the hall mirror.

'I did get the literary prize at school,' I began, but it was no good. Enid's enthusiasm would tolerate no interruption.

'You did say the last two weeks in August?'

'Well, yes, that was the time we'd thought, but of course there was nothing. . .'

'Well, then, Katy can come here. Oliver will be back from Rome. I'll be back from Yugoslavia. I forgot to tell you I was going, didn't I? Well, I am. Royston and some of his equally batty friends are chartering a private plane, flying over to Canada, then working their way from coast to coast. Make a change from pot-holing, won't it? And Serina mentioned something or other about joining a working party in Israel. So you see, darling, there's absolutely nothing to prevent Katy coming here, and I'll devote myself to her entirely. You know, zoos and things.'

Even Enid has to pause for breath sometimes and I spoke quickly, 'But it was just a vague, silly idea. . .'

She completely ignored me. 'Well, that's settled then. Must fly now. We've people coming to dinner and all I can think of is spaghetti and tinned milk pudding – separately, of course, but a bit colourless. . . 'Bye, Liz.'

And the telephone went dead.

Katy wouldn't want to go, I told myself. Whenever she met Enid she seemed to dissolve into nothingness – completely devoid of personality. I couldn't remember her ever uttering a really intelligent remark in Enid's presence. And Oliver! He'd terrify her, popping in and out of his studio-bedroom in his paint-smeared dressing-gown and chain-smoking through a chipped black holder. Still, Katy would refuse to go. I could be sure of that. Katy was the conventional, three-meals-a-day kind.

'How absolutely smash, Mummy!' she said when I told her. 'Enid will let me go all day without shoes or stockings on, and we'll eat things like nettle soup and have dandelion leaves in the salad, and perhaps Oliver will paint me. . .'

'He doesn't paint little girls,' I said shortly, 'and you'd better start liking yoghourt, because they almost live on it.'

Katy wrinkled her blob of a nose.

'It's the smell,' she said. 'Does Oliver paint things like fish on a plate, then?'

I laughed and thought of Oliver's huge canvases splashed with fierce daubs of orange, vermilion and angry reds. And his nudes, with skin tones the exact colour of the cream from a pint of Jersey milk.

'You'll see for yourself what he paints,' I told her, 'and now I must get on or dinner won't be ready when Caroline and Daddy come in.'

I peeped at the casserole of liver and bacon simmering away on the centre shelf of the oven. Below it, the meringue on the top of the rhubarb sponge glistened in pale amber, sugary peaks.

That was why I never had time to give rein to my creative urge, as Enid called it. I ought to be scribbling away in Bill's study, only emerging flushed with triumph five minutes before my family came in, to thrust before them yoghourt and chopped dandelion salad. I just wasn't 'dedicated' enough. My mind seethed with domestic trivialities.

After dinner, I watched with misgivings as Caroline wrote a letter to Odile and ran breathlessly to the post-box to catch the last post. The die, as they say, was cast.

When after ten minutes she didn't come back, I looked through the window. . . She was standing across the road, talking to a tall and painfully thin boy whose ears stuck out. I saw her look up at him through her eyelashes and laugh vivaciously at something he had said.

'You've been a long time,' I said carefully when she came in.

She leaned towards the steamy mirror over the sink and gave microscopic attention to a freckle on her nose.

'I walked very slowly,' was all she said.

I said nothing, but decided to talk things over with Bill when we were alone that night.

'The lies they tell!' I exploded. 'Caroline obviously knew that boy well, and he looked about eighteen.'

Bill adjusted the contrast control of the television, settled himself in his chair and gave me an indulgent smile over the top of his distance glasses.

'Just what you need, lovey – a fortnight from us all. Let you get things more into perspective. . . I was telling old Ted this morning that you were a bit "off", and he agreed with me that a couple of weeks on your own might set you up for the winter.'

'Most considerate of him,' I said dangerously, but Bill went on unperturbed.

'Naturally, I didn't tell him about the book. I mean to say, it sounds a bit, well, you know . . . saying I'm clearing off for a fortnight so that my wife can write a dirty book.'

I wished I'd been the type who threw things.

'It isn't dirty. It's real. True to life. It's the only kind of fiction that sells nowadays. Life's too grim for people to be fobbed off with trite little romances that merely skim the surface. They know that life is far from being like that. . .'

But Bill wasn't listening. His whole attention, his entire being, was riveted to the television screen where a great man with muscles as big as melons half battered the life out of a smaller man wearing satin trunks. I went disgustedly through into the kitchen and brooded over the coffee percolator.

What a lot had happened in one day, and all because I had whispered a half-formed idea sleepily into Bill's pyjama jacket.

I hated the idea of him going away with old Ted.

Old Ted wore hairy tweeds, smoked Whiffs and told jokes that were all against women. Old Ted's pale blue eyes held a permanent leer and he thought it was funny to pinch me when Bill wasn't looking. Old Ted could drink all night and then recite *The Village Blacksmith* backwards.

Bill thought old Ted was wonderful.

I passed him a cup of coffee.

'Sugar in?' he asked. I nodded.

'Stirred?' he asked.

I nodded again, and decided to go to bed.

In Caroline's room, a large framed photograph of Cliff Richard sat solidly on her dressing-table between the hair lacquer and complexion cream. Caroline, her dark hair tortured into bristly rollers, lay fast asleep, holding her head awkwardly on the pillow like a person recovering from a broken neck. She looked young, utterly defenceless and about twelve years old.

In the box-room Katy slept with the abandonment of a week-old puppy, her hair clinging damply to her head and her thumb, flattened and moist with constant sucking, an inch away from her waiting mouth.

And I had promised her to Enid for two whole weeks. . . Enid who ate when she was hungry, slept when she was tired and believed that mothers should be like the birds who push their children out of the nest at the first opportunity.

Katy sucked her breath in and let it out on a gentle snore. I leaned over her and kissed her forehead. She smelled of apple blossom and spring, I thought tenderly.

Then, on the way out of her room, I paused, remembering.

So did my best talcum powder. And, sure enough, a trail of it lay like a discarded paper-chase from the bathroom to her door.

I didn't care if she hadn't passed her eleven-plus, I decided; I didn't care if Caroline never learned to speak French fluently; and I didn't care if old Ted had to roam the golf-links alone. And I decided, finally, I didn't want to write a book.

But I knew there was no turning back now. What had to be, would be. The girls would come back more independent. They would come back to a mother fulfilled, with the manuscript of a book in her desk drawer – the first draft, anyway. And Bill, well, I had to face the truth. . . He would come back bleary-eyed, soaked in beer, with a complete repertoire of old Ted's awful jokes.

I heard his footsteps on the stairs and got quickly into bed, pretending sleep. . .

Next morning the sun was shining, full of promise of golden days and holidays spent lazing on a sandy beach. . . And I had decided to dedicate myself to higher things! But August was a long, long way off, I comforted myself, and all our plans might well turn out to be mere flights of fancy. The four of us, after all, would go as usual to the Isle of Wight for a cramped fortnight in the caravan of a friend of a friend of Bill's.

I saw the postman coming up the path with a buff-coloured envelope. I hurried out to meet him and opened it eagerly; this was what we had been waiting for.

'In our opinion,' it baldly stated, 'your daughter, Kathryn Margaret, is not considered to be a suitable candidate for a Grammar School education. If you will complete the enclosed form, further details of Myrtle Lane Comprehensive School will be sent to you.' A cloud covered the sun as I went into the house and closed the door.

But my Katy was intelligent, bright, full of promise! How dare they suggest that she wasn't a suitable candidate! I choked with disappointment, close to tears, then despised myself for being the kind of mother I had always convinced myself I wasn't!

This would be, I knew, the prelude to long and earnest discussions with Bill as to whether we could afford to send Katy to the smart private school by the Park gates, or whether it must be the doubtful portals of the comprehensive school.

Katy herself, after one swift glance at my face to see how I had taken it, was only mildly concerned.

'Would you like to go to Myrtle Lane?' I asked, and she stopped chewing for long enough to give the matter a second's consideration.

'They have washing-machines there. Better than yours,' she said. 'And ovens with windows in the front so that you can see what's going on, like at the launderette, except that it's food instead of washing.' She chewed reflectively. . . 'But at the Park School they wear those simply smashing little sailor hats – you know, with ribbons hanging down the back. But then, they haven't got washing-machines and ovens. . .'

Her brown eyes reproached me for bothering her with such a problem.

'I'll talk it over with Daddy,' I said wearily.

Caroline barely glanced at the letter when I passed it to her.

'Well, of course, I never thought she'd pass. She's hopeless, Mummy, honestly. She'll like Myrtle Lane. It's mixed, you know, and you're allowed to wear one frilly petticoat underneath your uniform skirt. Imagine! Miss Reynolds would have a fit if we did that. She hasn't the faintest idea of style. But she's about fifty, so one can't blame her really. She's just past it. . .'

I interrupted her. 'Miss Reynolds gets wonderful scholastic results and that's what matters really, isn't it?'

Caroline looked pityingly at me.

'Well, don't expect me to get even a single subject in GCE next year, Mummy. I'm just not the type, that's all.'

I hid a smile. For weeks before any examination, Caroline always warned us of the certainty of her failure. And every time her results delighted us. She wanted to be a doctor and Bill and I had decided, if it were humanly possible, to help her achieve this.

Bill has a good salary as a senior draughtsman, but like so many families today we live, almost literally, hand to mouth – what with the mortgage, the car, television, the washing-machine, spin-drier, record-player. . . Only last week Bill came home with a transistor radio, Caroline having told us almost daily for three months that every other teenager for a radius of miles was able to listen nightly to Radio Luxembourg!!

As soon as I heard Bill's key in the lock, I hurried into the hall to meet him.

'Katy didn't pass,' I whispered urgently, 'but don't say anything, we don't want to upset her, we'll talk about it later.'

Bill dropped his briefcase with a thud, and pulled me to him. 'Poor little devil,' he said. 'And what a system. We're as solemn as if we'd had a death in the family.'

Just then the sitting-room door opened with a flourish and 'the poor little devil' burst into the hall.

'Guess what? I failed, Daddy,' she said in her matter-of-fact little vóice, hurling herself at him. Then, pressing her mouth into a thin line, she mimicked Miss Anderson's voice with uncanny accuracy. 'No, Kathryn! You haven't failed. You have missed the final selection, that's all.' And she collapsed against the wall, helpless with giggles.

Bill's eyes met mine briefly. . . So much for our tactful regard for her feelings, they said.

Over coffee he brought up the subject of holidays again. At least, of *their* holidays.

'How would you like to fly to Paris?' he asked Caroline. 'That way we could put you on the plane and know that someone would meet you at the other end.'

Stars danced in her eyes. When she smiled she was really quite beautiful, I thought with pride.

But Katy broke in. 'It isn't fair. I've never flown. She gets everything; she's your favourite. I'm not going anywhere. . .'

The telephone rang and thankfully I went to answer it.

Old Ted's smoky voice breathed into my ear. 'That you, Liz? How are you, gorgeous? Still blossoming?'

Wearily I assured him that I was.

'Just been getting the "gen" on our August trip. Jolly splendid of you to let Bill off the leash for a couple of weeks, Liz. But not to worry. I'll see he doesn't do anything that I wouldn't do!'

And the line vibrated with the hooting sound that old Ted used for a laugh. I could almost smell his beery breath down the telephone wires.

'I'll get Bill,' I said quickly and tried not to feel hurt when I saw the eagerness with which he sprinted to the telephone. I groped underneath a pile of serviettes in the tablecloth drawer for my hidden cigarettes.

Katy's brown eyes accused me. 'If you smoke, you have a ten times bigger chance of dying a lingering death. We had a lecture about it at school. Barry Greenhill decided to cut his down to two a day.'

I stared at her, astonished. Barry Greenhill was all of eleven years old!

'Do his parents know he smokes?' I asked, fascinated against my better judgment. I was treated to a glance of withering scorn, and Katy's eyes rolled ceilingwards.

'I have a friend who smokes a pipe,' Caroline confessed, 'but he thinks that girls who smoke lose all their femininity.'

'Bully for him!' said Bill, coming back into the room rubbing his hands and beaming at us all. 'Well, old Ted really gets things done. All we need now is a spot of the old sunshine, then whacko. . . !'

He clutched an imaginary club and made a practice shot towards the television. 'Fore!' he shouted.

'You sound just like old Ted already,' I said as I went out into the kitchen to start the washing-up.

'Go and help your mother with the dishes. She looks tired,' I heard Bill tell them.

'I wish I could help,' Caroline said regretfully, 'but I have three subjects of homework to do tonight.'

'And I have to go to Susan's to tell her that I won't be at church next Sunday,' said Katy.

It was time, I decided, that I did something to assert myself – something to show them I wasn't just a domestic slave. . . Now, if I *did* write that book and have it published, they'd have to regard me in a somewhat different light.

Their three faces swam before me in a sentimental haze, unrecognizable with fawning respect. I was being interviewed on television by an earnest big-eared young man, with a slight lisp.

'And how did you, a busy housewife and mother, come to write such a brilliant first book?'

I smiled at him. There was not a trace of nervousness in my manner. 'My family co-operated marvellously,' I told him, 'even going their various ways for a few weeks, so that I could write undisturbed. . .'

'They must be very proud of you.'

I smiled modestly. 'I'm very proud of *them*,' I said.

The kitchen door was banged back almost to the plaster; 'Daddy has stopped us twisting because he says it shakes the television tube up,' said Katy.

Back to earth again, I wiped round the sink but afterwards, instead of joining the family circle round the television, I went nobly into the dining-room and sat before one bar of the electric fire, ball-point pen clicked at the ready and a virgin notebook open on my lap.

I stared at the pseudo-logs, memorized their position, drew them on the top of the page, checked for accuracy and proceeded to shade them in. Then I stared out of the window. Maureen Oliver, in the house opposite, was weeding her front garden. She looks about twenty-five, although I've calculated from the age of her eldest boy that she can't be a day under forty.

That week her hair, if it was her hair – she is a wig addict – was the exact colour of the laburnum by her front porch. Her turquoise slacks fitted her bottom like the plastic skin of a well-developed sausage and her scarlet sweater moved up as she worked, showing a good three inches of bare flesh.

Maureen Oliver, tanned as an unpeeled walnut all the year round, is rumoured to sunbathe in the nude on her back porch, and every summer Bill trots out a well-worn joke about wishing he had binoculars that could see round corners.

Before long, as I expected, Roger Byrom came out of the house next door and soon they were carrying on an animated conversation over the privet hedge.

Roger Byrom is a beige-quick-knit-pullover, yellow-spotted-cravat type of man, his eyes the kind books refer to as 'bold', the exact colour of home-made blackcurrant jam. He said something to Maureen and she laughed and put her hand up to her hair, revealing another two inches of midriff. Her husband goes away all week selling spare parts of something mysterious and Roger's wife, a thin shadow of a little woman, would I knew be sitting in their brown-painted house feeling depressed.

Everyone in the avenue is vaguely sorry for her, no one knows quite why, and calls her 'that poor little Mrs Byrom'.

Reluctantly I bent my head over my notebook again and tried to concentrate on Elvira.

For a moment, a fleeting moment, I had her there, imprisoned in my imagination. Dirty, misfit, lying there on her unmade bed . . . I could sense the despair in her heart, actually hear the gentle hiss of the gas-fire as she tried to put an end to it all.

Feverishly, I began to write:

'Last night, a young girl tried to put an end to her life. Somewhere out there in the teeming heart of London's metropolis she lay alone, her unborn baby kicking in her womb . . .'

Or was that last line a bit much?

No, I decided firmly. Realism was what the reading public wanted, and realism was what they were going to get. The whole thing would be a flashback, showing what had led to Elvira's utter despair. And her lover . . . what of him?

Closing my eyes, I could see him clearly. All six feet of demanding virility. Thick, well-cut hair. Hawk-like nose, burning eyes . . . It was only when I got to the yellow-spotted cravat that I realized I had just described Roger Byrom from across the road in meticulous detail!

Caroline put her head round the door. Every inch of her scalp sprouted a coloured roller, bristling with lethal porcupine quills.

She gave me a vague smile, passed palely over to the electric power-point in the corner, plugged in the hair-drier and sat down opposite me, slowly passing the hot air in rhythmic circles round her tortured head.

'Caroline! I'm writing!' I remonstrated, but gently.

Lately, any attempt at honest-to-goodness protestations

could reduce Caroline to a quivering nervous wreck, with crocodile tears pouring down her cheeks. The little ghost of a smile quirked the corners of her mouth again, and her voice over the hum of the drier was all sweet reasonableness.

'My hair only takes about half an hour, Mummy,' she pointed out.

Sweetly, I drew her attention to the fact that she had washed it only three nights previously. At that, Caroline promptly clicked off the drier, bent her head and showed me a portion of her prawn-pink scalp just visible between the rollers.

'Chronic dandruff,' she told me solemnly. 'That was the reason for my face being a mass of spots last week.'

I recollected the three red spots on her chin and gratefully saluted their passing . . .

For the next few minutes, only the soft hum of the drier and the more distant hum of the mower across the road broke the silence. I tried to will myself back into Elivra's little room but, every time I looked up, Caroline smiled a pathetic brave little smile. It was the smile that unnerved me. Lately, Caroline had so rarely smiled.

I smiled back and put my pen down. The very atmosphere breathed understanding, the touching loveliness of a perfect mother–daughter relationship. I really was lucky. Two daughters, two lovely daughters, growing up into young womanhood. A devoted husband.

Then suddenly, the first sentences of my novel reproached me:

'Last night, a young girl tried to put an end to her life . . .'

Like a dash of cold water, the truth hit me. I couldn't write what I wouldn't want my own daughters to read. How could I wallow in kitchen-sink dialogue when my two young daughters were at such an impressionable age? Why, at their age I was reading *Anne of Green Gables* and *The Lady of Shalott*.

Caroline frowned, and patted the middle roller into

position. 'A boy I know thinks I am the image of Elizabeth Taylor,' she told me.

I looked at her round face, grey eyes, guileless expression. 'Well, yes, there is a resemblance, lovey!' I lied.

She resumed the drying process, a small secret smile of satisfaction on her face.

I bit the end of my pen . . . There was always the camouflage of a pseudonym. I practised a few signatures:

Dare to Love, by Dawn Garland. Too fancy! *Dare to Love*, by Marguerite Hanley-Makeson. Select, but a bit to 'uppity' for a kitchen-sink novel. *Dare to Love*, by Liz Brown.

Yes, that was better. Of course, there would be no television interviews, no public signing of copies. Regretfully but firmly, I sacrificed my place in the spotlight . . . I could, however, water Elvira down a bit. She could still be poor and proud, but not pregnant. I could change her lover from a married man to the boy next door. All muscles and masculine dimples, with a job at the library, and captain of the local tennis club.

And that way no one, exactly no one, would want to read it. The trend of fiction was reflecting the anxieties of a troubled and uncertain world. Sighing, I bent my head to write the next torrid phrase.

Katy burst into the room.

'Just because the man on the television says the play isn't suitable for children or nervous people, Daddy says I'm to go to bed.'

I closed my notebook and put it away in the locked part of my desk.

'Daddy's right,' I said firmly and pushed the protesting Katy into the kitchen. I made her take her glass of milk and three biscuits up to her bedroom, knowing that she could make them last the full length of the forbidden play. Her voice spiralled down over the banisters. 'Let me know if anyone gets stabbed.'

I promised, and joined Bill and Caroline round the glow

from the fourteen-inch screen. I sank down into the worn springs of my arm-chair and watched Caroline and Bill following quite unperturbed the saga of a sailor with a wart on his left cheek who shot his mother, framed his hard-working Lancashire father for the murder, chewed gum all the way through the trial and, as the old man tottered to the gallows, mouthed the last lines: 'Seems the old so-and-so had it coming to him. Well, that's the way it goes. . .'

I went thoughtfully into the kitchen to make coffee. The play had, of course, been set in Lancashire. Why was kitchen-sink literature set in Lancashire so much more acceptable than kitchen-sink literature from south of the Wash? I was born in Lancashire and grew up to know and love the people there for their open-hearted sincerity. True, its 'dark, satanic mills' still pointed black fingers to the sky, but the girls dressed up for their Saturday dates, carrying their shoes in grey Marks & Spencer's bags to the dance halls, were as pretty as any of the typists swinging their hips along Oxford Street.

No, I decided firmly as the milk in the pan sneaked up on me and boiled over, my kitchen-sink would be installed well away from the North!

Bill was grumbling at Caroline as I carried the tray in.

'You ought to have been in bed a good hour ago.'

Caroline departed with the expression of a French aristocrat on the way to the guillotine.

Bill filled his pipe, felt with his thumbs for matches in the pockets of his grey cardigan, and I knew that he was all set for a 'husband-and-wife' discussion. He waited until his pipe was drawing nicely, then said apropos of absolutely nothing, 'It isn't that I'm a snob or anything like that, you know.'

I said I knew.

He blew a perfect smoke ring up to the ceiling. 'But I feel that we ought to give Katy every chance of a good education.'

'But wouldn't she get that at Myrtle Lane School?'

Over the stem of his pipe, Bill's eyes reproved me.

'Of course she would, lovey. Of course. But we have two daughters, you know . . . and the fees at the Park School aren't all that impossible. A little pinch here, and a doing without there, and we'll manage.'

I tried not to look as doubtful as I felt.

Bill knew, and I knew, that almost every penny of his salary was spoken for . . . mortgage, superannuation, insurances, HP on the car, and now Katy's school fees. But by the time we went up to bed it was all settled – and I'd promised to ring the headmistress the very next week and arrange an appointment.

Like so many other parents, we were doing the 'best' for our child. Or was it the best? I felt the issue was questionable, but was too tired to argue, too unsure of my facts.

Bill, on the other hand, had made up his mind and was, as usual, sticking to it. He breathed deeply before the open window – the whole subject obviously dismissed from his practical mind.

'Looks like we're in for a lovely hot summer, Liz,' he said. 'Look at that sky. Red enough to delight the hardest-to-please shepherd.'

And, chuckling at what he obviously considered the joke of the year, he got into bed and switched off the light.

But that was the year of the summer that never was. June went by in apologetic drizzle. July continued half-hearted; and August came in with a downpour that turned the golf-links into a paddy-field.

Caroline was due to fly to Paris from London Airport at the end of the second week. She had packed and re-packed her case at least three times. I had forcibly removed from it a large, incredibly heavy bottle of green setting lotion; a giant economy-size hair-lacquer spray; every pair of shoes she possessed and her precious, weighty copy of *Gone with the Wind*.

I had sewn four ten-franc notes into the lining of her blue poplin raincoat – 'Just in case, darling,' I told her – and tried to warn her about the possible dangers of young girls travelling alone in foreign parts. Every fresh instruction was received with raised eyebrows and, 'Honestly, Mummy. Anyone would think I was a child!'

I re-read the kindly letter from Odile's mother. It was written in French and Caroline and I translated it into rather peculiar English. But the fact emerged clearly that Odile's mother was a very warm-hearted person. She was, it seemed, looking forward immensely to having Caroline to stay with them, and would 'take of her the utmost care'. Then she went on to tell me that Marie, her eldest daughter, married at eighteen, was expecting a baby. Her husband was in the Army, stationed abroad, so Marie was living at home. 'So we shall have the full house,' the letter concluded.

I folded the letter up, thoroughly reassured. However, with only four days to go, the blow fell. Katy complained of a headache, sore throat, tender neck muscles, aching eyeballs, vague pains in limbs, nausea and intermittent diarrhoea. But I wasn't too perturbed – until the spots appeared.

She exhibited them proudly to us, sitting on our bed and pulling her pyjama jacket up and her trousers down so that we would get the full effect. I reached for the telephone.

'It can't be measles,' I told the sympathetic ear of Dr Williams' wife. 'She's had them. And chicken-pox. In fact, come to think of it, she's had the lot.'

'Don't you worry, now,' the lilting voice advised me soothingly. 'The doctor will sort it all out. Just keep her warm.'

I promised, and pushed a protesting Katy back to bed. Strangely enough, now the spots had come out all her alarming symptoms seemed to have vanished. Sitting up in bed, she airily demanded breakfast, something to read and the transistor radio.

When the doctor arrived, his diagnosis was swift, brief and

to the point: 'German measles!'

As I'd just spent a hair-raising five minutes with the medical dictionary and come to the terrifying conclusion that smallpox was the only disease her symptoms fitted, this verdict was almost an anti-climax.

'No need to keep her in bed more than a couple of days,' the doctor continued, 'but of course, if you have any friends who may be pregnant don't allow them to visit you for the time being.'

I smiled and promised, ticking off my friends mentally. Not a pregnant one among them, as far as I knew.

And then I saw Enid coming up the path. . .

The Yugoslav sun had done wonders for her. Her skin glowed. She wore tight washed-out jeans, with her feet thrust into sandals our Guides' Jumble Sale would have scorned. The top part of her was enveloped in a voluminous, circus-marquee, blouse affair.

'What a gorgeous maternity smock, Enid,' I said without thinking.

After a startled moment, she laughed so heartily that I pulled her into the house, closed the door, and explained.

'It's just that Katy has German measles, and if it were, you couldn't come in,' I told her crossly.

Enid smoothed the smock down over her hairpin silhouette and groped for a cigarette in the pocket of her jeans.

'But I've come to collect her stuff,' she said. 'Her room's all ready. Oliver found the old sleeping-bag he used on his walking tour of the Andes, or was it the Scottish Highlands, and we just knew that she'd have fun sleeping in that. I remember Royston, when he was small, insisting on sleeping on the billiard table in the loft for a whole summer.'

'I'm sorry,' I said, 'but I'll have to resign myself to ministering to Katy in between chapters, that's all.'

Enid sat astride a kitchen stool and puffed morosely at her cigarette.

'Trouble with you, Liz, is you're too good a mother,' she

said. 'Why can't you be a bit bloody-minded like me now and again? Stop being so noble and self-sacrificing. A child thrives on a bit of neglect. . . I remember we once took Serina all the way to Scotland by train when she was just getting over whooping-cough. Every time she whooped we stuck a caramel in her mouth and, by the time we'd shinned up and down a couple of mountains, her cough was gone. Now you'd have sat at home on a little hard chair by her bedside, reading a Noddy book to her.'

I laughed, but she was absolutely right.

'We'll have a coffee,' I said.

'Good,' said Enid. 'Now your best plan is to push Caroline aboard that plane before she starts anything – although I expect she's already had German measles.'

I stopped spooning instant coffee into two cups.

'No, she hasn't had it, at least I don't think so,' I said slowly.

'And probably never will,' Enid said firmly. 'Oh, for goodness' sake, Liz, just for once in your life take a chance. Trust your luck. You can't disappoint Caroline now, at the last minute. Have a cigarette and relax.'

I took the cigarette and sat down at the kitchen table and stared at Enid across the expanse of red Formica. There was something niggling in my mind – a fact I didn't want to face. . . Some important reason why Caroline couldn't go to France.

Then I remembered. Odile's married sister was in the early stages of pregnancy, the most dangerous time to come into contact with German measles.

'Poor little sausage,' Enid said, referring to Caroline when I told her. 'This will just about break her heart.'

And by the time Dr Williams' advice had been sought and a wildly expensive telephone call put through to Paris, I was very near heartbreak, too.

'They say that you can go next year,' I repeated over and over again to a Caroline half-dazed by disappointment. She looked at me through swollen eyelids.

'I don't want to go next year. I want to go this week.' And that night, for the first time in years, she got her old teddy-bear down from his seat on top of her wardrobe and slept with him snuggled in her arms.

Had we done the right thing, I wondered aloud to Bill? Had I, as usual, been far too conscientious?

I turned my pillow over, banging it into a more welcoming shape. I tried to lie still, but my thoughts whizzed round in my head like a moth caught in a light fitting.

And what would Elvira have done? I hadn't thought about my heroine for a long time. Was there, after all, something to be said for Elvira's way of life? The path of easy virtue might not be smooth, but at least Elvira's problems were all her own – no coping with examination nerves, no wondering how school fees were going to be paid, no lying awake in the dark because a daughter was almost grown up and had to learn how to face up to things.

Why was it, I wondered, that a mother could cope with the most appalling setbacks and take disappointment in her stride, yet when one of her children was hurt and upset her whole world, too, fell to pieces?

Determined to stop thinking about it all, I curled into Bill's broad back and roughed out in my mind the details of Chapter Three.

I saw no reason why my original plan of writing non-stop for a fortnight need be very much curtailed. The whole thing was, I convinced myself, written down, practically word for word, in my mind. There was only the simple job of transferring my thoughts on to paper.

I'd let the housework go. We'd wallow in dust and eat salads. After all, there would only be the three of us.

Bill's voice came muffled from his pillow: 'I think I'll tell old Ted I can't get away with him. Seems all wrong, Liz lovey, leaving you at home with the girls. . .'

I didn't remind him that his original scheme was to leave Liz lovey at home on her own. I told him that on no account must be dream of cancelling his holiday, that it wouldn't be fair to old Ted. He agreed with me immediately and, comforted, fell fast asleep.

The next two days were spent getting him ready. The equipment he assured me was necessary for two weeks' golfing would have seen an expedition through a month's safari in the jungle. Old Ted was picking him up just before dawn, at an hour chosen by most people to die. Shivering in my housecoat, with ill-concealed distaste I watched Bill make short work of a plate of bacon and eggs, washed down by strong coffee.

Old Ted arrived, as breezy as if he'd slept the clock round. He wore a puce-coloured knitted cap with a pompon on top. It clashed abominably with his ginger moustache, and long after they'd gone the smell of whisky and Whiffs lingered like incense in the hall.

'Have a cup of tea, Liz. You look a bit peaky round the nose. And by the time you've drunk it, we'll be half-way up the M1.'

I thanked old Ted for his solicitude, but I was too tired to put the kettle on and took myself and my peaky nose back to bed. I slept for one short hour, then Caroline woke me to ask me if you started German measles with a headache and a stiff neck. I opened my eyes to see her standing palely by my bed, her spotty face ludicrous beneath its inevitable crown of rollers.

As I staggered downstairs to get a drink and the aspirins, I thought about Bill and old Ted eating up the miles on the M1. If I knew them, and I did, they'd be singing slightly bawdy songs at the tops of their voices and behaving generally like overgrown schoolboys.

When I got back upstairs, Caroline had been sick before

she could get out of bed. As I got clean sheets out of the airing-cupboard, I remembered what Enid had said.

'Trouble with you, Liz, is you're too good a mother. Why can't you be a bit bloody-minded now and again?'

Standing there, stripping Caroline's bed in the cold grey light of dawn, even Enid would have been proud of my bloody-mindedness!

Then I decided to get dressed and make a start on what was obviously going to be a 'difficult' day. Dr Williams confirmed that Caroline had indeed got German measles, and said he liked to see young girls getting it over with so nicely.

'Why?' asked Katy.

I explained without mincing my words, because Katy had known the facts of life from about the age of six and probably had more obstetric details at her finger-tips than I had after two difficult confinements. She took a tissue from a box by her pillow, touched her nose with it once and dropped it daintily into her waste-paper basket by the other side of her bed.

'Well, I'm having it for nothing then,' she informed me. 'Because I'm not getting married. Ever!' She eyed me over her breakfast tray, her eyes ringed with black circles and her wrists protruding from the bedjacket with painful thinness.

I made a firm mental note. The next time Dr Williams called, I would have a serious talk with him about those tonsils.

'You don't have to get married if you don't want to, do you, Mummy?' Katy pleaded.

I gave her a swift kiss on a forehead that felt sweetly cool to my touch, and reassured her that there wasn't the slightest obligation.

I left her sniffing and sorry for herself, but before I closed the door saw her stretch out her arm and turn up *Housewives' Choice* to full and resonant strength.

*

In the next room Caroline lay, resigned to the inevitable.

'In a way, I'm terribly glad I've got it, Mummy,' she said. 'You see, I might have started it in Paris and it would have been much worse having it there. And besides, now I know I wasn't *meant* to go.'

Her eyes went opaque with dramatic intensity. 'Do you believe in things happening for a purpose? I mean, somewhere there is some reason why I shouldn't have gone to Paris. . .'

One look at her spotty face was reason enough, but I pretended fascinated interest. She folded her hands across the frilly front of my best nylon nightie and addressed the ceiling.

'Something will happen to prove I'm right. The plane I should have come back on will disappear over the Channel, never to be seen again; or the car that was meeting me at the airport will crash. Or the reason may only be revealed years and years later. . .'

By now I was way out of my depth, so I said wasn't that the window-cleaner knocking at the back door and made my escape.

'Light and nourishing meals,' Dr Williams had said, so I spent all morning concocting a light and nourishing lunch for the girls.

I looked at it and knew that they would hate it. Katy's taste runs to chips and strong tea, and Caroline's to the exotic, like mushrooms and steak done in brandy. They had scorned jellies and blancmanges from about the age of three.

I spent the afternoon running upstairs with milky drinks to keep up their respective strengths. Katy dealt with hers by leaving it on the beside table where it lay cooling and stagnant, a leathery skin forming on its wrinkled surface. Caroline said that what she really fancied was a glass of tonic wine, and I went back downstairs to think up a light and nourishing evening meal.

I was hesitating between coddled eggs and banana custard when there was a timid knock at the front door.

Poor little Mrs Byrom from across the road, looking more depressed than ever, stood holding out at arm's length a white basin, covered with a white table napkin which hung in depressed folds all around it. 'I heard about the girls being so ill, and your husband going off on holiday, so I thought I'd bring this across. Roger is away too. . .'

She stared wistfully into the hall, so I asked her in, took the basin and noted its contents – blancmange of an indefinite shade of beige. I whisked away my writing things and pulled up Bill's armchair for her. She sat there looking depressed, and I could sense her disappointment when I said that the girls would probably be up and about in a day or two.

By the time she'd trailed her scuffed flatties down the path again, I felt as depressed as she did and understood why her husband had taken to yellow cravats and animated conversation over the privet hedge with Maureen Oliver.

It was eight o'clock before I had a chance to get back to my writing and Elvira's dilemma, which was mounting to a climax in Chapter Six. Katy and Caroline had planted the transistor radio on the landing and turned the volume up to full, so that they could both enjoy the programme from Radio Luxembourg.

Against a background of the strong timbre of some female pop-singer's voice, I wrote a page of blush-making dialogue between Elvira and her lover, and was just moving her back to the dinginess of her basement room when the telephone rang. From what sounded like the other side of the world came Bill's voice, thin and almost unrecognizable.

'Everything all right at your end, lovey?' he was asking, and I decided not to tell him about Caroline.

'Everything's fine!' I assured him, and he spent the rest of the three minutes telling me about the splendid journey they'd had; their average speeds, and the way old Ted had talked his way out of a well-deserved parking fine.

The pips caught up with them somewhere up Shap Fell and with a hasty 'good-bye', Bill replaced the receiver. I went back to Chapter Six, but somehow the urge to write had gone.

'I've lost the "flow",' I told Enid when she rang up half an hour later. 'I'm afraid I'm not dedicated enough, somehow. I mean to say, a real writer wouldn't have let a little thing like German measles in the house put her off.'

That night I came to a decision. I would put my notebook away until the girls were well again. Like the good mother Enid said I was, I would devote myself to them.

I slept soundly, and for the rest of the week cooked, cleaned, washed, shopped, pandered to the girls' increasing appetites and got a three-minute weather report from Bill every evening from Scotland. It appeared that up there the sun was shining from cloudless skies and he and old Ted were in fine form.

'How's the writing going?' he would shout into my ear.

And I would shout back, 'Oh, just fine, darling, just fine.'

At the end of the first week I told him that Caroline had been ill, but was much better, and he was silent for a moment, wasting seconds of his precious trunk call. He was going to say something else, I know he was, but the first of the pips went and from sheer force of unbreakable habit he said an immediate good-bye.

The next night he didn't ring, and when I went to bed Caroline had the radio underneath the bedclothes and was listening enraptured to Radio Luxembourg.

Katy lay curled up, her fine hair fanned out on the pillow, her thumb at the ready an inch away from her mouth. She snored gently and I tucked the sheet in round her neck.

I lay awake for a long time. The bed was cold and empty without Bill.

About ten o'clock the next morning I was out in the garden hanging out a load of washing when I heard footsteps on the gravel path by the side of the house – then the unlatching of the back gate and a familiar voice. I turned round, and there was Bill! He was brown, and his eyes were tired and he needed a shave, and I had never loved him so much.

'Breakfast, a bath, and bed. In that order, lovey,' he grinned, and as I prodded three rashers of bacon in the frying-pan he explained.

'I'll never live this down with old Ted. But suddenly – no, not suddenly, gradually – I started to wonder why I was up there in Scotland playing golf, drinking beer in the club-house, listening to old Ted's corny jokes, flirting a little with a girl called Avril. . .'

I held my breath.

'Yesterday morning I woke up and I said to myself, "Bill, you want to go home. So why *don't* you go home? Now. Today. Old Ted won't really miss you. He'll carry on with Avril with much more aplomb than you are capable of. . ."'

He chuckled and as I walked past him to get the butter his fingers closed over my wrist, and he pulled me down on his knee. From upstairs, the radio blared out and the ceiling vibrated as Caroline and Katy got in a twisting session.

'The invalids?' Bill asked, and I nodded.

Then he kissed me, and it wasn't at all the kind of kiss that a thirty-five-year-old wife and mother ought to expect.

'I'm not going to write that book,' I whispered into his stubbly cheek. 'I can't. It's true what Enid says about me; I'm too respectable.' Bill kissed me again, and the way he held me pressed closely against him left me feeling far from respectable!

And all at once it was as though I were seeing things clearly for perhaps the first time.

What was happening to Bill and me wasn't unique. There were hundreds and thousands of married couples just like us – hard up, bringing up their children in a difficult world and still remaining deeply and passionately in love with each other. Their stories were kitchen-sink stories, too. . .

I looked across at mine, then, piled high with unwashed dishes.

'Some day I'll write stories about people like us. About you and me, and Caroline and Katy, and Enid, and old Ted, and poor little Mrs Byrom from across the road. . . And no one, exactly no one, will want to read them.'

'It's Daddy! He's home!' shrieked Caroline and Katy, and hurled themselves downstairs. . .

But not before Bill had said, 'You never know, lovey. You'll never know until you try it. . .'

JOBS FOR THE GIRLS

ENID Beverley is my best friend. She lives in a house at the other side of the Heath and, compared with her, I am totally decadent, a cabbage living in a morass of dull-as-dishwater domesticity.

That morning, in the Blue Lagoon coffee bar, she asked me why I didn't consider taking a part-time job. 'Take you out of yourself, Liz,' she said.

I tried not to look smug. 'Bill doesn't believe in wives working,' I told her.

She gave me a pitying glance from underneath her Cleopatra-style fringe. 'What on earth has it got to do with Bill? Pity, Liz, it would suit you to emerge from your suburban cocoon.'

'It would?'

She nodded into her coffee. 'Bill would come home to a wife who would entertain him with witty anecdotes about her day at the office. Poor dear, he must get tired of hearing about Katy's tonsils and Caroline's school reports.'

In a deeply reflective mood, I said good-bye to her and started the long walk home. . . Was that really all I talked about? Perhaps there was something in Enid's suggestion after all; we could certainly use the extra money.

We had more or less scraped the bottom of the barrel to pay a term's fees in advance at the select little private school by the Park, not forgetting the 'extras' which, according to Katy, *everybody* had. *Everybody* had piano lessons, *everybody* watched television for at least two hours each evening, and *everybody* wore frilly knickers instead of the grey uniform kind.

Caroline, attending the local grammar school and with impending O levels hanging over her head like the sword of Damocles, seemed to ask for money every single week. That day was no exception.

'We have to take half-a-crown for school funds and five shillings if we're going to see *Macbeth*,' she told me the minute she got in from school.

'And how many are going to see *Macbeth*?' I asked, knowing full well what the reply would be.

'*Everybody* is going, of course,' Caroline told me earnestly. 'We are reading it for English Lit., and if I don't go I'll be sure to fail – not that I won't, anyway.'

Upstairs Katy was doing her homework to the twanging of electric guitars relayed at strength from her transistor radio, and Caroline went through into the sitting room to write an essay in French, with the volume control on the record-player turned up as far as it would go. . . My head had begun to throb and I was in the hall, yelling at them to turn down their respective volumes, when Bill's key grated in the lock.

His startled face appeared round the door. 'I could hear you all the way up the avenue, lovey,' he exaggerated, and I put my arms round him and leaned against him, and smelled the familiar smell of tobacco and after-shave lotion.

Bill was home, all was right with my world again. He was all that was gentle, all that was kind and understanding. He would see my point of view about finding myself a job; especially when we had discussed it in a calm and civilized manner.

'I wish we had melon every day,' Katy said, coming into the dining room and measuring Caroline's portion against her own. She had just changed them over when Caroline appeared, the transistor radio hugged to her bosom, as much a part of her as if it were a second skin.

'Why don't we have melon every day?' she asked, sliding sideways on to her chair.

And we could, too, I thought suddenly. Melon could be our

staple diet if I took Enid's advice and went out and found a job.

'I've decided to find a job,' I announced, *apropos* of absolutely nothing.

Three faces looked up from their slices of melon.

Not in front of the children, Bill's expression seemed to say.

Caroline's eyes grew round. 'I'll be able to have a dress allowance then, won't I? Jennifer Drayton has one. Her mother is a middle-aged model; she's quite old, you see, about thirty-eight, but she's a lot slimmer than you are. . .'

'Will you be out when I come home from school, Mummy?' asked Katy, her brown eyes almost opaque with anxiety.

Bill's eyes merely sparkled with anger. 'You know my feelings about mothers who go out to work,' he said, and he went on in the same vein long after the girls had gone their reluctant ways to bed.

'You aren't lonely, you *can't* be; the girls are in just after four o'clock, and you have Enid and the Women's Institute.'

'I'm considering resigning from that,' I said. 'I found out a long time ago that I wasn't the bottling and pickling type, and I put the glove-making class to shame by making a pair of right-hand gloves, if you see what I mean.'

Bill threw back his head and laughed out loud. He was 'jollying me along', which was always a bad sign, and he was beginning to look triumphant already.

'If you were out all day, you wouldn't be able to economize by baking and sewing, and you'd miss having coffee with all your friends.'

'You make me sound like Mrs Dale,' I said crossly, and the very next morning got out the local paper and trailed my finger down the Sits Vac. columns.

I had decided to stick to secretarial work, although I had a secret longing to work in a launderette, or on the sweets counter at Woolworths, or even to be a middle-aged model like Jennifer Drayton's mother. That remark of Caroline's had stung a bit. I may be a stone or so overweight, but I'm not exactly in the cross-over, Paisley-patterned class yet!

I quite realized that it was almost seventeen years since I had taken down as much as a single sentence in shorthand, and as for typing – well I never had got the hang of using all fingers at once. But surely shorthand and typing were like swimming or riding a bicycle; once you knew how, you knew how for ever?

I was hesitating over a firm which required a competent, efficient secretary, and a gentleman who wanted an attractive, genial companion, able to type, when the phone rang.

It was Enid, bursting with her usual enthusiasm at only nine o'clock in the morning. 'Isn't it a simply gorgeous day, in spite of the mist,' she began. 'Makes one feel mellow and fruitful just to look through the window.' There was a breathy pause. 'I was breathing on the hall window, Liz; cancel the mist, it's pure muck as usual! It's still a gorgeous day though, isn't it?'

Smugly I gazed through my sparkling clean window, to where russet leaves hung motionless on still-life trees. The sky was amber-tinted, and there was a smell of wood-smoke in the air, and but for Enid I would have missed it all. . . She probably hadn't done a stroke of work; her black hair would be tousled, her dressing-gown minus most of its buttons. She would have breakfasted with her Oliver on black coffee and cigarettes . . . whereas I had cooked bacon and eggs, washed up, made the beds and dusted the sitting room; but I hadn't found time to look at the sky.

'I was telling Oliver about you needing to be taken out of yourself, and I think I've found you a job,' she was saying. 'I told him how fed up you are with the sordidness of balancing a budget, and he said thank goodness we've never had one to balance. . .' Pause for maniacal shout of laughter, in which I joined, because the idea of Enid balancing a budget was ludicrous.

When they had money, that was when Oliver had sold one of his paintings, or Enid one of her pots, they spent it. When they had no money they did without. It was as simple as that.

'You've to ring this number,' she was saying, trilling it out with the careful enunciation of a well-trained telephonist. 'It's a firm of spare-part manufacturers, I haven't a clue what of, though, darling; Brewster & Sons Ltd. The Managing Director needs a private secretary straight away, there's some sort of flap on. He's a friend of Oliver's, and an awfully good bod.'

Well! I had met many of Oliver's friends, but couldn't have described any one of them as an 'awfully good bod'. Mostly they were the arty-creative type, with beards and lean and hungry expressions. . .

'Ring them straight away, Liz. It's a heaven-sent opportunity, darling.'

As usual, Enid's sheer *joie de vivre* carried me along on a reluctant wave of enthusiasm. 'All right, then,' I promised weakly. 'I'll ring them this morning.'

'Straight away?'

'Well, all right, and thank you for thinking about me.'

'Don't mentch!' said Enid, and the telephone went dead.

Half an hour later I dialled the number with a finger that shook a little, and in two minutes flat had arranged with a nicely-spoken young lady to meet their Mr Simmons at half-past two the next afternoon. Enid answered her telephone so quickly that I could only conclude that she had been sitting on it, waiting for me to ring back.

'It's all been too quick,' I complained. 'I like to talk things over with Bill, and change my mind perhaps, and even call the whole thing off.'

Her exasperated sigh floated down the wires. 'Liz! You must be more go-getting, more adventurous, more reckless, more. . .'

But I didn't want to be told what I should be any more of. 'Bill will be furious! I daren't tell him, he'll think I've gone behind his back.'

'Well, you have, haven't you, and isn't it a nice feeling? I'm always going behind Oliver's back. Goodness, darling, if he knew all the things I've been up to, he'd never sleep easy in his bed again.'

Her suffragette-type voice sank to what I knew she considered to be a conspiratorial whisper, but I was sure that Oliver, painting away upstairs in his bedroom, would be able to hear every syllable. Still, like the coward I am, I promised not to tell Bill until I'd been for the interview.

When, in all innocence, that evening he asked, 'Going anywhere special tomorrow, lovey?' I jumped a mile. It appeared that he wanted me to call in at the bank and cash our first-of-the-month cheque, and I calculated that I could do that easily *en route* for my secret assignment.

'If I don't happen to be in this afternoon, I'll leave the key,' I told the girls as they left for school.

At the gate they turned, and their answering voices were as loud as trumpet fanfares. . . 'On the hook behind the garage door, then,' shouted Katy.

'Why don't you leave the back door unlocked, like you always do?' bellowed Caroline for all the avenue to hear.

I comforted myself that there weren't likely to be many aspiring burglars hanging round our quiet avenue at such an hour on a wet and miserable morning.

And it *was* wet! It rained non-stop, and in spite of all my plans to look the part of the well-dressed secretary, lunch-time found me standing in a queue at the bank enveloped in pale green pearlized plastic, with a hood like a transparent bag tied over my best hat.

Rubbing frantically at the mud splashes on the backs of my nylons, I waited until the clerk had counted out what seemed like a hundred pounds in pennies handed in by the spotty boy from the butcher's.

At last the clerk, who had a bad cold and looked as if life didn't come up to his expectations, counted out the notes, checked them and passed them over to me. . . I decided not to undermine his confidence by re-checking them, smiled at him and put the notes away in a leather wallet in my handbag.

In the train I peeped at them to make sure they were still there, then spent the rest of the journey persuading myself that I wasn't nervous and got out of the train as nervous as a neurotic kitten.

The imposing offices of Brewster & Sons Ltd were a little way down a side-street, and glancing at my watch I saw that I was over half an hour early.

I decided to while away the time by sauntering round the Junior Miss department of a big store, only recently opened. There was a huge notice just inside the door: SWEATERS DRASTICALLY REDUCED FROM TWO GUINEAS TO TWENTY-ONE SHILLINGS. GET-WITH-IT STYLES FOR TEENS AND SUB-TEENS.

That was enough for me!

Peeling off my plastic raincoat, I made for the counter like a homing-pigeon with a one-track mind. . .

Caroline had long wanted a black polo-necked sweater. Apparently *everybody*, apart from her of course, spent their weekends clad from throat to knee-caps in black wool, and there, just out of reach, was a sweater as long and as black as the cloak of Mephistopheles!

A lady with a purple mouth and hat to match seized it, and I watched her in agony until she discarded it in favour of a mustard bolero – short-sleeved version. Triumphantly I snatched the black number and anchoring it underneath my chin, opened my handbag. . .

At least, I intended to open my handbag but someone had opened it for me. Aided and abetted by the swarm of pushing women, they had opened it and taken out the first thing that came to hand.

The leather wallet.

The black sweater dropped from underneath my nerveless chin as I grabbed a passing pin-striped floor-walker. . .

He was quite nice about it all.

'By now they will be well away, madam,' he soothed. 'Why,

at our West End branch as many as twenty customers have their money stolen, on Saturday mornings alone. . . It's very difficult, I agree,' he said kindly as I began to cry.

He snapped his fingers and a stout lady wearing a Red Cross arm-band appeared, carrying a tumbler and a little hard chair. Behind a rack of 'Only slightly soiled' wedding dresses they sat me down. The stout lady patted my shoulder and murmured that nothing was sacred any more, and I slewed my eyes sideways and saw the time by her man-size wristlet watch. A minute after half-past two!

I had let Mr Simmons of Brewster & Sons Ltd down. I had lost a month's housekeeping money and let Bill down. There wasn't even a black sweater to atone for my afternoon's work. . .

I turned to the stout lady who was trying not to look as if she wished I would go. 'I'll have that now,' I said, and taking the tumbler from her drank the water in one grateful gulp.

Then, like a woman half-demented, I pushed my way out into the street again. To be late for work was bad enough, but to be late for an interview showed no sense of what was right and proper at all.

Mr Simmons' office was at the top of a flight of stairs covered in rubberized carpet the exact colour of a nourishing cup of meat extract, and I almost whimpered with relief when a small fair girl stopped reading a magazine for long enough to tell me that Mr Simmons was not yet back from his lunch.

She watched from beneath blue-frosted eyelids as I wiped the rain from my face, the splashes from my nylons and the mud from my shoes.

'You look all right, honest you do,' she said kindly, and at that moment kindness was the one thing that could unnerve me.

'What time do you think Mr Simmons will be back?' I asked as the door opened and a tall, willowy dark girl came in, followed at a discreet distance by a pink and balding little man in horn-rimmed spectacles.

He shot out a hand from a dazzlingly white starched cuff, then smiled at me with two rows of sparkling dentures.

'Mrs Galway? Yes? Sorry I've kept you waiting so long. Come along in. Come along in.'

Leading the way into his inner sanctum, he preceded me over a sea of dark grey carpet, round a desk as big as a billiard table, and motioned me to a chair strategically placed at one corner. From across the expanse of polished mahogany came the elusive but definite aroma of good cigars and brandy. Mr Simmons had the pinkly satisfied air of a man who had dined expensively and well. He had a high flush on his cheekbones, and I was wondering how long it had been since his blood-pressure was checked when he spoke.

'Now, Mrs Galway, let's get down to business. Oliver Beverley tells me you're keen to take up your career again?'

I said yes as a matter of fact I was.

He pushed his horn-rimmed spectacles half-way down the bridge of his nose, a surprisingly small blob of a nose, and gave me a speculative stare.

'I might as well be frank,' he went on and my heart did a downward flip. When anyone prepares to be frank I've found that what follows is usually unpleasant.

'My present secretary, Miss Wilkinson – you saw her just now – has given me every satisfaction. She is quick, efficient, tactful and completely in command of any situation that may arise.'

I sat forward, trying to look all of these things.

'Unfortunately, her mother has collapsed up in Yorkshire, and this necessitates the immediate presence of Miss Wilkinson.'

He obviously thought it most inconsiderate of Miss Wilkinson's mother to collapse, especially in such an outpost of civilization as Yorkshire.

'However, Oliver Beverley spoke of you in the most glowing terms. His wife came on the phone and positively extolled your virtues, Mrs Galway.'

I swallowed hard, and if there is anything in thought

transference, Enid must have felt pretty uncomfortable at that moment. To get her own way Enid would stop at nothing; not even at embroidering the truth.

Mr Simmons was pushing a lined pad towards me.

'Just a short letter to give us an idea of your potentialities. Ready?'

I nodded, gripping my pencil hard as he began to dictate . . . I managed the 'Dear Sir' without the slightest trouble, and 'in reply to yours of the fifth inst.' came with fluent accuracy. Then he went on about firms going into liquidation, and delinquent accounts, and my outlines became wavy and unsure of themselves. By the time he remained yours faithfully I was in a depressed, but not hopeless state. If I was allowed to type it out straight away, my memory would fill in the gaps, but Mr Simmons was taking a printed sheet of paper from a drawer and passing it across to me.

'Just a few calculations to work out first,' he smiled. 'Nothing to worry about, Mrs Galway, nothing to worry about at all. Miss Wilkinson will look after you, and if everything is in order we'll come to what I'm sure will be an amicable arrangement to us both.'

The telephone gave an apologetic burr and he picked it up with one podgy hand and held the other one over the mouthpiece.

'Thank you, Mrs Galway.'

'Thank you, Mr Simmons,' I replied, dropped my gloves, fished underneath the desk for them, forgot the list of calculations, turned back for it, then walked with what I hoped was studied grace from the room.

Mr Simmons was blissfully unaware that the word calculations had struck chill into my very bones.

Calculations in any language mean sums, grand totals, interests, percentages, credits, debits, and figures that must balance . . . and I was born without the ability to grasp the unalterable fact that two and two make four.

I *believed* that they did. As I grew older I became *convinced* that they did, but I never knew *why* they did. And what was worse, I didn't care!

However, in her little office Miss Wilkinson was kindness itself. She made me comfortable at her own desk and tactfully retired to a filing cabinet.

'I can't tell you what it means to me, you coming along like this at such short notice,' she murmured. 'To advertise my job would have meant delay, and I can't let Mr Simmons down – never have – and yet my poor mother is all alone.' She blew her nose into a lace-edged handkerchief, obviously quite overcome.

I told her that everything would work itself out, then immediately felt my choice of words had been inept as I looked down at the first question.

It asked quite reasonably enough what the accumulated interest would be on £5,867 at 9*d*. in the £ over a period of 47 years.

Stunned and disbelieving, I went on to the next question: Quite innocently it asked me to divide 79.567 by 1.348. . .

Soon the wide margins were covered in scribbled hysterical figures, and I began to feel a heart-rending sympathy for Katy, who had failed the arithmetic part of her eleven-plus examination. What hope had she had, descended from a mother like me?

I was in the middle of an unkind question about stocks and shares when I remembered the lost money. It didn't help at all, and I arrived at an answer that even to my impractical mind seemed to be almost a mathematical phenomenon.

Feeling acutely depressed, I pass on to the letter. After one false start, when Miss Wilkinson kindly pointed out that the carbons were the wrong way round, I began to type.

The first part I hammered out as quickly as the staccato spit of a machine-gune, then a dubious-looking outline with very fancy curves brought me to an abrupt halt. I typed a g instead of an e, and rubbed a neat hole in the top sheet and two thick smudge marks on the carbon copies.

'Not to worry,' said Miss Wilkinson, all solicitude, but by the time the letter was finished, every other word was a wild guess and I was worried half-way to death.

The door to Mr Simmons' inner sanctum remained ominously closed after she had taken my papers in, and when at last she came out her eyelids were surprisingly red.

'You've got to go in, Mrs Galway,' she said, obviously trying hard not to blame me too much.

Mr Simmons was equally charming.

'Well, I'm sorry we can't offer you the job as my secretary, Mrs Galway,' he beamed. 'Our shorthand's a bit rusty, and our typing somewhat erratic now, isn't it?'

I said something about it being a long time, and he twinkled at me through his bi-focals. 'However, we do happen to have a nice little vacancy in our accounts section – on a temporary part-time basis, of course.'

I must have turned pale, because he grinned widely, showing a rim of pink plastic gum. 'Everything down there totted up on the old adding machine,' he comforted, then he clasped my hand in a warm spongy palm and promised that further details would be posted on to me.

Miss Wilkinson was at her desk, sobbing quietly to herself, her satin-smooth composure gone.

'He's going to advertise, and it will take days and I can't let him down, I never have, and yet my mother. . .' She took out the lace-edged handkerchief again and screwed it into a sodden ball.

I patted her shoulder and had a sudden mental picture of her mother – grey-haired, crippled, marooned in a stone cottage on the Yorkshire moors, milk bottles piling up on the doorstep – the police breaking in to find her lying there at the foot of the stairs, a pathetic broken lonely old lady. . .

'I'm the one who lets people down, not you,' I said, but she didn't hear me.

'The neighbours are kind to her, but it's not the same as your own flesh and blood,' she was saying, her careful

Kensington accent broadening into Yorkshire dialect, when suddenly I had a flash of inspiration.

'Enid Beverley! She's the one! Fantastic shorthand speeds – she "sat in" at the Nuremberg trials – goodness knows, she's told me about it often enough, and she types fast enough to set her machine on fire. Yes, she's the very one. Here's her telephone number,' I said firmly, and patted her shoulder again. 'Her husband's a friend of Mr Simmons, so you're half-way there already.'

A faint glimmer of hope shone from beneath Miss Wilkinson's swollen eyelids and, altogether forgetting to thank me, she disappeared into her boss's room with the speed of light.

I tied the plastic hood over my hat and went back down the brown stairs into the street. It was still raining, and I missed a train by one minute; then, sitting on a pew-shaped form in a bottle-green waiting-room, I tried to justify what I had done.

Well, at least Enid was all those things Mr Simmons had hoped *I* would be; quick, efficient, hardly tactful, but certainly in complete command of every situation. . .

But feeling unaccountably guilty I followed a homely little body, whose feet were obviously killing her, into an empty compartment.

She was hemmed in by four massive paper bags, all bearing the name of the new store. She was glassy-eyed and replete after what must have been a positive orgy of shopping, and I stared at her suspiciously, wondering if my money had been used to replenish her wardrobe. . . She smiled at me and said wasn't it a dreadful day after the dreadful summer, and what on earth would people do if they had another dreadful winter when their resistances were so low?

Well, she wasn't to know, but my resistance was so low already that even a sudden return of the Ice Age couldn't have lowered it by as much as a single notch. . . So I wasn't in the least surprised to see the bus just disappearing, and to have to walk home through the wet and winding avenues.

The key dangled unused from its nail in the garage, and as I let myself into the empty house I felt as though I had been away for a long, long time.

Hastening on the thawing of frozen fish fingers, I remembered how often my mother had said to me, 'Have a bit "put by" in your own name, Elizabeth; it gives a wife that little bit of confidence to feel she has something to draw on in times of crisis.'

How smugly I had answered her:

'Bill and I have a joint account – we prefer it that way –' and now because of my stupidity, we would have to live for the next few weeks as frugally as dedicated monks on a starvation diet.

Caroline and Katy came up the side path together; Katy with her brown hair curling damply over her forehead, and Caroline with her black hair hanging like wet rope almost to her shoulders.

'I got nought out of ten for French verbs today,' Katy told me proudly.

'I got a detention for not wearing my hat, if you can call it a hat,' Caroline told me sadly. Then, shedding gaberdine raincoats, hats, satchels *en route*, they made straight for the record-player.

To a background of pulsating rhythm, Caroline told me that Jennifer Drayton had got a suède three-quarter-length coat. '*Suède*, not suèdette like mine,' she told me bitterly through a buttered crust.

Katy came and leaned against me as I mixed an apple crumble – a crumble as opposed to a sponge, because in that way I saved one whole egg.

'The girl sitting next to me at school went home today. She had a very, very sore throat.' Pause for full dramatic effect before she led up to the punch line. 'She was breathing on me all day!'

'Well, that doesn't mean to say you'll get it, lovey,' I soothed without much hope.

'You *promised* me I could have my tonsils out, you really promised,' she complained, scraping her bottom teeth along the strips of apple peel and dipping her finger into the sugar.

'I didn't *promise*,' I said. 'I only said that if Dr Williams thought it was necessary, and he doesn't think so. . .'

She sighed as deeply as if I'd dealt her a mortal blow.

'It isn't all that nice having tonsils out,' I went on, but she was throwing a strip of apple peel over her left shoulder, then going down on hands and knees to see what letter it made. Apparently the letter indicated the Christian name of one's future husband, and both girls took this prophecy quite seriously. At one quick glance I could see that it was clearly an S, but she declared it to be a J and retired, well satisfied.

When Bill came in, he put his arms round me.

'All right, lovey?' he asked, and I closed my eyes and leaned against him.

That was the moment I could have told him, sobbing with relief on the broad comfort of his chest, but Katy came in, swallowing with experimental hope. Proudly she told Bill all about her close proximity to the germ-laden one at school, and he listened gravely.

He went on being kind and sweet all evening, showing the patience of a placid plaster saint as he helped Caroline with her algebra. Usually, if he deviates in the slightest from the method used by her maths teacher, she goes into a sort of mild hysterics, accusing him of not understanding, of not trying and even of deliberately leading her astray; then he retaliates by throwing the pencil down in disgust and telling her that any method is the right one if the answer works out correctly.

But that evening he was gentle, he was the veritable soul of understanding, and when Katy said that all she fancied was a glass of fizzy lemonade and an aspirin, preferably two aspirins, he laughed and chased her upstairs to bed.

There was a sort of musical programme on television, and a little man with sad cow-eyes played 'our tune' on his violin.

It's a sugar-sweet melody. Bill and I had heard a street musician play it one wet and windy Saturday as we queued for the cinema on our very first date.

So now and for ever it was 'our tune'.

Grinning sheepishly, Bill knocked out his pipe and came and sat beside me on the settee. With a new and sentimental perception, I noticed the shabbiness of his dark grey office suit – the suit he had decided would 'make-do' for another year . . . I saw the little tired frown between his eyes and I remembered all the plans we had made, the countries we had meant to visit, the mountains we had never climbed. I remembered the look of awe on his face the night Caroline was born, and the way he had hidden his disappointment when Katy, and not the son he had longed for, was put into his arms.

'I love you, Liz,' he whispered into my hair.

But he won't when I've told him about losing the money and about the job he doesn't want me to have, I told a toasted crumpet as I buttered it for his supper. When I've told him he won't love me any more.

'Today,' I began, as he took the first unsuspecting bite, 'today I got a job as a temporary accounts clerk, and on the way to the interview I lost . . . I lost . . . oh, Bill, I lost *all* your money, and if you never speak to me again – well, it won't be any more than I deserve. . .'

He was staring at my face as though he'd forgotten what I looked like.

'Say all that again,' he said, and so I did.

'I'm sorry,' I finished inadequately and then I began to cry. I cried as though all the tears of my life were draining my heart, and Bill began to shake me gently.

'Liz! Liz, lovey, you're afraid of me! Say you're not afraid of me!'

'Oh, but I am,' I choked. 'I'm petrified!'

He held me close to him and gave me his handkerchief. It smelled of gear oil, but I blew hard and snuggled my head into his pullover, and a great and blessed peace seeped into my heart.

Later, much later, when all was said and settled, and he had rung the police and made me retrace verbally every one of my steps from the moment I left the bank, we went to bed.

He was husband, father, lover, all rolled into one, and I drifted into sleep, a soaring violin playing 'our tune' in my ears. . .

The telephone jerked us both awake. Bill sat up in bed, knocked over the lamp and swore. He listened impatiently as Enid's voice screamed excitedly at him, with no regard for the midnight hour, then he passed the telephone over to me.

'Liz!' she shrieked. 'I'm here on my own having the screaming ab-dabs, waiting for Oliver to come home. I've rung twice, but you were engaged.'

'Why, Enid, what's happened? I asked, like the hypocrite I was, but once started Enid would brook no interruption.

The telephone crackled as though it were alive, and I held it a foot or so away from my ear.

'They rang me up from Brewster & Sons this afternoon around three o'clock – I know I was just thinking it was time I made some lunch – and that friend of Oliver's, you know, Mr Simmons – an awfully good bod, at least I used to think so – said that they had allocated you to their accounts section as you didn't want a full-time job. . .'

Silently I congratulated Mr Simmons on his tact.

'And it seems they're in an awful flap. His secretary has an ailing grandmother somewhere ghastly like Stoke or somewhere, and he needs a private secretary absolutely straight away.'

Bill moaned and put the pillow over his head.

'And who do they want for the job, but me! And, oh, Liz, I've promised to go tomorrow morning as ever was. . .'

Even Enid has to pause for breath, and I spoke quickly.

'Well, why the panic then? It's a heaven-sent opportunity. You must be more go-getting, more reckless. . .'

She didn't wait to hear what she should be more of.

'Don't you see, Liz, it's Oliver! He hasn't come in yet, he's gone to Serina's flat and you know they always have to throw him out, and he'll be furious. He *must* be the bread-winner or he goes to pieces – he has a "thing" about wives who go out to work, he doesn't mind me messing about with my pots, but women who go out, well, it *demoralizes* him, it's some sort of complex, all his family have it. I should have said I would have to consult him.'

'But I thought you were always going behind his back?' I said unkindly, and Bill appeared from underneath his pillow for a second to switch off the light.

Enid gave a convulsive shriek. 'Liz! He's here and it's a bad sign, he's overshot the driveway. Pray for me, Liz. 'Bye. . .'

And the telephone went blessedly dead.

'You look like the cat who's eaten up all the cream,' said Bill as I snuggled back into his arms again.

'You aren't like Oliver, you don't mind my little job, do you, love? We need the money now,' I whispered, and he kissed me and said he guessed he knew when he was beaten.

The next morning the idyllic mood persisted, and I actually sang as I poached, scrambled and fried respectively three eggs to suit three capricious appetites. I walked to the gate with Bill and waved lovingly until he turned the corner. Then back in the house I told the girls that they had the best, the kindest, the most understanding daddy in the whole world.

'We have?' said Caroline, dipping a finger of toast delicately into her egg.

'*Sometimes* he's quite nice,' said Katy, painstakingly picking every shred of peel from her marmalade.

I poured another cup of tea, and feeling the most blessed among women, sat down and took a blissful sip.

HAPPY DAYS

ONCE a year, even after my father's cotton mill had closed and he had died of a broken heart, according to my mother, we went to the seaside for two weeks at the end of August.

Our hotel was on the promenade but not, of course, at the centre where the pier with its slot machines and Palace of Variety stretched out to sea. There the 'common' people stayed (not that my mother ever used that actual word), strolling about in their holiday outfits. These consisted of beach pyjamas, flared-legged and flowered, for the women and flannel bags for the men, topped by shirts with their collars turned down neatly over sports jackets.

Our small hotel was called, rather grandly, *The Albany*, and it was run by the Misses Higgins, two spinster sisters who charged a shilling a week extra for the cruet. Most of the work was done by a sixteen-year-old girl called Edna, who wore spectacles with lenses so thick that her eyes had a jellied look about them, as if she had drops put in prior to having them tested.

My mother and I shared a room at the back of the hotel which looked straight out at the red-bricked back of another hotel. The wallpaper was the colour of shortbread biscuits, stippled with currants of gold, and an enormous white chamber-pot was hidden away discreetly in a mahogany cupboard between our beds. The linoleum was brown, the exact colour of a cup of beef tea, a beverage highly thought of in those days. We were in the early nineteen-thirties and the country in general, and Lancashire in particular, was in a state of depression so acute that it would seem we would never recover from it.

That year, the year I fell in love, I was left much to my own devices, my mother having found a friend – a widow like herself, who read Warwick Deeping's novels and played a companionable game of two-handed whist.

The object of my affections was the comedian of a Pierrot Troupe, a tall, sad-faced double-jointed man by the name of Bobby whose pallor was accentuated by the thick layer of white greasepaint he wore. The days of Tommy Handley and his war-time catch-phrases were far off on the untroubled horizon, but Bobby would come to the front of the stage, stand for a moment while all the children in the audience held their breath in delightful anticipation, then call out: 'Hallo kids! Are you there?'

And with a roar that almost blasted the grown-ups in the audience out of their deckchairs, the children would shout: 'Yes, Bobby! Here we are!'

There were five members of the Troupe, all known to us by their Christian names. There was Bert who played the piano, raising his podgy hands at least a foot from the keys before crashing down with such gusto that I was sure the ends of his fingers would be blistered; Arnold, the tenor, who sang *Come into the garden, Maud* and *The Old Rugged Cross* with such feeling that tears would fill my eyes; Betty, the contralto, who always had the words of her songs written down in a notebook so small that it was lost in the folds of her enormous bosom; and Cherry, the comedienne, a dancer with a small smudged face who thought she was as good as Anna Neagle, and better.

And, of course, Bobby. . .

The children were allowed to sit on the sand in front of the deckchairs for twopence and, although I was almost thirteen, I was small for my age and never once paid the full price of sixpence for sitting in a deckchair.

There was another advantage in sitting on the sand, far more important than that of saving money. It meant that I was so close to the stage I could see the doleful expression in Bobby's eyes when he sang songs like *When father painted the parlour* and *Ain't she sweet?* and it came to me that he was, in effect, a modern Rigoletto, laughing when his heart was breaking and going home, I was sure, to a dingy attic to fry cabbage over a spluttering gas-ring. A Noël Coward who had somehow missed his way.

I spent the whole of my holiday spending money on going to the first three performances of the day, the last one at seven o'clock being considered late for me to be out alone.

'One can see the Pierrots from my balcony,' my mother's friend assured her one day when my mother worried aloud about the advisability of my going off alone so often. 'I wouldn't worry about Winifred, dear. She seems very *sharp* for her age.'

I looked at mother's friend and wondered if her hair was real. She wore sloping dresses which dropped from her sloping bosom, and she told mother that she hadn't had a family because she was barren, and I saw the way mother's eyebrows raised themselves as if she were a trifle put out, but not quite enough to mention it, at the use of such a word.

My mother's friend would see me going off to the morning performance and sigh and say 'What it is to be young! Ah, happy days!' Then they would settle down together on the balcony before the sun got round to it and pore over their crossword puzzles, staring out to sea thinking of words which began with 'o' and had nine letters.

On Wednesday and Friday afternoons there was a Talent Competition for the children, when little girls of six or seven wore spotted organdie dresses and sang loud songs about unrequited love into the hand microphone held by Bobby. Little boys recited poems which always seemed to be about shipwrecks and I burned with desire to enter and be in the Grand Finale on Friday evenings.

I didn't have a spotted organdie dress and my hair was too short to be tortured into ringlets, but I did know, off by heart, a whole passage of *The Ancient Mariner* and I saw myself reciting it so beautifully that Bobby was moved to tears.

There would be a London agent sitting in a deckchair in the third row, a fat man with a greasy nose, and he would invite me to appear in a play in the West End, and I would only agree to go on condition that Bobby went with me and was given a part also, and we would live together in delicious sin, and my mother would almost die of shame but come round to our way of thinking when she saw how famous I had become.

I was very hazy about the actual rudiments of sex. There was a 'fast' girl in my form at school who bleached the front piece of her hair yellow and went with the boys from the Grammar School into the pavilion of the Corporation Park. But for what I didn't know. I was very plain with bosoms that made no more than a slight bulge in the front of my box-pleated gym-slip, and no boy had ever kissed me or even looked my way.

Bobby's wink when he spotted me towards the end of our first week, sitting there on the sand, wearing my school panama because Mother had a great mistrust of the sun on the top of the head, meant more to me than the most impassioned love letter or the most ardent of embraces. From then on it seemed as if he sang his songs just for me, and told his jokes with a sideways glance in my direction, as if to say: 'Well, here I am just marking time till I'm asked to play King Lear, but that's life, and as such we must get on with it.'

Day after day the sun shone, burning little angry triangles of sunburn in the women's necks and causing the men to knot their handkerchiefs at the corners and wear them on their heads. I made friends with a girl called Dotty, a twelve-year-old who had won her heat in the Talent Competition singing *Ave Maria*. She seemed to have an inside knowledge about the private lives of the Pierrots which sent me almost wild with jealousy.

'Cherry and Arnold are married,' she told me, her small mouth pursed up into a corrugated rosebud with importance. 'And Bert drinks. That bottle by the other side of the piano has whisky in it, not lemonade. I bet you thought it was lemonade, didn't you?'

'Why should I think it was lemonade?' I asked her haughtily, and waited for her to tell me something about Bobby, but she said she had to go back to her digs for her mother to wet her hair with sugared water and wind it into rags. 'For the Finale,' she said and I swore I would clap her until my hands were blood raw, for the judging was based on the applause of the audience.

My mother told me that, as it was our last evening, we were going to ride on the top of a tram all the way to Southshore and watch the sunset, and when I explained why it was essential that I should be there to clap for Dotty, she lost her patience with me and said that I was far too interested in those tatty Pierrots and she couldn't see what I saw in such third-rate performers.

Her friend smiled at me and said she, for one, could remember what it was to be young, and I decided there and then that she wasn't after all too old to know what life was all about. I even gave her the benefit of the doubt and decided that her hair was real.

I must have looked an incongruous sight with my nose peeling from too much exposure to the sun on account of sitting facing it for long periods three times a day, my little round spectacles slipping down my nose and the pudding basin hat worn straight on my head, but my appearance didn't fit into my scheme of things at all. What I felt inside was what mattered and I had come to a decision.

After the performance was over I was going to go behind the stage, through the little door marked 'Artistes Only' and I was going to speak to Bobby and ask him for his autograph. I

would tell him how much his acting had impressed me, and if
he asked for it (and he simply *had* to ask for it), I would give
him my address which I had written out on a slip of paper and
placed for safety in the pocket of my blazer.

They played to a packed audience that night because all the
children entering for the competition had brought their
families and friends along. Dotty waved to me from a
deckchair, sitting between her mother who was showing
powder-blue directoire knickers, and her father who smoked
a cigarette held neatly between his thumb and forefinger.

'Good luck!' I mouthed over my shoulder, and Dotty
fluttered her hand in front of her chest to show me that she
had what she called the palpitations, and I could have told her
I had them myself, but for a different reason.

There was no curtain, and at the appropriate time Bert
ambled on in his white satin trousers and loose tunic with red
bobbles down the front, and sat down at the piano, flexing his
fingers before going into the opening chorus of *Here we are
again* which I knew off by heart, even to the exaggerated
gestures which went with its rendering.

Bobby came on at the end of the line looking sadder than
ever, and when the music stopped and he came to the front of
the stage, the children in the audience went wild.

'Hallo kids! Are you there?'

'Yes, Bobby! Here we are!' we shouted, but he cupped a
hand over his ear and swore he couldn't hear a sound.

'They've all gone home,' he told the rows of deckchairs.
'I'll try once again.'

And this time the response was so resounding that a small
boy sitting next to me jumped to his feet, overcome by the
excitement of it all, and waved his arms about to indicate his
presence.

'Here we are!' he screamed.

I knew I was really too old to take part in such childish play,
but I couldn't bear to see Bobby standing there, his face
creased into lines of sadness, and so I shouted with the rest.

'Here we are!' I shouted, and what I was really saying was, 'We'll always be here, Bobby. We'll never let you down because we love you so.'

And after the first chorus the Pierrots changed into nautical gear: white flannels, dark blazers and peaked caps for the men, and white skirts and red blazers for the women. Cherry and her husband, Arnold, sang a song about love, but the applause was only thin, and I knew that everyone was waiting for the Talent Competition to begin.

All the children taking part were ushered round the back of the stage by Bobby, and the first act was a piano duet by two sisters who played *The Bluebells of Scotland* not quite in unison. A tall girl with a look of desperation recited '*I must go down to the sea again*' in an elocution kind of voice, and I studied the buckles on my sandals until she had finished. Being recited at always embarrassed me greatly. Then it was Dotty's turn.

Again it was to be *Ave Maria*, and she belted it out with all the verve and confidence which seems to afflict many of today's newly-fledged pop singers, and I wasn't surprised that at the end, when all the competitors were lined up on the stage, she had won.

Bobby presented her with a doll in a box and kissed her on both cheeks, pretending to faint with the emotion of it all. Flushed and triumphant, Dotty acknowledged the applause, each ringlet seeming to dance with excitement, and I discovered that jealousy can be a physical pain – a sort of sharp stabbing beneath the ribs, coupled with a mist before the eyes.

I did, however, find it in my heart to congratulate Dotty when it was all over, but was more than a little gratified by the fact that the doll in the box had a hideous vacant face.

'She won't even take it out of the box,' her mother told me. 'She's like that. Keeps her things nice. Always has.'

'Come on then, Jeanette Macdonald,' said Dotty's father, rolling his eyes skywards. 'There'll be no doing anything with her now.' And off they went, leaving me knowing that now my own moment had come.

I glanced back to the promenade and fancied I saw two figures on the balcony of my mother's friend's room at *The Albany*. There they were, waiting for me to take a ride with them on the top of a tram to see the sun set over Southshore, and I knew that there was no time to lose. . .

Going round the back, I almost bumped into Bert, Arnold and Betty, still wearing their nautical outfits, making their way over the beach to the steps leading to the promenade.

'Heavens, but I could murder a pint,' Arnold was saying and, although my mind was in a turmoil, I couldn't help but think how much at variance his demeanour was with his recent rendering of *Christopher Robin is saying his prayers*. Betty seemed to have diminished; yes, that was the word, now that she had come down off the stage, and Bert, without his piano to thump, looked like the kind of little fat man you could see any day waiting for a bus.

But I wasn't interested in them. It was now or never and, clutching the little piece of paper in my blazer pocket, I knocked on the door marked 'Artistes Only', and hearing no reply, opened it and walked in.

It was a tiny room, hung around with costumes, with a mirror propped up on a table and a screen down the centre with photographs pinned all over it. Bobby was sitting on a chair facing the mirror and lying across his knee was Cherry, her arms round his neck, her white pleated skirt up to her thighs, and her copper-red hair falling back over his arm.

Bobby was kissing her, not the kind of kiss that I had read about in my secret reading of forbidden romantic novels, but a shaking, searching, *greedy* kind of embrace that seemed to go on for ever.

I couldn't move. Something had happened to my legs. I wanted to turn around and run, but my legs didn't belong to me and would not obey the screaming sound that was coming from my mind. And yet I knew that I had made no sound. . .

Then Bobby raised his head and saw me through the spotted, time-worn mirror and his face was terrible with anger.

'What the hell!' he shouted. 'What the hell!'

I won't say that, from then on, my whole life was ruined. With the resilience that the young have, I soon managed to put the shattering episode behind me. I wrote in my diary that night: 'Men are beasts,' and for a long time the shattering scene was imprisoned in my mind, an image that wouldn't go away, which came to haunt me when I least expected it.

What I *will* say is that the sun going down over Southshore that evening filled me with such consternation that I burst into tears, to the astonishment of mother and her friend.

'I never *dreamed* she was so sensitive,' I heard my mother murmur, and her friend patted my arm.

'What it is to be young,' she said, then she, too, patted my arm. 'Ah, happy days!' she sighed.

THE PARTY

SYMPATHY, when meted out to a drooping, chip-on-the-shoulder teenager, is often unwarranted or downright unnecessary.

Not that my sixteen-year-old twins have mere chips on their young shoulders; they have logs, whole forests of mighty trees.

All that beautiful early summer they had dragged themselves wearily to school each morning. Napoleon went into his long, bitter exile with more enthusiasm than they caught their early bus. According to them, the GCE that year was the hardest in the whole history of human endeavour.

'Don't expect me to pass in a single subject, Mummy,' said Debbie, skimming some imaginary tea-leaves from the surface of her cup.

'Or me,' said Jane, slicing the top from her egg with the precision of an Indian brave scalping his first victim.

'It wouldn't be so bad if we were going abroad when we break up,' said Debbie. 'Sharon's going to America, and Linda's going on a Mediterranean cruise.'

'Well, we're going to the Isle of Wight,' I said cheerfully.

They looked at each other briefly, then raised their eyes as if searching for enough patience to tide them over my next remark.

'Just think how we feel,' Debbie went on, with Jane nodding agreement, 'having to tell our friends at school that we're having a measly ten days in the Isle of Wight.'

'And in a caravan,' Jane said mournfully into her egg.

'Sharon is flying to America for six weeks,' Debbie said.

'Linda's got an evening dress, strapless, with five petticoats to wear on the cruise,' Jane said.

'Well,' I said cheerfully, 'a strapless gown wouldn't be much use in a caravan, would it? And there isn't room for more than one petticoat each. Daddy says it's so small we've got to start practising breathing in and out together.'

They scraped their chairs back from the table and stared at me with huge reproachful eyes of an identical blue.

I knew to a syllable what was coming.

'You just don't understand,' they said together.

I followed them into the hall. I was beginning to feel acutely depressed, and the day had hardly begun.

They each took a navy-blue beret from the cupboard and squashed it into a fashionable shape being worn at all the best schools that year. Pushing and jostling at the mirror, they puffed their hair out into the required shape underneath.

Between them they slept in twenty-four lethal looking plastic rollers, made even more diabolical by the addition of small porcupine bristles. Most nights, when I watched them lay their tortured heads gingerly on their pillows, I would say 'It must be agony sleeping in those.'

And most nights Debbie would say, 'You don't understand the first thing about hair fashions, Mummy. Honestly, just because you wore ringlets at our age. Times have changed, you know.'

'Ringlets indeed,' I'd say. 'I'd have you know I had the niftiest "page-boy" you ever saw when I was your age.'

'Page-boy!' they'd shriek, and the beds would shake with their helpless giggles.

I watched them cram their books into already bulging satchels and check their purses for dinner money and bus fares. Already the sun was climbing high in the sky, and through the open door the air seemed to shimmer with the promise of the heat to come.

It was hard to be going to school on a day like this, in a blazer made of hot navy serge, and it was all wrong to be cramming for exams, when the sky was a cornflower blue and the birds sang their hearts out in the branches of the leafy trees outside.

I looked at their pale, morning faces, greasily innocent of powder, and it was then that my sympathy began ever so gently to run away with me.

'Would you like a party?' I said. 'The week you break up perhaps, to celebrate the ending of exams.'

They looked at me as if I'd asked them to have a double gin each before they left for school.

'It isn't our birthday until next January,' Debbie said cautiously.

'I know,' I said.

'What kind of party?' they asked together.

Recklessly, I said, 'Oh, you know, a grown-up mixed party, with records and so on.'

Jane looked at her watch and yelped, and started to walk backwards down the path. Debbie did the same.

'You mean we can ask *boys*?' they said incredulously.

I nodded. 'You know some, don't you?' I smiled.

Again the well-known furtive exchange of glances.

'We know hundreds,' said Jane.

I laughed. 'Well, three or four will be enough to be going on with, but we'll talk about it tonight. Hurry, or you'll miss your bus.'

Wearing expressions of stunned incredulity, they turned and gave me their usual half-hearted waves. They trailed wearily out through the gate and disappeared.

I sighed and looked at the lilac bush by the gate for consolation. It hung low, weighted with heavy mauve blossoms. I couldn't resist the impulse to pick an armful, and as I stood on tiptoe to reach the highest branch I saw the twins turning the corner.

They were chattering and laughing excitedly to each other. Debbie was tossing her satchel up in the air and catching it as she ran. The bus lumbered round the corner, and as I watched they hurled themselves aboard.

I walked back into the house, arms full of the sweet-smelling lilac, shaking my head in bewilderment. I lit a cigarette and poured out my fourth cup of tea. As I took a comforting sip, I felt the first faint stirring of apprehension.

However, being the eternal optimist, I planned all day. By the time the twins came home from school I had every single detail of the party neatly tabulated in my mind.

Section one was who to ask.

'I thought about four girls and four boys,' I said innocently as I watched them prop their homework up on the kitchen table and take a 'snack' each from the larder to sustain them.

Debbie took a scornful bite from a huge wedge of fruit cake. 'We've already asked ten girls,' she said.

'Well, you can just un-ask them,' I said. 'This isn't the Locarno Ballroom, you know.'

'When Sharon has a party her parents hire a special room,' Jane said, looking at me reproachfully over a buttered crust.

'I expect you'll ask some of the boys from the youth club?' I ventured.

Almost hysterical laughter greeted that remark.

'We'd rather die than ask any of that lot,' Debbie said at last, when she had recovered enough to speak.

I decided to make myself a nice cup of tea and move quickly on to section two.

Section two was food for the party.

Casting my mind back happily to the days when I had set out the dining-room table with egg and cress sandwiches, red and yellow jellies in individual glasses, biscuits with names piped in icing across their middles, paper serviettes made like rosettes with sweets nestling in each petal; and Debbie and Jane resplendent in frilly party frocks, presiding over all, I started off.

But halfway through my recitation, Debbie stopped me.

'You aren't serious, Mummy, are you?' she said, her

eyebrows disappearing into the fringe she swore she hadn't tried to cut.

'Jellies,' Jane said. 'Egg and cress sandwiches. Oh, really Mummy, you don't understand.'

I poured out my cup of tea and sat down. 'Well, what do you suggest?' I countered, remembering the talk given at the Townswomen's Guild by a lady in a purple hat. She'd said that the opinions of adolescents should be respected.

Debbie produced a bruised apple from her satchel and bit into it thoughtfully.

'Wipe it first, Debbie,' I found myself saying automatically.

They then went into a delighted discussion about tiny sandwiches spread with anchovy paste, black and green olives, pickled gherkins, cheese and crisps, and sausages by the thousand speared on to little cocktail sticks.

Looking at their shining eyes and carried away by their sparkling exuberance, I couldn't damp their enthusiasm. So 'We'll see,' I said, resorting to cowardly evasion.

Section three was games for the party.

Now, I am firmly convinced that Bill is a second Russ Conway; he has the same foot-tapping style. 'I thought perhaps we could start off by a session round the piano,' I said.

There was a small, strained silence. 'You're not serious, are you, Mummy?' I was asked for the second time.

They couldn't have looked more shocked if I'd said that I'd do a striptease while Bill accompanied me on the mouth organ.

I hurriedly moved on to section four: the date of the party. That was fixed without the slightest preamble for the following Saturday. They convinced me that it was better to celebrate the exams before they started, as they would be too depressed afterwards.

Pouring myself another cup of tea, I drank it quickly, then went through into the dining-room to lay the table.

Section five, under the heading of 'What shall we put on?'

was well under way when I got back to the kitchen. Debbie looked up at me with indignation sparkling in her blue eyes.

'Pink is far too girlish for us now,' she said firmly.

'You thought those dresses were beautiful at Christmas,' I said.

She stared mournfully at her 'French into English' dictionary. 'That was ages and ages ago,' she said, 'and fashions change, you know.' Or did you know? her expression seemed to say.

'Sharon says that people who wear pink have no personality,' sighed Jane.

I began to scrape the potatoes, trying to hide a smile. They were both in such deadly earnest. 'And what kind of dress does Miss Personality herself wear?' I inquired.

Both girls spoke at once, their faces rapt and their eyes clouded with emotion. 'Black,' they said, 'with a deep plunge at the back, and her shoes are red, with four-inch stiletto heels.'

'No girls of mine,' I said primly, 'are wearing black at sixteen, or stiletto heels. They'll distort your spine, or something.'

'Sharon's spine isn't a bit distorted,' Jane said.

'She has a gorgeous figure,' Debbie said dreamily. 'She has a twenty-one inch waist.'

'And a thirty-seven-inch bust,' Jane whispered.

'I expect she's one of those you've asked to the party?' I said, without too much hope.

'She was the very first one to accept,' Debbie said proudly. 'And she'd like to stay the night, if it's all right with you, Mummy, because her parents are having a cocktail party the same evening and the car can't be spared.'

'You've no idea how rich she is,' Jane breathed.

'I'm getting the idea,' I said, 'and I'm truly honoured that she will share our humble abode.'

Debbie jumped up and gave me a bearlike hug. 'We'll get her room ready, Mummy,' she said. 'You'll be really surprised when you see how nice we can make it look.'

I was, too. Especially when I saw they'd put the pink scalloped sheets on the bed. Those sheets were a wedding present, and were made long before drip-dry materials came in. I only use them on very special occasions.

It wasn't that they were so terribly precious, but they were the very devil to iron, each scallop curling round the iron and refusing to co-operate.

Jane had placed a huge bunch of lilac in a jug on the dressing table. I knew it would be dead before Saturday, but I said nothing. Three blood-red peonies bloomed on the bedside table, and the room began to resemble a shrine.

'May we put your silver hairbrush out?' Debbie asked.

'May we hang your new flocked nylon dressing-gown behind the door?' Jane pleaded.

The night before the party the house was filled with the warm, spicy smell of baking. The twins are grand little cooks, and spare nothing in the way of ingredients. Not for them the economical cake with one egg and a substitute spoonful of vinegar. Not for them the scones made with one ounce of margarine. All their recipes contained half a dozen eggs and best butter, and their walnut cakes were perfectly bristling with walnuts.

Bill was watching a sports programme on television, but every now and again he'd walk into the kitchen and sample whatever was laid out neatly on the cooling tray.

'Daddy,' they wailed. 'It's not fair.'

'Wish I were coming to the party,' Bill said. I sniffed. A committee meeting had unexpectedly and conveniently cropped up at the golf club, and the girls almost hugged themselves with relief when he told them about it. I'd a feeling they would like to get me out of the house, too, but I stood my ground. Whatever deep plots were being hatched for Saturday night, I was going to be there to see them through.

*

It had been a week of whispering in corners and the telephone was hot from constant handling. There was much giggling and hissing of instructions as each fresh number was tried.

All the boys were unknown quantities to me, and when I asked if that nice boy from round the corner might be coming, Jane's eyebrows disappeared into the blonde fringe that, like Debbie's, had miraculously made its appearance overnight.

I gave up and went to add another pound of sausages to my shopping list.

The first batch of sausages went under the grill about the time the twins disappeared into the bathroom the following afternoon. They had allowed two hours in which to bathe and deodorize themselves and coax their hair into the style currently in favour. Highly scented steam began to drift in clouds over the banisters.

I was spearing my forty-third sausage with its stick when the doorbell rang. I hurried down the hall and, opening the door, came face to face with five feet seven of teenage sophistication.

'Sharon!' I said, holding out my hand, then hiding it quickly behind my back. Sausage grease and this vision definitely did not match. She wore a cream silk duster coat and her dark hair was pulled back into a perfectly symmetrical French pleat. Her eyebrows were so beautifully groomed I thought she must have used a slide rule to get them that way.

As she graciously accepted my invitation to enter I saw that Jane had been right. Her spine was most definitely not distorted and she clicked along on stiletto heels like a veteran.

'Sharon's here,' I carolled upstairs. I began to be glad my pink scalloped shets were on the spare room bed.

'Why, hallo, Sharon,' the twins called out, as if she was the last person on earth they expected to see. I noticed their accents were as false as my own.

I crept back to the sausages, but the doorbell rang again

and I let in three girls with bouffant hair-dos exactly like Jane's and Debbie's to the very last hair.

The dress of the smallest one stuck out so much that she had to come through the door sideways.

I decided that must be Linda, wearing all of her five petticoats at once.

Soon the sitting room was filled with gay, excited twittering, until the boys began to arrive and then a heavy embarrassed silence took its place.

The first two masculine arrivals had thick, well-oiled hair and spotty pallid complexions. They answered to Jimmy and Pete, and slouched across to the window seat where they sat glaring out into the garden. They talked to each other in furtive whispers out of the sides of their mouths, and occasionally shot terrified glances at the girls.

Sharon was swaying glassy-eyed to a Cliff Richard record, and Debbie and Jane were trying to imitate her, so I went through into the kitchen and began to set out the sandwiches.

The doorbell kept on ringing, and I caught a glimpse of two youths in well-worn tight jeans and orange pullovers, being greeted hilariously.

I thought my eyes must be deceiving me when I saw one with a beard and a velvet waistcoat disappear into the sitting room, but they weren't.

'Who's that one?' I whispered to Jane.

'That's Mortimer,' she said. 'He's madly in love with Sharon, and he writes poetry about her.'

'Does she love him back?' I whispered, fascinated.

Jane, hidden discreetly behind the punchbowl, pointed to the far corner.

'No, that's the one she loves.'

I looked across and saw a boy lounging against the wall, a cigarette in his hand. His dark, wavy hair fell in a neglected way over his forehead, and he looked as dissipated at seventeen as some men look at forty.

'Do you and Debbie know him well?' I asked worriedly.

'Oh, no, we don't know any of these boys, really,' said Jane.

'Well, why on earth. . ?' I began, then stopped as a boy in a black leather jerkin came up to ask if Jane had any traditional jazz records. He had a crew-cut and a squashed-in evil face with little piggy eyes.

I went back rather unhappily into the kitchen. Bill found me there, sitting alone staring at the boiler, while the house vibrated to the beat of rock 'n' roll.

'There's a gang of boy beatniks in the dining room,' he said, with a grin. 'The girls are in the other room listening with rapture to Adam Faith. It's a queer set-up for a party, isn't it?'

'I know it,' I said miserably.

I served the girls their supper in the sitting room, where they were thumbing through our snapshot album.

'You used to be quite pretty really, Mrs Hampton,' Sharon said, spearing a sausage daintily on its little stick.

'Thank you, Sharon,' I said sweetly, and went through with the second lot of food into the dining room. The boy beatniks fell on it like starving wolves.

The girls were dancing together with solemn and dedicated faces, so I said to the boys, 'Why don't you go and dance instead of lying on the floor?'

'Catch us,' the one in the black leather jerkin said.

'They're doing all right without us,' a furtive oily-haired one said.

'But it's a party,' I said to Bill over the washing-up. 'They're here to mix and play games, and did you ever see such clothes?'

Bill began to laugh.

'What's funny?' I asked him.

'I was thinking of myself at sixteen,' he said, wiping the same plate for the third time. 'I wore my school scarf wound round and round my neck, summer and winter, and held an empty pipe clenched between my teeth. I think I wore large horn-rimmed glasses, too, just to add to the effect.'

I put the dishcloth down and stared dreamily at the soap-dish.

'At sixteen I wore long woollen stockings at school, and a hat like a pudding basin. At the weekends I curled my hair at the sides with the curling tongs. I had a "pash" on Nat Gonella, and at weekends I would paint my nails purple. My girlfriend adored Bing, and we'd lie on the floor in the dark listening to his records.'

'See what I mean?' Bill said, and put his arm round me. 'We were just crazy mixed-up teenagers, too.'

He was kissing me gently when the dissipated one appeared in the doorway. He leaned against the wall and leered at us through heavy eyelids. I pushed Bill away and blushed.

'Yes, dear?' I said. 'Did you want another glass of lemonade?'

He flicked imaginary ash off his cigarette, which was still unlit.

'No, thanks,' he said. 'Mind if we push off now? We have to be in by ten o'clock. Our mothers worry. They worry all the time, you know.' He shook his head sadly.

'Well, of course, if you have to go,' I said uncertainly, and they trailed down the hall in a shifty-eyed, sad little troop.

The girls condescended to peep out of the sitting room and wave goodbye. Then they got to the real business of the evening.

Jane produced a large fat bottle of sticky green setting lotion, and Sharon proceeded to give them all fresh hair-dos. The television was switched on for company and they all sat with their backs to it, holding mirrors up and admiring their changed appearances.

When, an hour later, cars began to arrive, each and every one of them disappeared into the darkness sporting a French pleat, exactly like Sharon's to the very last hair.

Debbie and Jane vaguely offered to clear up, but I looked at their faces, pinched into lines of fatigue, and sent them off upstairs.

Sharon looked as fresh as a daisy and thanked me prettily for a charming evening.

'Not at all,' I replied, in the silly accent her superior attitude made me automatically adopt. 'I hope you sleep well.' Her poise for a sixteen-year-old was shattering in its effect, and I breathed a sigh of relief when she was safely tucked in between my best pink scalloped sheets.

Bill was nearly asleep and I was climbing wearily into bed when the twins came in. They perched on the end of my bed, long legs sprouting from their baby-doll pyjamas.

They were shining clean, freshly deodorized for the night, with imaginary spots on the rounded cheeks lavishly coated with strong-smelling ointment.

'Why don't you have your hair tinted, Mummy?' Jane asked with a yawn. 'You'd look much younger if you did.'

'Why do you wear that awful bed-jacket?' Debbie asked. 'It makes you look like Red Riding Hood's grandmother.'

I laid my head wearily on the pillow and closed my eyes. 'Good night,' I said in a tone of voice implying dismissal.

Instantly they were on their feet. Debbie tucking me in with strenuous precision and Jane puffing up my already puffed-up pillow. I heard the click of the electric light switch and then the darkness lay like velvet against my closed eyelids.

Young arms were tight round my neck for a fleeting moment and wet kisses were softly imprinted on my cheek.

'Thank you for a smashing party,' said Jane.

'Sharon says she wishes her mother was just like you,' Debbie confided.

Then all was quiet as their bare feet padded away.

'Well, was it worth all the hard work, love?' Bill said sleepily into his pillow.

'Worth every precious minute of it,' I said happily into mine.

WAVE AT AN EMPTY WINDOW

ONE sunny morning when I come back from shopping to find that we have been burgled, the first person I telephone – after dialling a shaky 999 – is Beth.

Beth is the friend of my bosom, and has been ever since we were at school together. It must be a classic case of opposites attracting, because everything I am not, Beth *is* – a fact she points out to me with irritating regularity.

I know she is having a few days off work with her sinuses, and when I tell her the news she immediately orders me, rather nasally, not to touch a thing.

'I'll be straight over, darling,' she says.

To tell the truth, I do not feel like touching a thing. I am, I suppose, in a mild state of shock, and so after the police have gone I pour myself a naughty eleven o'clock gin and tonic and sip it as I sit on my bed and stare around at the chaos.

Every drawer has been pulled out and overturned. All the most intimate pieces of my underwear are scattered with abandon, and all the little boxes containing a lifetime's acquisition of jewellery are lying opened and empty, their velvet linings pathetically bare.

'Right!' says Beth, arriving pronto and looking, in spite of her sinuses, as if she has spent three hours getting ready. She has just returned from a fortnight in the Bahamas, topping up her tan with her friend of the moment, a man with a traumatic divorce behind him and a hairy chest which he embellishes with a sliver medallion. Beth's own divorce is ten years old, but she still talks about it and sometimes regrets it, I suspect.

'The first thing is to put everything back,' she tells me. 'So I'll set to in here.'

And set to she does after I have pointed out the three hard objects the police have told me to leave untouched until the arrival of the CID and the fingerprint expert.

'Do you *really* take a size 38 bra, Maggie?' Beth asks me as she dangles a rather tatty one from her fingertips. 'And a C cup too! Now that is surprising when one considers what a narrow back you have.'

'I'm a freak,' I tell her, but she isn't listening. Beth has discovered Don's Y-fronted underpants and is busy telling me what irreparable damage he can do to a certain part of his person if he insists on wearing them.

'They could render him sterile, darling!'

'At my age I don't want any more children,' I tell her, and am given a scathing look from Beth's oyster-grey eyelids. As we were in the same form together my age is Beth's age, and she does not like to be reminded of this.

We move into Don's study, and the disorder there is indescribable. Papers, files, books, even his visiting cards are scattered over the carpet like wanton confetti. Beth gets down on to her exquisitely trousered knees.

'I hope you have a comprehensive insurance, darling,' she murmurs, holding up what looks suspiciously like our Last Will and Testament. She skims through it with interest, then asks me have I telephoned Don as yet?

I shake my head. 'He's up in Scotland on business for three days, but I'll tell him tonight when he rings. There's no need for him to rush back. There's nothing he can do.'

The doorbell rings before she can answer back and, jumping up, Beth lets in one tall dark detective and a girl with long fair hair who reminds me of the young Mia Farrow in *Peyton Place*.

Beth ignores the girl and concentrates on the man, taking him straight through to the sitting room to show him the broken window.

'He cut himself on the glass as he climbed through. See, there are blood stains on this cushion cover. Shall I whip it off so you can take it away to be analysed? To ascertain his blood group,' she explains.

When we troop through into the kitchen, she pounces on my solitary pork chop, taken from the fridge and left on the dresser.

'They must have been disturbed. They always take the *meat*,' she tells the CID man and thrusts the chop into his hand. 'See, it's still cold, so that's another clue for you. Maybe you can deduce from that the exact time of entry. From its state of thawness,' she goes on. 'They always take the meat to throw at any dog that might appear,' she added.

The tall young man is obviously bewildered by Beth's enthusiasm, and he leaves us to go back into the sitting room where he stares at the empty place where the television used to be.

'There must have been two of them,' says Beth, coming up behind. 'Marching straight down the front path as if they were little men come to repair the television. It goes on all the time.'

By sheer persistence the policeman manages to take down a few details from me and, giving me a number to ring in case of doubt, leaves with Mia Farrow, telling me that the fingerprint man will be along at any minute.

'Double-glazing would have prevented this happening,' Beth tells me as we pick up sheets and pillow-cases and stuff them back into the rifled airing cupboard. 'Did that never occur to you, Maggie?'

'It occurred, but now that both girls are coming up to university entrance we thought. . . .'

But Beth does not wait to hear what we thought.

'*Priorities*, darling,' she tells me, and then she says she is going to ring a little man who will come round and replace the broken window within the hour.

As Beth knows more 'little men' than I have had hot dinners, I do not doubt this, and sure enough a man in tight jeans and a grubby tee-shirt arrives on the scene and tacks up a temporary filling in the space where the window used to be.

Beth flirts with him from the inside, then makes him a pot of tea and hands me my cup laced with sugar.

'For your nerves,' she says, and I notice that as usual Beth is drinking hers with a slice of lemon and no milk. She has still kept the figure of a teenager and I note this without rancour, having come to terms a long time ago with the fact that I never had a teenage figure anyhow, and it's far too late to acquire one now.

'Where are the girls?' she asks, and when I tell her they are spending a week of their school holidays with their grandmother in Devon, Beth says she is glad she has her overnight case in the car outside.

'But I'll be perfectly all right,' I try to say, but she is adamant.

'We can share the chop,' she says, and when the fingerprint man arrives she holds out her immacuately manicured hands to him.

'So you can *eliminate*, darling,' she tells him. He blushes and says that will not be necessary as his preliminary examination has shown that the intruders wore gloves.

'That little man is sex-starved,' Beth tells me when he has gone on his bewildered way. 'There was a bulging sadness in his expression.'

'Perhaps he was wearing Y-fronts?' I suggest with a laugh, and she tells me to go ahead and have hysterics if I feel like it, that my calmness isn't healthy.

I put Beth in our elder daughter's room, and she wafts in to say good night to me on a wave of Chanel Number Five.

'Darling, why do you have such an obsession for pastel-shaded nighties when your own colouring needs a warming boost?' she wants to know. 'Your trouble is you are too passive, Maggie.' She runs her fingers through her shaggy perm. 'You should be having the screaming ab-dabs at what's happened, and as far as I can see you've already quietly accepted it. If my things had gone I'd go berserk, especially at the thought of nameless faces and groping hands in my flat.'

'*My* blessings come on two legs,' I remind her, then at once am ashamed. In spite of her self-satisfaction Beth is a lonely woman, always searching for the tenderness and love that I wish to God was every woman's right. I am thinking of something I can say to wipe out my tactless remark when she catches sight of my soap-clean shiny face.

'Cleanse, tone and *nourish*, Maggie. 'You'll regret it some day. . .'

Off to bed she goes, and I lie down and think about my Lancashire grandma who washed her face with the same soap she used to wash the kitchen floor, and died at seventy-eight with an unwrinkled complexion of roses and cream. Then I worry for a while about Don who works too hard, and I remember how defeated his voice had sounded when I told him what had happened. I ponder for a while on the faceless strangers stalking around my house on a sunny Tuesday morning, and I wonder will they feel just a teeny pang of regret when they tear my mother's photograph out of my Victorian locket before they sell it to a fence? This does not bear thinking about, so I switch to the nice kind fingerprint man and wonder why Beth thought he was sex-starved when I hadn't noticed anything unusual about him at all?

The next morning Beth announces that she will stay another night. We go shopping, and she makes me stop at the end of the path and turn and wave to a mythical person we have supposedly left behind us in the house.

'Always do that, Maggie. They lurk about waiting for housewives to go out,' she whispers, and I stare at a small man standing at the bus-stop and see him turn into a latterday Al Capone before my very eyes.

We grate our vegetables raw instead of cooking them for our supper, and Beth puts me on a diet to cleanse my system. I go to bed feeling inwardly spotless, but outwardly so hungry she catches me buttering a cream cracker as midnight strikes.

When Don arrives home from Scotland she has gone, and I

tell him how kind she has been, but he says he wishes she had left his study untouched as he has just found a note for the milkman filed with his income tax returns.

It is almost two months before I see Beth again. I answer my telephone one day and her voice comes over in a wail of anguished despair. I say I will go over straight away.

Beth's burglars have been more thorough than mine. Everything portable and valuable has been taken, and amid the chaos she strides about, actually wringing her hands as she mourns the loss of her jewellery.

There is nothing I can say, because what Beth has lost is all that she in all honesty possesses: material things and memories. The engagement ring her husband gave her many years ago, and the string of pearls he gave her the year before he left to live with someone else.

I try to comfort her, but it is impossible and I wish I could put my arms around her and rock her as I do the girls when awful things happen to them.

So I drive home at last, and if I say I am counting my blessings and aching with pity for Beth, it will sound complacent, so I shall not say it.

Instead I will prove what a nasty side there is to my own nature, by admitting that when Don and I are in bed I tell him with glee that while helping to put things away I have spotted the fact that Beth wears a size 34 bra, with so much padding in it there would be enough foam rubber to stuff a sofa cushion.

'Friends of the bosom, indeed,' says Don, and falls asleep with a smile on his face. . .

SAM

OUR BABY, Sam, otherwise Samuel Adam Mortimer – the last two names given in respect of two doting grandfathers who, because I am thirty-two years old and have been married ten years, had given up hope of ever being grandfathers – is the most beautiful, the most wonderful baby ever born.

I know in my heart that this isn't strictly true, but both my husband Kim and myself believe implicitly that it is so.

Often when we unwrap him to change his nappy, or bath him, we gaze at his perfect little body and his pot-belly and his firm bandy legs, and we ask each other – what have we done to deserve a baby like this? We who are quite ordinary, myself too tall and thin and Kim of average height, his brown hair already receding at the temples.

'And they say that miracles don't happen,' Kim says, and we tickle Sam and touch his wobbly chin, and swear that he recognizes us and smiles.

The truth is that Sam doesn't smile all that often. The truth is that Sam, in spite of his beauty, is no according-to-the-book baby.

He cries during the night when he should be asleep, and sleeps during the day when he could be awake; and at the clinic they say he is a windy baby, prone to colic, and it may take some time before we have found the right formula of milk for him.

So we are discovering that sleep isn't all that necessary, and there is even something to be said for being wakened up when the rest of the world is fast asleep.

Sam, at the moment, is suffering from what the kindly ladies at the clinic tell me is a heat rash, or a milk rash –

apparently it is of such little consequence that the definition isn't all that important. But his little red face is undeniably spotty, covered in angry patches and blotches, which in no way detracts from his breathtaking beauty.

Around four-thirty in the morning, when I hear the first whimper and know that any time now it will change into an experimental roar, I try to slip quietly from our double bed, hoping that Kim, who has to leave the house before eight, will stay asleep and undisturbed.

I am becoming quite clever at lowering the prepared bottle into its heater and switching it on, and I convince myself that I am as silent as an Indian stalking his prey as I pad over to the cot by the wall and lift Sam from his cocoon of blankets.

But Kim always wakes up, and as I sit in my chair over by the window of our eleventh-floor flat, and see the lights of the city far below already beginning to disappear in pinpoints of light, we talk in whispers.

'He's supposed to sleep until six o'clock,' I tell Kim. He says not to worry, that our baby isn't going to follow any old rules. Our baby is unique, a rebel. Anyone can see.

The bottle is ready and I hold the baby, newly changed and smelling of spring and apple-blossom, close in my arms and guide the teat into his wildly searching mouth.

At the first touch his eyes roll ceilingwards in a positive ecstasy of delight and the milk goes down at an alarming rate.

'He's too greedy,' I tell Kim, who laughs.

'Maybe he'll grow up to be an all-in-wrestler,' he says, 'or a member of the Olympic team.' Because, of course, in spite of the fact that our baby is a full five pounds heavier than the books says he should be for his age, we know that in no way could he be described as fat.

'He's very intelligent. You can tell that already,' says Kim from the bed. 'Just look at the way his eyes can focus, long before they are supposed to, and the way he knows our faces and the sound of our voices. . . .'

'And he's trying to talk,' I say, knowing full well in my heart that if this were true, then our baby would be written up in the medical journals as a biological miracle.

Already the bottle is half empty and in spite of our son's vehement protests, I take it away from him and sit him up to wind him. He objects strongly to this, but I am firm.

'He is very self-willed,' I tell Kim seriously, 'and this is the way we are going to be, right from the beginning. Firm.'

Sleepily Kim agrees with me.

'For Christmas,' he says, his voice disappearing into the pillow. 'For Christmas I'm going to buy him a train-set. With lines that cover the floor. He'll love it.'

I rub Sam's back and imagine how they will both love it, and I see my husband and his little son crawling about on the carpet, coupling and uncoupling the engine, setting up stout little bridges and signal boxes.

Then I give the unwinded baby back his bottle, and the silence settles all around me and I know that Kim has gone to sleep. I am glad, because his job at the factory is a hard and demanding one, and I don't like to see dark shadows round his eyes when he staggers into the bathroom to shave.

It is going to be a lovely day. I can see that by the way the sky is already changing from black to a soft velvety navy-blue. The stars are beginning to fade, and I think how lucky we were to get this flat, even though the rent means that our budget has to be planned to the last penny.

Samuel Adam Mortimer is almost asleep but still, by a determined kind of reflex action, is sucking valiantly at his bottle. I take the teat away and wonder, in quite an agony of indecision, ought I to wind him and risk waking him up again, or shall I put him back unwinded hoping that he will sleep?

I sit there, quiet and content, and I bend my head and kiss the baby on his rounded and spotty forehead. My whole body aches with love for him and I, who thought that I would never be a mother, count myself immeasurably blessed.

I remember the years when to see a pram standing outside a shop in the High Street filled me with a sense of inadequacy, and even bitterness and uncontrollable envy.

I know that outside in the city just waking to another day, there will be strikes and strife, and deep unhappiness; that people will soon be waking to despair and pain, and the unfulfilment of their cherished dreams.

But for me, there is only this quiet content.

The baby stirs and in the big bed, my husband changes position and stretches out a pyjama-clad arm, reaching for me.

Carefully and slowly, I get up from my chair and lower the baby into his cot. I hold my breath in case he wakes and I tuck the blue blanket round him, and smile as I see that he is trying to guide his tiny thumb into his searching mouth.

Although the room is warm, the bed is warmer and I snuggle down next to Kim, and we move at once into our familiar position like spoons in a box, facing the same way, with his arm heavy and comforting round my waist.

'I love you,' I say, and he says something I can't catch in his sleep, and his arm tightens round me.

I take his hand and hold it and, not for the first time, I lie in the dark and wonder about the young girl whose baby lies sleeping in the cot by the wall.

Will she ever get over the anguish of giving up her baby for adoption? Does she wake in the night for no reason at all, with no husband to hold her close and comfort her?

And I pray that in some way she knows that her baby is loved and cared for, and that somewhere he is growing up fine and strong. And in my happiness I turn my head into the pillow and spare a small sad tear for her. . . .

SUCH SWEET SADNESS

EXACTLY at half-past-seven, Mrs Levison from flat sixteen lowered herself painfully into the chair facing the chintz-covered sofa, looped her stick over the arm and pulled at her long black skirt so that it hid the heavy caliper on her left leg. She'd come to babysit.

'Well!' she said. 'Now that we know each other, mes enfants, and now that your mama and your papa have gone out to their dinner and left us alone together, what shall we do? Would you like it that we watch the television?'

The two little girls, identical to the double crown on top of their shiny blonde heads and the freckles that marched like a river of ants across their respective noses, stared at her with duplicated fascination.

'No, thank you.' Emma, the younger of the twins by ten minutes, spoke politely, her eyebrows ascending as she saw a hairpin dislodge itself from the side-slipping bun at the back of the old lady's neck and disappear down the neckline of her blouse. If Sara had seen it too and nudged her, all would have been lost.

They were at the age when to giggle about nothing at all, sometimes for as long as ten minutes or so, was quite commonplace. She moved an imperceptible inch away from her sister.

'We are only allowed suitable programmes,' said Sara, very smug. Mummy always said so.

What she didn't add was that it was far more interesting just sitting there staring at the old lady from flat sixteen. She thought she must be the fattest lady in the whole world. Part of her flowed over the edges of the chair, and one of her legs was stretched stiffly in front of her. It never moved.

Sara narrowed her eyes and hoped fervently that the leg was false, but she knew that under no circumstances must she ask. Their mother had made that quite clear.

'You can stay up until half-past eight as it's Friday, but remember it's very rude to make personal remarks,' she had added for the benefit of Emma, who had said that Mrs Levison's hair looked as if it had been knitted on curly needles.

'She has huge bosoms,' said Sara, who always went too far.

And they had fallen on each other, giggling helplessly, snorting and hooting, until their mother – who was tying a nappy on their screaming seventeen-month-old baby – yelled at them to be quiet!

'I suppose that for eight-year-olds they're quite normal really?' she had asked their father in the privacy of their bedroom, but he was torn between a blue tie with a faint stripe and a grey one in a muted paisley design, and didn't reply.

'If Alfredo from upstairs hadn't caught mumps, and if your mother hadn't been speaking at the Townswomen's Guild, then I wouldn't have had to ask old Mrs Levison to babysit. She's eccentric and a bit of a recluse, but I'm sure they'll be okay.'

Turning round from the mirror, her husband stared at her as if wherever she was it wasn't there standing right behind him.

'I think I'll wear the paisley tie. Cheerful, but hopefully not too gaudy,' he had said.

'We could play Monopoly,' Emma had suggested kindly, but the old lady's attention had now wandered. Sitting upright in the too-low chair, she was pointing to the picture rail and the two frilly dresses hanging side by side.

'You are going to a party another day perhaps?' she asked.

Solemnly Sara shook her head. 'Oh, no. We always go to parties in our long dresses. Those are our flower costumes for the ballet display tomorrow afternoon. We're sweet-peas.'

'In a garden,' Emma added. 'And we have to wear the dresses tomorrow, but Mummy hasn't had a chance to sew the frills on.

'Because of our brother. He's teething. He had a blood blister on his gum and every time Mummy tried to sew he screamed and tried to climb on her knee.'

'Because he was jealous,' Sara explained. 'He just wanted attention, you see.'

Mrs Levison's eyes were shining like tar in the sun and the end of her long nose seemed to be twitching with excitement.

'To think I have lived in the flat across the way all this time without realizing I was so near two ballerinas,' she said. 'If you would like to pass me your mama's work-basket from over there and hand me one of the dresses, I will sew on a frill.' She smiled. 'It is all right – really. I am what you can call an expert at sewing frills on to sweet-peas, I can promise you that.'

She wasn't really like a witch, Emma thought as she handed over a dress with a tacked-on-frill, and the work-basket from the topmost bookshelf. She was much too fat for a witch, anyway, and she smelt quite nice close to. Like an orange left on a window sill to soften in the sun. 'Will you tell us a story, please?' she asked. 'Grandma tells us a story when she babysits.'

The old lady was searching with podgy swollen fingers for the needle-case which had become tangled up with a reel of cotton.

'A story, you say? Well . . . Maybe. . .'

Emma hugged herself with that secret delight which she always felt when a story was just about to begin. Sometimes she even forgot herself enough to suck her thumb. She sat on her hand, just in case; she mustn't be a baby.

Mrs Levison had found the needle and was threading it, squinting at it with her black eyes almost hidden in envelopes of pink flesh.

'Once upon a time . . .' she said, and even Sara was still.

'Once upon a time, a long, long time ago, there was a beautiful young dancer, and her name was Adeline. She was a ballet student at the Opera School in Paris.

'Because all she wanted to do was dance, she grew up just as if she was a princess in an ivory tower. She worked all the days so hard that even her ballet-master would worry about her.

'"Adeline," he would say, wagging his finger at her, "the chestnut trees are in blossom. Did you know that? The sun sparkles on the Seine. Did you know that also? You must take time off."'

'But she would smile at him and shake her head, because for her springtime was in her heart and in her feet when she danced.'

The old lady reached for the scissors and snipped off a piece of thread and Emma held her breath, waiting for her to go on.

'Adeline was so advanced in her learning that once, when she was just a student, a visiting German ballerina was taken ill and the choreographer . . . you know choreographer, what it means?'

Two fair heads nodded in unison.

'He entrusted the leading role in the ballet *Coppelia* to the young Adeline. Just for the once, you understand? She was a magnificent success and all the audience stood up and shouted and clapped . . . and the flowers . . . oh, the flowers. . .

'They came in great baskets on to the stage, and they came tied with long ribbons, and some were thrown from the balconies; she was so happy that there were tears running down her cheeks.

'When little Adeline went to bed that night she promised herself and God that she would work harder than ever, so that one day she would be the most perfect dancer in the whole world.'

The old lady's head bent nearer to the dress, so that a tiny pearl earring did a little dance of its own against the drooping jowls of her cheek. When she spoke again it sounded to Emma as if her voice was suddenly coming to them from a far-off place.

'Then five years went by, with Adeline keeping her promise of shutting everything out of her life but the ballet, and then one day a new dancer came to join the company. He had been with the Imperial Ballet in St Petersburg. Mischa was his name.

'He was the most beautiful young man Adeline had ever seen. He wasn't very tall, but when he moved she could see that every single one of his muscles was tuned to his wishes. His skin was pale and his eyes were huge.

'When he danced he soared, and all the girls in the company fell in love with him. Yes, every single one. It could not be helped, you understand. He was so kind and so gentle and so charming and so beautiful.

'There was never a time when Adeline saw him with the corners of his mouth turned down. Even when he was serious – and he was always serious when he practised – his mouth seemed to laugh.'

Sara started to say something, but her sister's hand shot out and gave her a fierce nip.

Mrs Levison's podgy fingers started pleating the second frill. . .

'Mischa had eyes for no one but Adeline. He danced with her and it was as though they had been born for each other. Their bodies flowed into each other and instead of going home alone to her attic flat, Adeline would walk with him hand in hand, and now she saw the chestnut blossom and the river dreaming in the moonlight.

'But she saw them with her heart as well as her eyes because now, for the first time in her life, she was in love. She was twenty-three, and this was the first time, you understand?

"We will always be together," Mischa promised. "Wherever we dance – and we will dance in all the countries of the world

– we will insist on being together, on dancing together."

'She was thrilled, and when they were alone he would take the pins from her long hair and let it flow over his hands in the tiny waves which Adeline could never quite smooth out.'

Now the old lady was speaking so quietly that Emma slid to the front of the sofa cushion so she wouldn't miss a single word of it.

'His hands were so gentle, and yet when he held her in the dance they were like steel.

'My children, Adeline loved him so much that the late summer so very long ago seemed to be concentrated into just one day when the sun shone, and his pale blue eyes understood when she grew hot and her body ached with despair at getting even a tiny step wrong.'

She went on: 'She had been given the leading role in a new ballet, you see, and it was a difficult role, but Adeline was determined to be a great success. She *had* to be a success – for him now as well as for God and herself – because even though she loved Mischa so much there was a part of her that knew he would love her all the more if she was successful.'

Emma and Sara gulped as the sewing fell from the old lady's hands, as though she had forgotten what it was doing on her widespread lap.

'If the baby wakes, or the telephone rings, I'll die,' Emma thought in dramatic despair. . .

'The first performance was in September, and Adeline danced as she had never danced before. She wore a flowing dress which fell off her shoulders. . .' A rheumaticky hand demonstrated just how on the air. 'And there was a flower entwined in her long hair. The music was in her heart and in her feet, and it was as though Mischa was making love to her there on the great stage in front of the audience. . .

'The critics went wild with delight and Adeline read their reports sitting up in bed the next morning, clutching her throat, which hurt so much it felt as if a knife was scraping it raw inside. Her head ached and she was sick . . . oh so sick . . .

and when Mischa came and saw how sick she was he left the flowers he had brought on the bedcover and slipped away from her bedside very quickly.

'It was a sickness they called infantile paralysis in those days, and Adeline was one of the first victims in the city of Paris at the end of that long summer.'

'Did she die?' Sara whispered. Emma shot her a scathing look.

Mrs Levison jabbed the needle into a fluted frill.

'No, she did not die, ma petite, but she never danced again. Her legs were affected, the left one in particular, and for months she lay in a hospital bed and the dancers from the company came to see her, to talk of everything but their dancing – which therefore was of nothing – you understand?'

'Mischa?' Emma's voice came in a strangled whisper.

'Oh, he came, too. He was with a pretty young dancer, a solo artist with bright red hair as smooth as a scarlet scarf of silk. They left the company soon afterwards and went to America, and Adeline was offered a job with the company sewing the costumes.

'After a while, once she had accepted that she would never dance again, she was reasonably happy. You see, there was nothing to stop her still going on dancing in her mind.'

The black eyes twinkled. 'She danced in her mind until the war. A British soldier, who was almost as old and fat as she had become, marched past her window and saw her sitting there with the sewing. And he fell in love with her, and so they married.'

'And lived happy ever after,' said Sara, fidgety now.

Mrs Levison folded up the dress and put the needle away.

'Sometimes for ever doesn't last for very long, cherie, but for the time they were together it was as if all the birds in the sky sang in chorus together. He wasn't a bit beautiful, not like Mischa, and he smoked too much and he coughed too much, because of what the war had done to him, you understand? Poor man.

'But he would say "wotcher mademoiselle?" and tease Adeline about her accent, and when her leg ached he would make her sit up with it on the sofa. And he would shop and bring back all the wrong things. And his name was simply Fred.'

'Is that the end of the story?' Sara asked. 'We're allowed to make you a cup of tea, Mummy said. Do you take sugar?'

The old lady struggled to her feet and followed Sara's important-looking back into the kitchen.

'Would you like a biscuit?' Emma heard her sister say.

Mrs Levison had two cups of tea and four biscuits, and Sara told her all about Miss Bradley at school and about the time she dropped her recorder in the middle of an end-of-term concert.

And Emma listened quietly, and went to bed quietly, which was difficult because Sara was determined to talk; she kept bouncing about in her bed, switching the light on and off, and searching for a wrapped caramel she had seen at the back of her knickers' drawer.

'Wasn't that a funny story?' she whispered when at last she settled down with the duvet pulled right up beneath her chin.

'I thought it was very nice,' Emma said in a stiff little voice.

'You're crying!' Sara's voice was accusing. 'Why?'

Emma's denial was too indignant to leave the slightest room for any argument and in less than five minutes, with the tears on her cheeks, savouring the lovely sadness inside her, she fell reluctantly to sleep. . .

THE WAY IT USED TO BE

BY the time Claire was in her eighteenth year, Margo, her mother, was in her fiftieth and too old – *far* too old, she told herself despairingly – to cope.

All that year Claire had been convincing Margo that to send her back to school in September would be one sure way to hasten her early demise; that to get her values straight she would have to go out into the world and *identify*.

'With what?' Margo asked, with the defeated air of one who can stand no more.

'With what is *real*,' said her daughter, sighing with exasperation at her mother's lack of understanding. 'You went to Oxford, I know,' she added, dismissing Margo's degree with the contempt she obviously felt it deserved, 'but what did you gain apart from an academic qualification? You told me you had to take a commercial course before you could get a job. By starting work now I'll have been independent for five years before I'm twenty-three, and besides that, I'll know exactly where I'm going.'

'Where will that be?' Margo asked quickly, feeling the conversation could be taking a more hopeful turn.

Claire raised vivid blue eyes ceilingwards as if praying for patience.

'Nowhere!' she said promptly. 'That's what's wrong with your generation, Mummy. You always had to be *going* somewhere. I'm just going to live.'

And where Claire was going to live come September was Scotland, where she was going to be a very junior reporter and general dogsbody on a local paper, almost four hundred miles away from home.

'We must have been mad to agree,' Margo told husband

Bill one evening as the house reverberated around them to the sound of Glen Miller's orchestra playing a much amplified version of 'Little Brown Jug', while Claire and best friend Eloise, dressed Forties style, jived solemnly together on the hearth-rug.

'I'm sure he never used to play as loudly as that,' Bill grumbled. 'I swear they'll all be wearing hearing-aids by the time they get to our age. And did *you* ever wear such awful clothes? I don't seem to remember you in padded shoulders with your hair all frizzed out like that.'

'Rita Hayworth did,' Margo reminded him, 'but I wore my hair over one eye, like Veronica Lake.'

'Oh, yes, I remember,' said Bill, who did nothing of the kind. 'For heaven's sake, why can't someone answer the door? Someone's got their finger on the bell and left it there. Why can't they answer it when they know it's for them?'

'Because they don't want to appear *keen*,' Margo replied, going to the door and letting in three boys who if they hadn't been wearing tee-shirts and jeans could, from their flowing hair and drooping moustaches, have been mistaken for The Three Musketeers.

'Surely there's something not quite right,' she said, going back into the sitting room, 'with boys sitting at their school desks sporting moustaches and side-burns. It doesn't seem right somehow.'

Once, a few weeks ago, when a boy bearing an uncanny resemblance to John the Baptist had called to take Claire to a disco, Margo had remarked on this afterwards.

'Mummy,' Claire had explained, with the patience of a speech therapist talking to a backward four-year-old, 'if there *is* an after-life, I'm sure Saint Peter won't line everyone up at the pearly gates and ask all those men not wearing short back and sides to fall out. I don't know why your generation must always judge a person by his appearance.' She bent down to pull up a knee sock, ringed with all the colours of the rainbow – a sock at complete and utter variance with the black granny shawl tied round her shoulders. 'I expect it was because of the war. All that regimentation. It was bound to have an effect.'

'Yes, it did,' Margo retorted. 'It taught us a lot. For one thing, living through a war taught us never to take things for granted. Happiness, love, the fact that to get anywhere we had to study and get qualifications.'

'Qualifications!' said Claire, as if it was a dirty word, and when Margo told Bill that evening he drew on his pipe, which he didn't seem to have noticed was unlit, and said what mattered was that they had given Claire a foundation.

Foundations could crumble, Margo wanted to point out, but didn't. Bill's firm was doling out redundancies to men older than forty-five, as if years of experience and loyalty counted as nothing. She wasn't going to add to the worry frowns on his forehead.

'I feel,' she told her friend Joan across the road, a woman of her own age with children safely married and paying enormous mortgages on houses they could not afford, 'I feel that allowing Claire to take this job so far from home is parental irresponsibility taken to an extreme. Every time I pick up a newspaper I seem to read that we must let the young ones go their own way; that discipline is outmoded. But in some ways are we all that far removed from our Victorian ancestors who used to push their kids up chimneys and down mines to work when they were no more than children? Isn't their welfare just as much at stake?'

Joan, with the complacent air of a grandmother twice over, had smiled and said, 'My Manda was engaged at Claire's age, and a mother before she was twenty. Stop worrying so much, love. Young people these days know how to look after themselves far better than we did. At least the consequences of their actions are spelled out loud and clear; they've only themselves to blame if they make a mess of things.'

Sex, Margo thought, her mind buzzing with the frenzy of a bee caught in an upturned jar. Sex, drugs, abortions; films and plays on television, with lovers writhing in tumbled sheets and four-letter words used with abandon. Oh, dear Heaven, how could she cope? She was too *old* to cope, and so was Bill.

And the week before Claire was due to take the train to Scotland, the week coming at the end of what had seemed an endless summer of young people swarming round the house, eating miles of spaghetti, sitting on the floor when there were perfectly good chairs going begging, she found herself telling her daughter little anecdotes about how it had all been when she was young.

'There was a reliability about everything,' she said. 'Films and books and plays showed how *happy* marriages could be. The media (though we never used that word in those days) didn't dwell on the sordid. We were in the middle of a war, but we knew things would come out right.'

Margo's words tailed away at the teasing intensity of Claire's blue gaze.

'If only I knew what she was really thinking,' she told Bill, and he said she worried far too much; that Claire had her head screwed on all right and her feet firmly on the ground. And they laughed together at the ridiculous image his words conjured up.

'One thing we can be grateful for is that she doesn't seem to be wanting a "meaningful relationship" with anyone just yet,' Margo said after she'd let two Restoration dandies into the house.

'I shouldn't think the YWCA hostel up there is a centre for sexual orgies,' Bill said dead-pan, but she refused to be comforted.

'If only they didn't despise everything we held dear,' she said sadly. . .

Then, the evening before the day Claire was to catch her train to Scotland, there was a war film on television. Margo had seen it twice; once sitting in the back row of the cinema clutching Bill's hand and the second time on her own identifying with the characters and glorying in every minute of it.

Surprised and touched that Claire had, of her own accord, opted to stay in with them, they settled down to watch it: Margo with her knitting, Bill with his pipe and Claire curled up on the sofa.

And there it all was, in black and white. The soaring violins and crashing piano chords which accompanied the lovers' every utterance. The crunch of bombs; the bedroom scene when the lovers (married, of course) were never actually seen even sitting on the bed at the same time.

The middle of the night, when the war-shocked hero came down the stairs in immaculate dressing-gown, plus cravat neatly tucked into the revers of his striped pyjamas, to play a nocturnal concerto on a convenient grand piano, with an unseen orchestra swelling to a crescendo from the shadows.

And the bride in flowing uncreased nightgown, hair as smooth as if she'd just been combed out at the hairdresser's, trailing one hand on the banister, parting lips as shiny as if they'd been sprayed with varnish.

Margo, the knitting lying forsaken on her lap, felt the artificiality of it all; the crude sentimentality hit her sensibilities with the impact of a force ten gale.

Then the hero, eyes glinting with patriotic zeal through his flying goggles, had his plane shot down in flames, spiralling through the sky to a background music of the unseen orchestra still playing with frenzied fervour. The next shot showed him sitting up in a hospital bed with no more to show from the experience than a white bandage round his noble brow.

Disbelieving and disillusioned, Margo looked across the room at Bill, only to see that he had gone unashamedly asleep.

Claire, who had sat apparently unmoved through the entire film, uncurled her legs from the sofa and announced that she would go and make coffee.

Leaning back in her chair, Margo closed her eyes,

suddenly very weary. Were those the values she had tried to impress on her only child?

The glorification of war? Phoney romance?

Opening her eyes, she glanced across at the still sleeping Bill. Thinning hair, protruding stomach, chin settling itself over his shirt collar. Was this the dashing pilot she had clung to with innocent passion during his leaves? Too swayed by her puritanical background to give him the comfort his young body had craved, *saving* herself for the day when she walked down the aisle towards him, clad in well-deserved virginal white.

Suppose he hadn't come back from one of his flights? Would she have been proud of her principles, or ashamed? Could it be that the accusation of hypocrisy levelled at her generation by the young ones could contain an element of truth?

Tomorrow at this time, Claire would be gone. When Margo made a pie, it would still be there in the fridge when she went to get it out for their supper. The lid would be firmly clamped on to the biscuit tin, and after she had cleaned and tidied Claire's room it would stay that way. No clutter on the dressing-table, boots on the clean duvet cover and posters on the walls. And Claire would be fending for herself almost four hundred miles away, with no mother around to tell her how it was when she was a girl and how she wished it was now. . . .

But *did* she? Could she have been partially wrong all the time? Not entirely, but perhaps just a little? Then what was she supposed to do? Worry and say nothing?

Sighing, she went through into the kitchen where Claire was waiting for the kettle to boil, a dreamy expression on her face.

'Super film, Mummy,' she said, 'absolutely super; no wonder you saw it twice through.'

Margo held her breath. She had known her daughter for a long time, for almost eighteen years; far too long not to know when she was being kind just for the sake of being kind.

'I wish they made films like that now,' Claire was saying, gazing soulfully and with tender yearning at the dish-washer. 'That bit where she came downstairs in the night, and he was playing the piano, and the searchlights were making a pattern in the sky – that was really lovely. . .'

'Well!' Margo said. 'And would you believe it?' she asked Bill when Claire had gone to bed, floating up the stairs as if on waves of romantic longing. 'I've made a discovery. Young people today aren't the realists they make themselves out to be. At heart, they're just as romantic as we were. Perhaps nothing's changed really, apart from the hypocrisy, and it was time that went.'

She remembered the coffee that Claire had forgotten to make, and going back into the kitchen took three cups down from the dresser.

Tomorrow it would be two cups, and Claire would be far away. Being alone with Bill could, she supposed, be a kind of middle-aged honeymoon.

And when she carried the coffee through and woke Bill to tell him it was time they went to bed, she was smiling.

Perhaps there was hope after all. Perhaps things weren't all that different from the way they used to be. . . .

THE HONEYMOON

IT WAS RAINING when they got there. Not rain falling straight as pencils but a dreary drift of drizzle, and the railway station smelled of fish and cold damp stones.

He stood patiently by the newspaper stand as she tied a scarf over her hair, her wedding day hair whose bouffant splendour in the registry office that morning had turned her into an unfamiliar stranger.

'A pity to squash it,' she told him, knotting the ends of the scarf into a bow underneath her rounded chin. Then she giggled and squeezed his arm. 'But it'll be out in the morning anyway, so what does it matter?'

Yes, they could take a taxi, a passing porter told them, moving a wad of chewing gum from one cheek to the other. 'But it's not all that far to walk. Nobbut five minutes, just round 'corner really. Up to you, though, sir,' he said cheerfully.

He saw her blue eyes twinkle as she listened to the broad Lancashire accent. 'Thank you very much,' he told the porter grandly, and wondered if he ought to tip him. 'My wife and I will walk.'

And as he said 'my wife,' his throat swelled and the two words almost choked him with pride. Understandably, of course, because it was the very first time he'd said them.

The train from London had been on time, and with the new electrification the journey had flown. 'I wish we'd had dinner – lunch,' he corrected himself, 'on the train. The hotel won't have dinner until about seven I expect, and I'm sure you're hungry by this time.'

'I am,' she said, 'and why are you talking like that?'

He picked up the two cheap fibre cases, shouting aloud

their newness, just as her pale blue dress and jacket and his pin-striped lounge suit proclaimed to the world at large that they had been married that very day.

'Talking like what?' he said huffily, not meaning to sound huffy.

'As though you don't know me,' she said, hurrying along beside him on silly heels that made her almost as tall as he. 'I noticed on the train, you were so polite it made me want to giggle.'

'I'm always polite,' he said stiffly, 'and your mascara's running down your cheeks.'

She wiped it away on the back of her fabric glove. 'I think you are scared,' she teased.

Because she'd hit on the truth, he just went on walking, turning the corner the way the porter had said, feeling the weight of the cases dragging at his shoulders and the sharp-edged handles cutting into his hands.

Now and again as they walked along the busy Saturday pavement, with the rain puddles throwing splashes up the back of her long legs, he glanced at her sideways. At the purity of her profile, and the long, fair hair escaping from the blue scarf; at the ridiculous false eyelashes which she insisted on wearing, although at the beginning when she took to wearing them they always seemed to be falling off.

Once one sooty fringe – like a many-legged, magnified insect – had finished up on his shoulder as they danced. They'd laughed themselves sick about that.

'What was the name of the hotel?' she asked him. 'I think that porter must have been a gold medal sprinter if he thought it was only five minutes' walk away.'

'Sea Breezes,' he told her, 'a stone's throw from the sea, the letter said.'

'There it is,' she said triumphantly, 'across the street and thanks be to goodness – these shoes are killing me.'

He put the cases down on the pavement and stared unbelievingly at the shabby red brick house. For that was what it was – a detached house and not an hotel at all, with a swinging board above its rain-drenched porch, 'Sea Breezes' embellished on it in letters of gold.

How dare it call itself an hotel? he asked it silently. Advertising itself in the paper as if it were one of these posh places with a sweeping circular drive and a uniformed page-boy to help with the cases. And yet the very cheapness of its tariff should have warned him, but what with the licence and the orchid for Shirley, and the train fare, not to mention the month's rent in advance on their newly acquired bed. sit. in Balham, he was just about skint before they'd even set off on their honeymoon.

'Well, come along then,' she was saying. 'I don't know about you, but I could *eat* a cup of tea.'

Dodging behind a bus and narrowly missing being run down by a cruising taxi, he marvelled again at her bland acceptance of things. She would think the hotel was smashing, just as she thought their room in London was smashing.

He supposed he ought to be grateful, he told himself ungratefully; he could have picked himself a girl who was for ever moaning about something or other.

It was a long time before anyone answered their ring, and he had time to study the three umbrellas dripping disconsolately in a corner of the porch, the frayed and sandstrewn mat, the black and white tiled vestibule and the heavy oak door with its panels of ruby-red glass.

The girl who opened the door at last was tall, with mousy hair pulled straight back from her white face with a narrow velvet ribbon. Diamanté earrings dangled from her ears, at variance with the down-at-heel bedroom slippers which slopped from her heels as she led the way upstairs.

'Breakfast at nine, dinner at twelve-thirty, high tea at six, cup of tea and biscuits if you're in before eleven, and no smoking in the bedrooms.'

'Could we have something to eat now?' he asked her. 'You

see, my wife and I have been on the train since this morning and missed our lunch . . . dinner,' he corrected himself.

The girl shook her head, making the earrings do a little sparkling dance. 'Sorry, sir, nothing served in between meals, but there's a café straight across the street.'

'She talks like Elsie Tanner,' Shirley said, laughing but prodding anxiously at the bouffant hair-do at the same time. 'Come on. Let's go and get something to eat before we unpack. I'm famished, I'll tell you that for nothing.'

'Fancy giving us twin-beds,' he said, staring glumly at the two beds in their identical splendour of rose-coloured eiderdown and matching bedspreads.

'They weren't to know we were on our honeymoon,' she said.

She was at the dressing-table doing things to her face, adding another layer of pale lipstick to her mouth. He sat down on the nearest bed and watched her, noticing properly for the first time the faint swell of her stomach underneath the tight blue dress. He groped in his pocket for a packet of cigarettes.

'No smoking in the bedrooms,' she said in almost an exact imitation of the maid's north-country accent, and he said a rude word and blew a cloud of smoke straight up to the high ceiling.

Depression as clammy as the weather outside closed in on him and when she picked up her handbag and gave a final glance at herself in the mirror, he went over to the window and, raising it a little, stubbed out the cigarette on the ledge outside.

And in spite of the absence of tablecloths and carpeting on the floor, the food in the café across the street was hot and good.

'These chips are smashing,' she said, and he told her that only in Lancashire would she get chips cooked just like that.

He knew she wouldn't speak again after that until her plate was empty. That was how they were a lot of the time – not talking, just sitting together, or dancing together, without the need for words. Or was it perhaps that there was nothing to say? He stared across the table at her bent head.

But surely that was what had attracted him to her in the first place – the way she would dance with him, without saying a word? Not like some of the girls he'd known, for ever natter, natter.

She had no time for small talk. She had something to say and she said it, or else kept quiet thinking her own thoughts, like now.

'Penny for them?' he'd often said and the answer was always the same. 'They're worth far more than that.'

But were they? Watching her now, spearing one chip after another and reaching across the table for yet another piece of bread and butter, he wondered.

'Penny for them?' he asked aggressively.

The false eyelashes raised themselves, and her blue eyes smiled into his.

'They're worth far more than that,' she said.

Pushing his plate aside, he lit a cigarette. He'd thought she'd finished, but she was stealing a chip from his plate now and finishing off the last piece of bread and butter.

'Remember, I've got to eat for two,' she giggled, and he took a long drag at his cigarette.

It was bad for him, he knew, but what the hell? Everybody had to die of something, hadn't they? Look at his old man; he'd been wounded in the war and died of the wound four years later, and he'd never smoked.

Where was the pattern in that? Where was the pattern in anything, come to that?

And in six months from now he'd be a father. Him, Bob Yates, a father, with £5 a week to find for the room they'd rented with a cupboard for a kitchen and damp coming through the wall. Perhaps if he'd listened to his mother and gone to night school, got a trade in his fingers, he'd have finished his apprenticeship just about now.

Since he left school he'd been a butcher's errand boy, done a milk round, worked for a time in the furniture department of a big store, and now he had a job in the shoe trade.

It sounded better that way than saying he spent his days trying shoes on strangers' feet. Sometimes it seemed to him that his whole world was made up of feet, stockinged feet pointing their big toes up at him.

'We'd better go and unpack,' she was saying, dabbing at her mouth with the paper serviette. 'That was good. I feel better.'

He settled the bill and followed her out into the street again, and hand in hand they waited to cross over to the other side.

'Thought you told me that the sun always shone at this place,' she teased.

'It did,' he said, unsmiling. He could remember it almost as if it were yesterday.

Cheap day trips with his mother when he was a kid – coming out of the station into the sudden glare of sunshine, clutching tightly to his bucket and spade, coming out to the smell of sand and shrimps.

He'd remembered the clean concrete sweep of promenade, the steep steps down to the beach, the corrugated ripples of sand that hurt his feet, the gritty sandwiches produced from a carrier bag, the canvas deckchair with his mother's permed head lolling back against its canvas stripes.

It had been because of the memories that he wanted to come up north for their honeymoon, but he couldn't think why.

'You can have the chest of drawers for your things, and I'll have the dressing-table for mine,' she said, clicking open her case and laying a pink nylon nightdress across one of the beds. 'Which bed do you want?'

'You kidding?' he said and she smiled at him, and he felt the sudden longing for her – the longing that had got him where he was, he told himself grimly.

'Not now,' she whispered, struggling to free herself from his arms. 'Elsie Tanner might come up again, and there's a piece of confetti in your hair.'

It took him less than ten minutes to unpack. He hadn't brought much for four days, but Shirley seemed to have brought her entire wardrobe.

Defiantly he lit another cigarette and watched her take dress after dress from the case, smoothing them out, then taking them over to the big mahogany wardrobe where empty coat-hangers swung in its cavernous depths.

'Close your eyes. I'm going to change and put another dress on,' she was saying, and he opened his mouth to say something about it being a bit late for that now; then he saw that she meant it, so he compromised by lying back on the bed and watching her from beneath half-closed lids.

She was beautiful all right, the most beautiful girl he'd ever taken out. Her legs, long and slim, were as nice as any on the television advertising nylons, and the brief pale blue lace slip barely covered her rounded thighs. Her skin was white and soft, and as she reached into the wardrobe one strap slipped down, showing the lovely curve of her breast.

'Come here!' he said, and turning round she held the dress in front of her like a shield, her blue eyes watching him with an expression he couldn't fathom. She was scared, too, he thought. That made two of them.

Over by the window she struggled with the zip of her dress, but he made no attempt to help her, issues too complex for him clouding his mind.

'There's a patch of blue,' she said, 'and it's stopped raining. Everybody's taking off their plastic hoods down there in the street. Let's go down to the front.'

By the time he'd made his gesture to the seaside by exchanging shoes for sneakers and his jacket for a thick-knit pullover, the small patch of blue had widened and a watery sun had broken through.

Hand in hand, like children, they ran down the stairs,

slamming the door behind them until the ruby-red panels shivered in protest. They ran along the crowded Saturday pavement, round the corner, down a road of houses with BED AND BREAKFAST notices in their front windows; waiting for a tram to pass, across a zebra crossing, then at last, breathless by now, across the concrete promenade, and it was there.

All the things he remembered were coming to life now that the rain had stopped. The queue of people already waiting for deckchairs, the children pulling at their fathers' hands, dragging them over to the pier where a forlorn group of donkeys had sheltered from the rain. The ice-cream stall opening its shutters, and the tide coming in, with the last of the rain clouds disappearing over the town and out on the horizon the sky a clear, heavenly blue.

'Come on, Mrs Yates,' he said.

'That'll take a bit of getting used to,' she said, and they climbed down the steps to the beach, picking their way round the bodies already stretched out in starfish abandon, with faces upturned to the sun.

'Deckchair?' he asked, and she put out her tongue.

'You kiddin'? There's a place over there by the breakwater, and we can sit on my cardigan.'

And as usual everything delighted her, everything was smashing. She sat with her back against the low wall, drinking it all in childishly. That was all she was, he thought in sudden paralysing fear, a child.

He lay down, resting his head in her lap against the soft curve of her stomach, and closed his eyes, feeling the warmth of the sun seep through his eyelids.

They stayed quiet for a long time, as they often did, then he opened his eyes and stared straight up into her face. She was so close that he could see the recently healed scar of a spot on her chin, and she was so close that he could see the quivering stupid eyelashes and the tear trickling slowly down her cheek.

It fell on his forehead and he left it there.

'Don't cry, Shirley. I'll be a good husband to you. Honest,' he said, the words saying themselves, and surprising him. 'I'm sorry that we had to start like this, with the baby and everything, but I'll make it up to you, I swear.'

'It wasn't all your fault,' she said fiercely, the tears coming thick and fast now. 'I was there, too, wasn't I?'

He reached for her then, pulling her face down to his, heedless of the people around them, hearing only the beat of her heart and the soft lap of the waves and a seagull crying far out to sea.

'Everything'll be smashing. You'll see,' he said desperately, and he tangled his fingers in her hair and felt the unfamiliar stiffness of the wedding-day hair-do.

'It's up to us to make it smashing,' he said. 'It's all up to us, Shirley.'

Now his own eyes were wet with tears, and when she saw she rocked him gently in her arms as if he were a child. Then they were silent again, everything said that could be coherently said, holding each other close and staring out to sea.

'Penny for them?' he said at long last.

Against his cheek he felt her breathe a sigh. 'They're worth more. Far more than that,' she said.

THE REVOLUTIONARY

IN THAT year, the fiftieth anniversary of the Russian October Revolution, old Mortimer Francis came into his own. For years he had been telling anyone who would listen to him that he had been there – actually there, on the spot so to speak – when it all began.

And that year, when all three channels on television showed in dramatic documentary style their versions of what had taken place, he was one up, as he said, even on *Panorama*.

He'd seen it all; he'd been for a while a prisoner of the Bolsheviks; he'd been shunted on a train on a nineteen days' nightmare journey to Archangel. He'd actually heard some of the first guns firing on Kiev in the Ukraine.

'In fact,' as his daughter Edwina remarked waspishly to her husband James, 'one would think he'd started the whole thing.'

'Probably did,' said James. 'Trust your father to get mixed up in a thing like that. Typical, I would say.'

As well as that year marking the anniversary of the uprising in Russia, it also marked James's rise to directorship in his particular field of electronics. Roughly half a century after the peasants had exchanged their plough-shares for guns, James had been called into the office of his chief and told that he was to take charge of the new factory on the outskirts of London. He would be expected, his chief told him, staring across the expanse of virgin blotting-paper on his desk, to entertain important clients from abroad. VIPs, he stressed; but having met James's wife, he was quite sure that she would grace the position of hostess.

James was quite sure, too, and allowed his thoughts to wander for just a fleeting moment to Edwina.

In her early fifties, though she would never admit to a day over forty-five – with her slim figure, her dark hair with its grey parting ruthlessly obliterated every few weeks at the hair-dressers in the High street – Edwina epitomized the perfect hostess. Her dinner parties were the talk of the neighbour-hood. Invitations to her fork luncheons were angled for, and her cocktail get-togethers were organized with the attention to detail normally afforded a military tattoo.

The one snag, the fly in the ointment, as James remarked to Edwina later that evening, was Mortimer.

'Where is he, by the way?' he asked his wife as they sat together sipping perfectly percolated coffee in their tastefully decorated drawing-room and discussing the exciting news of the promotion and move to London.

Edwina sighed. 'Down at the village hall giving one of his little talks. They've had him at the Women's Institute and the Mothers' Union, and tonight it's the turn for the Youth Club.'

James sighed, too. 'What is it this time? Up the Steppes to Freedom or I was Lenin's Double?'

Edwina didn't laugh. She knew that her husband wasn't trying to be funny. Besides, there was worse news to impart.

'He went in his fur hat.'

James walked over to the window. 'The one that's defied the moths for over half a century?'

Edwina nodded, but he didn't turn round. 'You know what I'm going to say, don't you?'

'Yes dear, and I'm with you all the way,' said his wife with commendable loyalty.

James brought his fist down smack in the palm of the other hand. 'He'll have to go into a home. We couldn't have him holding forth about how he slept on a stove.'

'Next to that Ukrainian woman.'

James shuddered. 'He wouldn't be any more likely to keep

to his own room when we entertain down there than he does here.'

'He likes company,' said Edwina, rather wistfully.

'We'll tell him the minute he comes in,' said James before his wife changed her mind. . .

Old Mortimer came in flushed with success, the fur hat at a rakish angle on his head. It was a good mile uphill from the village hall, but he had done it at a steady pace, reliving his little triumph step by step.

Still well over six foot tall, there was no straining of his waistcoat buttons over his board-flat stomach, and although his teeth were depleted in number every one was his own.

'Fine lot of youngsters down there. Had them eating out of me hand,' he said, in a voice that had lost none of its boom. 'The old country can stand on its feet for a long time yet. Not a drug-addict among them, I'd stake me life on that.'

'Sit down, Father,' James said. 'Edwina and I want to talk to you. For your own good,' he added firmly.

'In your own interest,' Edwina said. 'It's our responsibility to do what we think is best for you.'

Mortimer's blue gaze disconcerted her for a moment and she twisted round to avoid it.

As they unfolded their idea, she fancied rather hysterically that there before their eyes, her father seemed to dissolve, to shrink into a little old man, and when he spoke his voice held a distinct quiver.

'So you want to have me put away,' he said, 'because I've lived too long. Oh, yes I have,' he quavered when James tried to speak. 'Longer than my allotted span, and now my own kith and kin are rejecting me.'

His shaggy head drooped on his chest and the hand fumbling for his cigarette case trembled.

Sternly Edwina reminded herself that her father was no mean actor, pathos being his speciality.

'We're thinking of your happiness, Father,' she said. 'What sort of a life would it be for you down there away from all your friends? At the Home you'd be surrounded by men of your own age.'

Mortimer's head jerked up. 'D'you mean you'd actually send me to an all-male establishment? Am I so senile that it's come to that?'

James patted the tweed shoulder. 'We'll see to it that you go to a mixed community, if that's what you want, Father,' he said gently.

Mortimer struggled up out of his chair. 'I shall go to my room,' he said pathetically and strode with his usual vigour towards the door, remembering his rôle half way and quickly changing the stride into a shambling gait.

They waited until a door slammed upstairs. Mortimer was, they knew from bitter experience, a past master at eaves-dropping.

'I'll start making inquiries tomorrow,' said Edwina.

The next morning her father behaved as though he'd gone feeble-minded overnight; mislaying his reading glasses and asking her three times what day it was. Around eleven o'clock, much to her relief, he set off for his walk.

He had decided privately whilst shaving to visit one of his lady friends and play on a little feminine sympathy. There was nothing like a pretty shoulder to cry on, he told himself as he marched briskly along the avenue.

By the roundabout he hesitated. Who should it be? Molly? No, she was a cold fish – never quite forgiven him for kissing her underneath the Christmas mistletoe. Irene? She was pretty enough, but a bit of a crank with her fanaticism for health foods and vitamin tablets. Last time he'd called she'd served him with an obnoxious concoction of herb tea.

Netta? Ah, that was better. He turned left towards a newly built row of bungalows and turned in at a gate marked 'Dun-Rovin'.

The small woman with grey curls and a neat waist topped

with a well-upholstered bust, gave a squeal of unconcealed delight when she saw him. 'Mortimer! I might have known. The coffee's just made, and I've a loaf of your favourite date and walnut.'

Removing his tweed cap and bending his head to avoid the low lintel, Mortimer stepped inside.

In the warmth of her cosy living room, sitting comfortably in her late husband's chair, Mortimer stretched out his long legs to the fire and enjoyed two cups of coffee and allowed himself to be pressed to a second piece of cake before he came to the point.

'So they're going to put me away,' he finished. 'To live like a monk, with nothing else to do but play dominoes until it's time for the television programmes to start. Just waiting for the end,' he added, wondering if he could risk another piece of walnut loaf.

Netta's reaction was all he could have hoped for. She actually groped for a lace-edged handkerchief and dabbed at her eyes. 'It doesn't seem right,' she said. 'Not after the life you've led. Not after coming through the Revolution and everything.'

She spoke as if it had been but yesterday, and Mortimer glowed. How pretty she was, sitting there opposite to him in her blue dress, with her cheeks flushed pink from the quite unnecessary heat from the electric fire. And a marvellous cook, too. Dammit, he'd have another piece of that walnut loaf if it wasn't for the fact that Edwina always had his lunch ready at one o'clock on the dot.

'Is there no way out?' she was asking. 'They wouldn't consider you staying on here by yourself?'

'Not a hope. Not the domestic type you see, me dear. Never boiled an egg in me life,' said Mortimer proudly.

Netta crossed the room to refill his cup. 'I know one way you could turn the tables on them,' she said, her cheeks growing pinker than ever. 'You could get married. That would show them.'

For probably the first time in his long life, Mortimer was at a loss for words. He actually felt his grey moustache bristle with astonishment. 'Me? At my age?'

Netta wagged a coquettish finger at him. 'You're in your prime, Mortimer. With a good woman to take care of you. . .' she leaned over and passed him the plate of walnut cake and too surprised to refuse he took another piece. 'There's Molly Graham,' she went on. 'She fancies you, that I know, and she's buried two husbands and they both left her a fortune.'

Mortimer sat up a little straighter in his chair. 'Does she now? And did they really?'

Netta nodded. 'And there's Irene Marsh. She's never been married, so she'd jump at the chance, and you'd soon get used to eating shredded cabbage and drinking nettle-beer.'

'Never!' said Mortimer. 'You can cross her off.'

Netta pouted prettily, apparently deep in thought. 'Then there's Mary Baines, the widow across the road. She's an ardent pacifist though, can't bear the talk of war, so you wouldn't have to upset her with any of your tales. You could always leave the fighting bits out, and tell her about the night you saw Pavlova dance at the Bolshoi Theatre in Moscow.'

Mortimer listened to Netta's soft voice prattling on; he studied the way she smiled and he noticed the way that the sun through the window touched her curls to silver.

'If I did marry again,' he said at last. 'If I did, I said, but it would take some thinking about, mind you – there's only one woman I could live with for the rest of my life. . .'

Netta's eyes, as blue as his own, widened in surprise. 'And who might that be, Mortimer?' she asked innocently.

At exactly ten minutes to one – Edwina didn't like to be kept waiting – he closed the gate marked 'Dun-Rovin' behind him.

Turning round, he raised his tweed cap in old-world gallantry to his fiancée. She responded by blowing him a kiss. With no regard at all for the neighbours he blew one back and, swinging his stick, started back up the long avenue.

Twenty years dropped from him as he walked along, and his blood stirred in his veins as it had stirred all those long years ago, when he'd heard the first firing of the revolutionary guns in the Ukraine. Squaring his shoulders, old Mortimer marched up the path to where Edwina waited with his cold lunch all laid out in the kitchen.

He carried on round the side of the house, going in at the back door as he'd been trained to do.

'Wipe your feet, Father,' said Edwina without turning round.

Mortimer started to obey, then remembering the way the Russian peasants had taken up the cudgels on their own behalf all of fifty years ago, he walked straight in, giving the mat a satisfactory kick to one side.

Edwina, rinsing a lettuce, was obviously bent on avoiding his eye.

'I think it can be arranged, Father,' she told him. 'I've had a long chat with the Matron of the Twilight Home and we shall drive out on Sunday and look the place over. Most of the residents are quite active, considering their ages. I think you'll be happy there, I'm convinced of that.'

Mortimer heard her out in silence, then drawing himself up to his full height his voice boomed out, filling every corner of the room.

'No need to be going anywhere on Sunday, my dear. I've made me own plans, y'see. I'm getting married to Netta Margerison, that bonny little woman down the avenue. Just as soon as it can be arranged. No need to worry.'

It was then Edwina turned round, water from the colander dripping unheeded on her polished floor.

'Just as soon as it can be arranged,' he said again, his blue eyes flashing almost tangible sparks. 'And I don't fancy any lunch today. Netta expects me back for tea.'

Then giving his grey moustache a twirl, he did an about-turn and walked with his purposeful stride towards the door. And as he closed it behind him he could have sworn he heard the mighty guns again, thundering in his ears.

THE LOVED AND THE LOVING

SHE saw me first, and fifteen years hadn't altered her all that much. Her obviously expensive classic-style, camel-hair coat was just that length that isn't mini, midi or maxi; her hair was cut in the same indefinite shape it had been at school, and her leather shoes and kid gloves were more utilitarian than decorative.

'Grace Barton!' she said, using my maiden name. 'Well, of all things!'

And she sat down opposite me at the table not yet cleared of its previous occupant's tea things, crumb-strewn plates and crumpled napkins.

'This is really a coincidence,' she went on, sliding a silk scarf from her neck. 'I never come up to town – well, hardly ever – but I've been trying to match some material for cushions and my feet are killing me.

'Now tell me everything,' she said eagerly.

'Which one did you marry? The Rugger Captain from the Grammar School or the one who was going into the Civil Service?'

'Fancy your remembering,' I laughed. 'And well, it was John.'

'John of the Board of Trade?' she asked, and I laughed again, and said how was Rupert. I didn't need to ask whom she had married.

For the last year at school, the year of our eighteenth birthdays, she had worn his engagement ring on a thin chain round her neck. I'd received a minute portion of wedding cake in a lace-trimmed box the year after, and slept with it underneath my pillow.

How we'd envied her her Rupert! Rupert of the fair hair,

the elegant sports jacket, the green sports car he'd park round the corner from the school. He was old, of course, at least twenty-five, and already the part owner of two antique shops with an interest in buying and selling anything that came his way. Amassing a fortune, we were all convinced, and the epitome of all that was glamorous and romantic.

'What *does* he see in Elaine?' we used to ask ourselves. Elaine of the mousy hair and pallid complexion, who had nothing – or so it seemed – to commend her but an enviable bust and an adoration of Rupert.

It was: Rupert said this, and Rupert said that, and some of the nastier girls said of course it was her father's money he was after. Then we'd giggle a little and say what else could it be, when he could have had anyone?

Any one of *us*, I think we meant. . .

A heavy-footed waitress hovered and Elaine asked for tea and a plate of cream cakes and I watched as she dropped two lumps of sugar into her cup. She was talking too quickly, the words tumbling over themselves, in the over eager way the lonely do – the women who haunt tea-shops in search of company.

'Have you any children?' she was saying, and I would have to have been completely insensitive to miss the wistful tone of her voice.

'Two,' I told her. 'Both away at school in Sussex. And you?'

She shook her head. 'Rupert never wanted children, and perhaps it's as well. He's away so much. Sales and things, you know.'

She speared a forkful of cake and held it half-way to her mouth. 'Five antique shops now, plus an interest in one in the Midlands and another in the North.'

'Daddy's money,' I thought uncharitably, and as if reading my thoughts she said, 'My parents died and I did take a job. Not for the money, of course, but to *do* something, but Rupert didn't approve. He likes to think of me being there when he comes back from his trips, and I agree, of course.'

She had finished the cake on her plate and was trying, but not too hard, to resist the temptation to take another one.

'He keeps urging me to join things you know – the Women's Institute, bridge clubs – and I did try, but either you're the type or you're not. I mean the joiner type. Rupert's a joiner. . . Remember at school,' she said, a second cake now on her plate. 'If you weren't the Form Prefect you were the Games Captain, and remember the year you won the bust of Molière for French speaking, and we had a form photograph taken with you in the front row next to Miss Larner?

'We didn't realize just how happy we were,' she said slowly. 'Do *you* still join things?'

I told her that I was the President of the local Townswomen's Guild, a committee member of the Red Cross Society, and that I ran a club for the disabled and was becoming interested in council work.

'Just like Rupert,' she said. 'Most of the evenings he's at home, he's out, if you know what I mean. He's often asked to give talks on collecting silver. . .' As she spoke she was pouring herself a second cup of tea from the silver-plated teapot. 'And what about John?'

I shook my head and smiled. 'Work, more work, television, then bed.'

It was meant to have been mildly funny, but she seemed to have taken me seriously.

'I liked John,' she said, surprising me. 'I only met him once or twice, but I liked him.'

'I like him, too,' I said, and we smiled at each other, but there was something in her expression – a *diminished* look was the only way I could describe it. I'm not a perceptive person – even my John, who thinks I'm more or less perfect, admits that – but I said, 'Elaine, you're happy, aren't you? I mean, when you said just now about not realizing how happy we were at school. There's nothing wrong, is there?'

She started to gather her gloves, handbag and the bill

together; mine, too, in spite of my protests. 'I'm happy,' she said slowly, 'but I often think about something my mother said to me before she died. She said that, in most marriages, there is the one who is loved and the one who does the loving. . .'

I waited for her to go on, but as she was about to say something an elderly couple came and stood by our table. And the moment of closeness had gone.

By the cash desk we exchanged telephone numbers and promised to get in touch, but as I watched her walk away I knew that neither of us would do anything about it.

Elaine was the kind of person one forgot, and I was too busy anyway. And yet, all the way home, strap-hanging in the tube, taking a taxi from the station, I couldn't forget her.

When John came home I told him about meeting her and I said it was obvious that Rupert the Glamorous had sapped what personality she had.

'I expect they're happy enough,' he said, then asked – as he always asked – was there time for him to go upstairs and change before I dished up the meal?

'Yes, but hurry,' I told him. 'I've got to be out by seven-thirty and it's my turn to pick the speaker up this month and keep her calm before the meeting begins.'

He smiled at me and touched my cheek gently with his finger, then went upstairs quickly because I'd asked him to.

'I liked John,' I remembered Elaine saying and suddenly, standing there at the sink draining garden peas through the colander, I knew a moment of uneasy truth.

John and Elaine, the non-joiners, two of a kind. And Rupert and me, the other kind.

What was it she had said?

'In most marriages there is the one who is loved and the one who does the loving. . .'

The moment when John had touched my cheek and smiled at me, his eyes had mirrored the same look that Elaine's had held, a *diminished* look.

John, the one who did the loving, and I, the one who was loved.

And the thought gave me no happiness – no happiness at all.

WHO AM I? THAT'S A GOOD QUESTION

BETH and I are on a boat called the St George, sailing to The Hook of Holland en route for Copenhagen, because I have had an hysterectomy and am depressed.

'Your hormones are all out of flunter,' Beth has explained and though I do not quite know what she means, I realize that sitting on the edge of my bed and staring at the wall for hours on end is indicative of something or other.

I would never have agreed to come if Don had not had a small legacy from a maiden aunt in Harrogate, and convinced me that to put it in the bank would be equal to throwing it away. And I would never have agreed to come if the girls had not greeted the news that they were to spend a week of their summer holidays with their grandmother, with loud cries of undiluted joy.

Beth has made me swallow two sea-sickness pills, even though the sea is like a hand-painted mill pond. And in no time at all we are slowly drifting into the harbour and busy sailors are busy throwing ropes to their busy counterparts, who are catching them cleverly.

I tell Beth, rather wistfully, that the girls have never been abroad, not once, and she tells me that if I as much as mention their names once more during the week to come, the whole object of the exercise will have been defeated.

'From this moment in time you are not Maggie, mother of two, but Margaret, a liberated woman in her own right with an identity all her own,' she tells me as we board the train.

Beth knows exactly who she is, and always has done. A

divorcee with a string of lovers to her credit, she wears sun-tan make-up and false eyelashes to breakfast.

Frankly I love Beth and have since we were at school together. I feel a sort of motherly affection for her, but would rather die than tell her so.

Our sleeping compartment is tiny, and I am rather gratified to discover that in spite of her perfection Beth snores in her sleep. In wonder if her lovers have minded. . .

After breakfast I stare through the window at the spanking clean houses with window-boxes gay with flowers. I wonder aloud if Don has started to paint the outside of our house as was his avowed intention.

'Who is Don?' asks Beth, with every line of her newly-tanned face expressing disapproval, and I feel that is carrying things a bit far. But she says no; the reason for my depression is because I have always identified far too much with my husband and children, so that now I am incapable of individual thought and action, living merely vicariously in their respective shadows.

'Women's Lib was invented for the likes of women like you,' she adds. 'The world is full of widows wandering around like lost space capsules revolving eternally in the dark realms of nothing, because they have lived in their husbands' pockets.'

The word 'widow' sets off my depression again, and I see a terrifying image of Don falling from the topmost rung of the ladder as he paints the guttering.

My gloomy thoughts last me nicely for the rest of our train journey, though I keep a brave smile on my face. Then we are in a cab speeding on the wrong side of the road towards our hotel, and I stare at the clean neck of our driver and wonder if I will be able to keep on our house, with the mortgage repayments still to run, or if it would be wiser to sell it and move with the girls into one of the new flats overlooking the bus terminus. 'Only one left,' the notice had said the last time I passed it, and I find myself hoping it won't have gone by the time I get back home.

'You must lie down for an hour,' Beth tells me briskly as we walk into the foyer of our small hotel. 'The journey has taken it out of you, darling. When we set off you looked pale and interesting. Now you just look pale.'

The young man who takes us up in the lift is so clean and shining he looks as if his mother has pressed him all ready for work that morning, and my room has a pale yellow carpet and a writing table adorned with a gold lamp, whilst through an open door can be glimpsed a bathroom so opulent I am convinced champagne will gush from the taps instead of water when I turn them on.

The french window opens on to a tiny balcony. As I wander out I notice that there's a sort of barrow with fire-fighting equipment on it down in the courtyard, and I see in my depressed mind's eye the headlines in the London newspapers the next day: 'Fire in Copenhagen hotel. One of the victims is believed to be from London'.

My doctor hasn't been much use. 'Anxiety complex, common after an operation such as yours, coupled with early menopausal depression,' he had told me.

Later, when I refused to take the tranquillizer pills he was prescribing, telling him that I was determined to sort myself and my out-of-flunter hormones out in my own way, he sighed.

'There are times when we all need a prop of a kind, even if only temporarily,' he said, but even then I wouldn't cash in the little slip of paper at the chemist, believing that someone as well adjusted as me couldn't possibly be in need of a biological uplift.

I hear a discreet tap on the door and, knowing it will be Beth coming to check on me, lie down quickly. Beth is now wearing white slacks, topped with a navy and white striped skinny vest, so I am not surprised when she tells me that, after she has unpacked for me, we are going on a boat trip down the canal to view The Little Mermaid sitting on her rock alongside Copenhagen's harbour.

I hope she does not notice that my dresses are all last year's and that my second nightie is an ugly shade of khaki from an episode in the hot wash with Don's brown tie that had sneaked in there by mistake.

And yes, that is the thing she looks at first.

'What a simply super shade, darling,' she cries, laying it over the end of my bed. 'Now that your hair is fading this is much more your colour than all those wishy-washy-looking pinks and blues.'

'Expensive though,' I murmur, keeping my fingers crossed that she has not seen the chain store label. She watches without comment – unusual for Beth – as I climb into my green slacks and top them with an over-blouse long enough to cover my bottom. It goes without saying that Beth's bottom is small enough to be revealed in all its neatness.

I follow her down the corridor to the lift, deciding as I do every day that from tomorrow I will stick to my diet.

We are lucky, and the open boat is waiting for us at a landing-stage. 'How the girls would have loved this,' I say as we sail slowly down the canal, with an American couple sitting in front of us photographing everything within sight.

'And who are the girls?' Beth asks. 'You must try, darling. You are a woman in your own right, here in Copenhagen, the most liberated city in the world.'

'Surely you're not expecting me to carry things that far?' I am remembering all I've read about the sex shops, the frankness, the lack of inhibitions.

'It would do you good,' Beth says, and I close my own eyes and see myself being seduced by the clean young man in the lift. I am wearing the khaki nightie and after it's over I tell him I'm depressed. The thought makes me smile and Beth looks proud of me. 'That's better, darling. I can see you're beginning to relax already. See, we're coming in to land so that we can see the Little Mermaid to advantage. Isn't she beautiful?'

And she is smaller than I imagined, sitting there on her little rock with her stone tail tucked neatly in beside her. The American couple take at least twenty-four snaps of her. 'Isn't she cute?' they say, and staring at the little figure I want to cry.

What is she doing all by herself sitting there? And what am I doing here? Why am I spending Don's auntie's money so selfishly when all we will be able to afford this year is a fortnight in a rented caravan down at West Wittering? What is she thinking about, that little stone maid, gazing so pensively at nothing? Is she wondering, like me, exactly what life's all about?

And the fact that she has no legs, and I have no womb, seems to strike me as being unbearably sad, and to my dismay I feel the tears begin to roll down my cheeks. I turn my head away, as she, the Little Mermaid, is turning her head away, but Beth sees and hands me a neatly folded wad of lilac tissues which, as I sob into them, give off the scent of Chanel No. 5.

'So emotional, the Italians,' I hear the American couple say and to my horror Beth turns on them and tells them that her friend, if they don't mind, is English and is having a little nervous breakdown. That is all.

'The statue reminds her of someone she lost very dear to her,' she goes on to say and the American man says, 'What, tail and all?' And I wish I could just slide peacefully into the dark brown water and let it cover me up as I sink out of sight.

'Uncouth,' Beth says in a loud voice, and when we get back to the boat she sees to it that we sit as far away from the Americans as possible.

That evening I am somewhat recovered, and after dinner we go to the Tivoli Gardens with its roses in full bloom, its illuminated fountains, its gay restaurants peopled with laughing tourists, and I wonder what the meaning of it all is.

Beth has insisted that we wear our long dresses, and the fact that the Germans, the French, and the Italian women are all wandering around in their sun-dresses doesn't deter her for a moment.

'You must remember that you are you, darling. An individual.'

'In my own right,' I say bleakly, and she nods into her glass of lager.

'That has always been your trouble, darling,' she goes on to explain. 'You are a mother figure, even to Don, and now that you have had this little operation, it is making you feel – very mistakenly of course – less feminine.'

I say I'll try to be sensible, and she grips my arm and walks me over to the Pantomime Theatre with its Chinese roof and peacock's tail curtain. Harlequin and Columbine are acting out the age-old drama, and when the children call out to them I try not to wish that the girls were there.

Beth reads my thoughts and leads me gently away down a winding path to a seated enclosure where, beneath the spreading trees, a band is playing a selection from *Carousel*.

'I am very fond of Don,' Beth whispers in my left ear as we sit down on two rather wobbly iron chairs, 'but he is just the teeniest bit possessive with you, darling. He hasn't allowed your own personality to develop. You have got to the stage where you can't be away from him without feeling bereft.

'You identify far too much with your husband and the girls; you take their troubles as much to heart as if they were your own, and what you must realize, darling, is that no one is indispensable. The graveyards are full of them,' she adds, taking a small mirror from her cavernous shoulder bag and peering intently into it. Then, obviously well satisfied, she puts it away.

'Full of what?' I ask, having lost the gist of her conversation in the sudden emotional swell of sound as the drummer goes berserk.

'Indispensable people,' she assures me, and then we wander back through the roses and the strings of fairy-lights, out of the Gardens back towards our hotel. As we walk along a wide boulevard lined with shops filled with magnificent furs and exquisite porcelain and cut-glass, I see my gravestone covered in clinging moss. 'A good mother' it says, and the terrible sadness fills me again. . . We take a short cut down a street of bookshops, with big-bosomed ladies displaying their bare charms, and Beth stands there saying, 'Fancy that!' in her carrying voice, and reminds me that liberated women, if they are honest, should be as frankly interested in sex as men.

At that instant, as we move away to turn out of the pedestrian street into the Main Square, she discovers that her massive handbag is missing and I see her turn pale beneath her sun-tan make-up.

'Oh,' she cries. 'Everything I possess is inside that bag. My passport, my foreign currency, my return train and boat tickets, my credit cards, my spectacles – everything! Maggie, I'm sunk!'

'But surely you could have left most of those things back at the hotel,' I say, and she tells me that ever since she had a paperback whipped from beneath her very nose in the Champs Elysées four years ago, she has never trusted a foreigner an inch.

'But we are the foreigners here,' I say, and her face disintegrates before my eyes.

Beth is wailing. 'My rings and my fob watch, and my gold fountain pen! Oh, Maggie, what are we going to do? Oh, tell me what to do!'

I fear she is about to burst into tears, and am reminded of the day my daughter Jane accidentally left her school satchel on the bus. 'I'll die if I don't ever find it, Mummy!' she had sobbed. 'I'll simply die!'

And all the motherly instincts, all the despicable traits Beth has sworn she will rid me of, rise to the surface. I forget

myself and my depression and tell her that everything will
come all right if she will just leave it to me.

'Could it have slipped from your shoulder without you
noticing?' I ask, and she shakes her head.

'Could someone have taken it as we stood outside the
bookshop, then?' I ask her gently and she shakes her head
again, incapable of uttering a single word.

'Right, then. We'll retrace our steps to the Tivoli Gardens,'
I soothe. But did we come up that little street, or did we walk
through that tiny alley? Neither of us can remember, so we try
both ways, then sprint as fast as we can, holding up our long
skirts, to the main entrance, and I try to tell a scrubbed-
looking man in the ticket office what has happened. 'Parlez-
vous français?' I say.

'Sprechen Sie Englisch?' I say, and in perfect and smiling
English he tells me that the Gardens are open until midnight,
and that if we go back to the restaurant where we had our
drinks we will probably find that the bag has been handed in.

'Copenhagen people are honest people,' he tells us, and I
don't like to remind him that in July the city is three-quarters
full of foreigners.

Beth starts to tell him about her paperback whipped from
beneath her nose in the Champs Elysées, and I hurry her
away towards the open-air restaurant; then as we go I
suddenly remember that she took a mirror from the bag as we
sat on our little wobbly chairs and listened to the band.

'If the worst comes to the worst,' I tell her, 'I will ring Don
and he will send us some money. And we can go to the British
Embassy,' I add. 'We won't be the first tourists to land
themselves in a jam like this. We're not in Siberia. No one is
going to send us down a salt-mine to work our passage back
home.'

She reminds me I wouldn't be able to lift my pick-axe if
they did. 'And how you can joke, I don't know. I always have
that bag sticking to me like a plaster, and besides, I promised
Don I would look after you, and now we'll be thrown out of

our hotel on the very first day because we have no money to pay the bill. You don't seem to realize. How can you be so calm?'

That is a question I ask myself as we try to find the spot where the band we listened to was playing, rushing first down one path, then another, with Beth actually wringing her hands and moaning softly to herself.

Why, in my present state of nervous anxiety, have I not dissolved into a psychotic jelly? Why am I at this moment in full control, when only last week I lay on my bed and sobbed because the washing-machine had stopped at the rinse and dry position? Why are my hormones back in flunter again? Why? Why?

And the answer is that I have served my convalescence. I have recovered whatever it was I had lost. And there, as we round a corner, is the bandstand, closed down now for the evening. And there, amazingly, still looped over a chair back, is Beth's bag, bulging with everything she holds most dear. As she falls on it with a whoop of delight and checks that everything is still intact, I take a couple of deep breaths and know that my recovery is complete.

Beth has recovered, too, and as we start back to the hotel she says that tomorrow we will search the old curiosity shops for a present for Don.

'Who is Don?' I say. Beth stares at me, then she laughs and I laugh. And as we pass the scrubbed man in the ticket office I am only the teeniest bit jealous when he stares with admiration at Beth and not me. . .

THE QUIET WORLD OF
BERNARD BRIGGS

GERTRUDE was saying something. But then Gertrude was always saying something.

Half-heartedly, Bernard watched the snapping movement of her thin lips.

'You've put your knife down again, and yes, I can see it – yes it has, it's left a smear of marmalade on the tablecloth. Do you know how many tablecloths I washed last Monday? Five! Oh, I know I've got a washing machine, but they've still to be ironed. I was ironing for two and a half hours. Two and a half hours, what with the tablecloths and your shirts, and why you can't wear nylon shirts like everyone else I don't know. . . Everyone else's skin manages to breathe through nylon; it's just one of your fads. Our Phyllis was telling me the other day that Gordon wears nylon shirts *and* uses paper tissues instead of handkerchiefs. Half an hour a week, she reckons her ironing takes. . . .'

By the simple procedure of averting his eyes, Bernard switched himself off and slipped into his quiet world.

True, he knew it was a world of his own making, far removed from reality. Reality was the radio on the dresser, belting out its early morning 'wakey-wakey' music. Reality was his son Edwin whistling between his teeth as he studied his long sideboards in the kitchen mirror, and reality was his daughter Janet complaining that her egg was either too hard or too soft.

But for a long time now, as his deafness increased, Bernard had possessed the gift of being able to shell himself in welcome solitude.

And paradoxically, instead of cutting him off from the world around him, it had made him more observant; it had sharpened his sense of perception, until he felt he sometimes knew more about his fellow creatures than they knew themselves.

Quite dispassionately he studied his wife's face. He observed her morning-grey skin, the hairnet preserving her set, her incipient double-chin, and her quilted dressing-down which cruelly accentuated her bolster-shaped bosom.

Janet said something he didn't hear, jumped up so that her chair fell to the floor with a crash even Bernard heard. With his increased sensitivity he almost saw his wife's nerve-ends jangle, but quite calmly he folded his newspaper, walked round the table, pecked her on the cheek and collected his bowler hat and briefcase from the hall-stand.

Edwin was already in the drive, kicking his motor-bike into life, and the ensuing roar as he shot off down the avenue was no more to Bernard than a muted and rather attractive hum. It was the same on the station platform as he waited for the eight-fifteen.

On the fast line, trains rushed through on their last rocking few miles into London. He felt the vibration and saw his fellow travellers wince as the sound smote their eardrums, but he remained aloof, wrapped in his own soft cocoon of calm.

He had to be extra careful crossing the busy roads because cars approached him silently, speeding along on soundless wheels; a jet roared overhead, flying low as it prepared to land at Heathrow Airport. But to Bernard it was no more than a silent silver bird, gliding in on noiseless wings.

And in the office of the big iron foundry where he had worked for twenty-eight years as a clerk, he knew that through the glass partition diabolical machines pounded the hours away, and conversation had to be carried on at shouting level. But Bernard sat at his desk in his own private cloud of isolated peace.

That morning, two of his co-workers were involved in an argument – something, he gathered, about an impending strike. The shop steward was there, wearing his oil-spattered khaki overall, waving his arms about and pointing to a sheet of paper, jabbing it with an angry finger.

Once he turned to Bernard asking for confirmation of his grievances, but Bernard resorted to the subterfuge of shaking his head, conveying sadly that his deafness made it impossible for him to join in the heated discussion. So he was left in peace at his desk, with the smooth pages of the ledger open in front of him and not even the scratch of his relief-nibbed pen to disturb his concentration.

At one time he had shared his lunch hour with Dai Jones, a fellow clerk, going round the corner with him to the pseudo-Victorian pub and being subjected to a non-stop narration of Dai's conquests of any female who came within the range of his bulbous blue eyes.

Over the surrounding clink of glasses and barrage of conversation, Bernard found it increasingly difficult to hear, his gift for lip-reading almost nullified by the fact that Dai talked through a cigarette dangling from his lips. Once the big Welshman had realized that his captive audience of one was only hearing one word in three, he had moved on to a more receptive table.

Now Bernard lunched alone, drinking his half-pint of beer and munching his pork pie – watching, observing the fascinating pantomime being enacted all around him.

That day he walked back to the office with Joe, an engineering apprentice, a boy of twenty forced into a marriage by the indignant parents of his pregnant girl-friend.

'It's the noise that gets me down,' Joe confided to Bernard. 'The everlasting noise. It's just like that record – you know the one I mean, Ravel's something or other.'

Bernard lip-read and nodded his understanding.

'There's simply no escaping from it. They say men don't gossip, but did you hear them in the pub back there?'

Like the hypocrite Bernard at times suspected himself to be, he nodded again.

'And when I get home, if it isn't the telly, it's the baby yelling his head off or the wife nagging. D'you know what I'd like to do? I'd like to be cast away on one of those lovely desert islands without even a record-player. It's the curse of our times, is noise. No wonder so many people are going round the bend. You just can't get away from it.'

'I quite agree,' said Bernard as they parted company at the foundry gates, keeping the fact strictly to himself that he had found his own desert island a long time ago. . .

The only thing that would have worried Bernard about his mythical sojourn on a desert island was the fact that he would have been allowed to take only one book – the Bible and Shakespeare excluded, of course.

A self-educated man after leaving school at fourteen, he valued his books as if they were personal and precious friends. Every evening while the television screen flickered and danced in the living-room, he sat in his chair in the pool of light from the reading-lamp, devouring anything from Chekov to James Bond; everything from Byron to John Lennon's contemporary off-beat jingles.

That night as he read a paperback on the loves and life of an exceedingly lecherous old man, there was a programme on BBC 1, a medical programme, and the subject was ears and their intriguing abnormalities.

His wife snatched the book from him, forcing him to watch. . .

It appeared that there was an operation which could be performed in certain cases of hearing loss. Gertrude was sure Bernard would come into this category and turned up the sound so that he wouldn't miss a syllable. It seemed that by removing two small bones the surgeon could give at least partial hearing to the sufferer.

'It doesn't follow that *I* would benefit,' Bernard said, but Gertrude was adamant and no one could be more adamant than Gertrude when her mind was made up. Bernard could tell by her expression that she was itching to set wheels turning.

And within a month Bernard had been led like a docile lamb to his local GP; then to the Out-Patients' Department – ear, nose and throat – of the hospital, to be told by a keen bespectacled specialist that his particular case was indeed operable.

He was put on the waiting list and within months a bed was found for him. So, clad in his back-to-front hospital gown, with his teeth left behind in a little white dish, Bernard was wheeled into the operating theatre.

Less than two weeks later he was back home, minus a goodly portion of his thick grey hair, a bit off-balance, but with his hearing miraculously restored, exactly as the television programme had predicted.

It was indeed a miracle. The surgeon had told him that only a couple of decades ago he would have been left in his little world of silence, growing steadily more deaf, an unwanted piece of flotsam – one of life's rejects in fact, he seemed to be saying.

Bernard was properly grateful because, as anyone knows, miracles don't happen every day.

Now indeed, his life could begin. He could hear every single word Gertrude said; he could hear her voice, trumpet-loud, he could even hear the ticking of the kitchen clock, the family arguments that seemed to go on non-stop, his son's motor-bike roaring into life, the perpetual motion of the machines at work, his workmates' discussions about the Pools and their impending strikes, argued at fever-heat every day in the overcrowded noisy Victorian pub.

From being a non-participant always on the fringe of things, now he was expected to join in, to air his views, to take either one side or the other. And in the evenings, when the blaring television made it impossible for him to read, he was subjected during the advertisements to a whining list of his wife's domestic grievances. A never-ending stream of complaints and carping was borne along on the tide of her whining conversation.

'It's a miracle,' Joe said at work. 'I bet you could hear a pin drop.'

Bernard agreed that in all probability he could.

'A miracle of modern science,' Gertrude said, whisking him off to the pictures and the Bingo hall. 'My husband's a new man,' she told her friends proudly. 'Doesn't miss a thing.'

It was all true, of course. It *was* a miracle of modern science; he *was* a new man, and he didn't miss a thing.

Now his world was peopled with voices and sounds – the noise of traffic, the everlasting pop music from the transistor radio his daughter wore like a second skin; the arguments that seemed to pervade every corner of his home and above all, his wife's voice, a voice that over the years had receded to a muted undisturbing drone until it became part of the background.

Bernard was grateful and he said so, over and over again whenever she mentioned the subject.

'I can't express how grateful I am. I'm a new man, there's no doubt about that!

And he would never have admitted to a soul, not even to himself, that somewhere inside his partly shaved head, a little voice that only he could hear was weeping sadly for the loss of his own private, his own peacefully quiet little world.

TABLE FOR FOUR

ALTHOUGH the Mastersons had promised they would get in touch if ever they came over to visit England, the letter still came as something of a surprise.

Aileen read it aloud to her husband, Tom, over their late breakfast. The baby, born on her thirty-eighth birthday, still slept in his cot upstairs and the twins, harassed and white-faced, had left for school and the history paper of their O-level examinations. Tom, unshaven, was reading the morning's headlines, a slice of marmalade-spread toast in his hand.

Since his redundancy and his reluctant acceptance that he wasn't going to step straight into another job, he had grown quiet and withdrawn – almost, Aileen thought angrily, as if he'd done something to be ashamed of.

She'd found herself trying to jolly him along, adopting a too-bright tone in her voice, assuring him almost every day that it wasn't the end of the world, that something in his line was bound to turn up.

The bill for the rates had dropped through the letter-box, along with the letter from the Mastersons, but Aileen wasn't going to let her husband see it. Not yet. Not until he'd finished his breakfast and smoked his cigarette, the first of the three he allowed himself each day.

'Yes, you do remember them, love. The Americans we met in Italy last year but one. They had a girl about the same age as our two. You must remember how kind they were, and generous – they gave our two a whale of a good time.

'And surely you remember how, after they'd left, the hall porter gave me a parcel and it was that lovely black shawl Betty wore in the evenings? I'd admired it and after they'd gone, there it was, all wrapped up with a little note saying she hoped I'd wear it and think of her sometimes?'

'He wore a red shirt with the laps out of his trousers, and insisted on giving me a bottle of rum because I'd let slip it was my favourite drink,' Tom smiled as he remembered.

'And *you* insisted on opening it that last night and you drank it between you,' Aileen said, blessing the Mastersons and their letter for the spark of interest in her husband's eyes.

She started to read aloud: 'We'll be in London for just two days, the 11th and the 12th, and we'd just love you and Tom to join us for a meal. Pattie is all grown up now and doesn't want to spend her vacation with her ma and pa. She's got herself a boyfriend and Hank says he wouldn't care if she married him. He's so nice, we can't believe it, especially after the selection we've had up till now.'

'A precocious kid who chewed gum and painted her toenails,' Tom said, and Aileen smiled.

'But so sweet and generous, just like her parents. Dinner in the West End . . . I can't take it in. I'll wear my long black skirt – it never dates – and the shawl. Betty would like that.'

But Tom wasn't listening.

'We go out with them on one condition,' he was saying, and his voice held a determination it hadn't held for months. 'That I pay. That I pick up the bill.'

Aileen forgot to think twice before she crossed him.

'You have to be joking! How on earth can we afford a meal for four in the West End? Don't talk silly, love.'

Tom folded his newspaper and stood up, tall, unshaven and dignified in spite of the pyjama jacket flapping over his gardening trousers and the bedroom slippers he always seemed to be wearing these days.

'You heard what I said. They are visitors to our country and it is my turn, my *right* to entertain them. Either that or we don't see them. I mean it, love. That's the way it's got to be.'

Aileen tried not to lose her temper, but her voice actually wobbled on the verge of lost control.

'Have you any idea just how much a meal in the West End costs these days?' She produced the rates bill with a flourish. 'And we haven't paid the electricity bill yet. Oh, love, be sensible. We have fifty pounds in the Post Office, that's all. They're loaded, Hank and Betty. See, it says here, they're going on to Greece, they won't *expect* you to pay. They would be horrified if you even suggested it.'

'Then write back and tell them it's no go. Make some excuse to them,' Tom said and left her there, the letter still in her hand, its envelope with the bright green tissued lining lying there beside his discarded slice of toast.

Never at the best of times a very perceptive person, Aileen was puzzled. She followed him upstairs to pick up the baby from his cot and dress the fat squirming bundle, issues too complex for her to comprehend clouding her mind.

She wanted to see the Mastersons again. Now that Tom had laid down his ultimatum she wanted to have that evening out with them more than ever. He was being unreasonable and stupidly proud, showing an obstinacy she wouldn't have credited him with.

It was mad, she told an unresponsive baby, stuffing him into his high chair in the kitchen and spooning cereal into his open mouth. That money in the Post Office was there for emergencies, only to be touched if the money from the State ever failed to stretch to cover the mortgage repayments, the food and the cost of keeping two grown children at school and the baby clothed.

It was outrageous, but she would have to write back that very night and tell the Mastersons that they were sorry but they couldn't manage either the 11th or the 12th. She'd find some excuse.

The last time she'd written was at Easter, just after Tom's firm had gone bankrupt, and she'd made light of it, saying that a qualified engineer was bound to find a job. Believing it.

So even if they accepted the invitation, Hank Masterson wouldn't let Tom pay. She remembered his open-handed generosity, the way he'd run them around in his hired car, showing them parts of the Italian countryside they'd never otherwise have seen.

When Tom came downstairs, he was whistling underneath his breath, a sure sign that he was in a good mood.

'You drop a note and tell them we'll be there, love,' he said. 'And get out that blessed black shawl, and have your hair done. You deserve a night out.'

And coming behind her he dropped a light kiss on the top of her head and chucked the baby underneath his double chin before going out into the garden to mow a lawn that had been mowed only four days before.

They booked a table for four at a French restaurant tucked away in the labyrinth of streets behind Leicester Square, a restaurant Tom had taken her to when he was in a job, the week she'd discovered she was pregnant again after so long.

'It will be a boy this time,' Tom had said, 'an unexpected bonus.' They'd drunk to that, feeling young and gay, and the next month he had received his redundancy papers.

Hank and Betty Masterson were delighted to see them again. In the cloakroom, Aileen confided that her husband was still out of a job.

'But that's dreadful, honey,' Betty said. 'It's the same back home. Come forty, and a man's reckoned to be past his prime. What on earth do you *do* with Tom around all day?'

'He decorates and gardens,' Aileen told her, keeping back the information that the way things were going Tom would no longer be able to afford the price of a tin of paint or wallpaper, even to keep himself occupied, much less to improve the house.

'It sure is nice to see you again, honey,' Betty said, giving her tinted hair a satisfied pat and adjusting the neckline of her elegant blouse. 'And I don't know about you, but I'm hungry. I've decided to give my diet a rest until we get back home. Thank the Lord, Hank says he likes his women to have plenty of meat on their bones.' She chuckled.

The men waited for them in the tiny bar, and Aileen noticed without surprise that Hank was quicker off the mark than Tom in paying for the round of drinks before they went in to the dining room to eat.

Their corner table was ready, and they got down to the serious business of ordering from menus as big as wind-breaks, with prices beside each item which made Aileen – conditioned to counting every single penny – actually close her eyes in horror.

It was so long since she'd dined out that she couldn't believe a steak could cost so much, and she found herself eyeing the hors d'oeuvre and calculating that they would have made a satisfying and complete meal at home for the whole family.

At first Tom was quiet, letting Hank and the voluble Betty do most of the talking. Then, after his wineglass had been replenished for the third time, he seemed to relax and they compared notes about the children.

Betty said they just couldn't wait to get their girl Pattie married off to her boyfriend.

'Before marriage as an institution dies right out,' she said, and she pronounced it 'institootion' and they laughed.

Hank said what a pity it was they had all been born too early to enjoy the permissive society, and he flirted with Aileen and she responded, slipping the black shawl from her shoulders and catching sight of her animated expression in the wall mirror on her left.

The sweets trolley was wheeled to the table, and Betty chose out-of-the-season raspberries, and the waiter smothered them in cream and she said that she'd have to starve herself silly when they got back home. The others had extravagant chocolate gateau.

They had liqueurs with the coffee, and Hank reminded Tom about the bottle of rum, and they were laughing again when the waiter, at a signal from Hank, brought the bill over and placed it, folded neatly, on the table between the two men.

Tom moved so quickly that Aileen thought she had
imagined it. Waving Hank's protests away and barely glancing
at the total, he reached in his pocket for his wallet.

For Aileen it was as if the whole room, with its shaded red
lights and gay scarlet napkins lying discarded amongst the
coffee cups and empty glasses, swayed and dipped out of
focus.

She had no need to guess at the amount involved. With her
mind attuned over the months to assessing every penny,
Aileen watched mesmerized as he took out four five-pound
notes and placed them on the tray.

She could feel an actual lump in her throat, a tightening in
her chest. Hank was saying something, and she stretched her
mouth into what she hoped would pass for a smile as she
turned to listen to the conversation.

Already her mind was screaming aloud at Tom, chastising
him, asking him why, why, why? How could he have done
this?

She watched the waiter return with the tray. And then, as
Tom waved the change away with a hand holding one of
Hank's large cigars, she saw the expression on his face.

It was as though all the long months of degradation, of
humiliation, of disappointment, had never happened to him.

The man who had picked up the bill was the Tom she had
known a long time ago. The generous man, the man of pride,
the husband the long months of unemployment and rejection
had taken from her.

And she knew she would say nothing to him about it . . .
nothing at all.

TRUE COLOURS

PERHAPS it's true that many a business deal is transacted on the golf course, but Mr Swales, my boss, doesn't play golf at all; racing is his 'thing', and he does it in style, with a hired private box on the top tier at Royal Ascot. He gives his guests the full treatment – starting with gin and tonic, then lunch, and finishing with champagne at five.

Usually his wife goes along with him to play hostess, but on that warm June day, when the sun shone down from a blue haze of sky and the turf was a coloured television shade of green, she woke up with a bad migraine.

'So you'll have to come along and do the honours,' he said.

The prospect scared me stiff, and in vain I pleaded that I had still to type the minutes of the last board meeting.

'Bruce Gordon will be going,' he said craftily.

And that was that. . .

I've loved Bruce Gordon, the firm's junior accountant, since I joined as a typist straight from commercial college three years ago. And even now, in my elevated position as personal and very private secretary to the managing director, he still treats me like a piece of office furniture.

Bruce came to the firm fresh from university, and Mr Swales says he'll go a long way. But it wouldn't be with me; that much was beginning to be obvious.

Mr Swales looked at his watch, and said that was that then, and gave me the morning off to 'pretty myself up'.

'It's going to be a beautiful day once this mist clears,' he said. Then he turned round and took out his wallet and flourished a ten-pound note. 'Here's a little something to play with, Anne, but don't put it all on the first race.'

And he patted my shoulder in a fatherly way, gave me strict instructions about my duties as stand-in hostess, and told me not to be late.

I promised, covered up my typewriter and went outside to the little courtyard at the back where I keep my car. To maintain it and pay the rent of my small flat means I am constantly near the breadline.

This time, I decided, I would make Bruce see me as a woman and not a piece of inanimate office furniture. So, back in my flat and remembering the Ascot scene in *My Fair Lady*, I chose a plain sleeveless shift dress, worn with white tights and *the* hat.

The hat is a sort of family heirloom. My mother bought it originally to wear at my brother's wedding, and when she told my father how much it had cost – dividing the truth neatly into two – he nearly collapsed.

It is red and the brim is about a yard wide, adorned with full-blown ruched white nylon roses. It is a once-in-a-lifetime kind of hat, and when I stared at myself in my full-length mirror my courage nearly failed me.

But there was no time to change either my mind or my ensemble, and at half-past eleven exactly I slid carefully behind the wheel of the Mini and started off for Ascot.

I saw Mr Swales's car right away, and was surprised to see that Bruce wasn't with him. I had taken it for granted that they would drive down from the office together, and for a quite dreadful moment I thought that perhaps Bruce wasn't coming after all and my heart sank right down into my white tights.

'Where's Bruce?' I asked him.

'He'll be along. He's picking Jane Gorman up,' said my boss cheerfully, adjusting the white carnation in his buttonhole slightly.

'And who's Jane Gorman?' I asked, feeling a pang of jealousy so acute that it was an actual pain.

'Daughter of old Gorman,' explained Mr Swales, his lips

twitching I'm sure at the sight of *the* hat. 'He's in Textiles, you know, but they've flipped over to Japan on some scheme or other. Thought it was a shame to waste the tickets, so I asked Bruce to do the honours with their daughter.'

'How old is she?' I asked grimly, but he was waving to the occupants of a car which had just driven in, and I had to smile and shake hands with a Mr Jameson in Plastics, and his fuchsia-velvet-hatted wife.

We waited for a few minutes, and I was introduced to a Mr Iveson in Light Engineering and *his* wife, who was wearing a hat in cream lace with brown spots, like a mushroom forcibly grown to gigantic proportions in some dark cellar.

'Where the devil has Bruce got to?' Mr Swales muttered, and with what I recognized as his delaying tactics he handed round our little striped badges and, dutifully, we all anchored them to our respective chests.

'Think we'll move on,' he was saying, and we were waiting to cross the busy main road when Bruce swung his car into the parking ground, positioned it with dexterity and handed out a girl who looked like a model from a London fashion house.

I hated her on sight. To begin with, she made the rest of us look like the chorus line-up from a third-rate revue. She was wearing a plain coffee-coloured linen dress, with tights and shoes to match, making her legs appear long and slim; her hat was a single rose in a tiny froth of net.

'Ah, here we are!' said my boss, and fresh introductions were made before we went through the Private Boxes entrance, manned by a bowler-hatted official, and caught the lift to the Top Tier.

Betty, the girl who 'does' for the firm on such occasions, had laid the table beautifully, and at a nod from Mr Swales she handed round gins and tonics.

Jane Gorman took her drink out on to the balcony, followed by Bruce, of course. He looked absolutely besotted, and seeing my boss giving me a meaningful glance, I asked

Mrs Jameson if this was the first Race Meeting she had attended.

That was a mistake, because it turned out her father had been a jockey and she went on about form and the decline in racing procedure, and I had to pretend fascinated interest and try not to watch Bruce giving Jane Gorman a preview of the course through his binoculars . . . and taking his time about it too.

Before we sat down to lunch, we all trooped downstairs to place our first bets and I chose a horse called Black Sorrow, because that fitted my mood; with a lot of giggling, and egged on by Bruce who fancies himself as an expert in these matters, Jane Gorman placed her bet on the favourite, a horse that went by the name of Night of Joy.

At lunch I sat between Bruce and Mr Iveson, Light Engineering, and as I ate my smoked trout, I heard all about his views on the permissive society. Bruce ignored me until the roast stuffed capon arrived and he was forced by politeness to offer me the Mexican salad.

Fluttering my carefully fixed-on eyelashes from underneath the rose-strewn brim of *the* hat, I asked him how things were.

'What things?' he asked, grinning at me; then he said, 'Do you know who you remind me of in that flowery outfit, Anne?'

'The bride's mother,' I said gloomily, and he threw his head back and laughed out loud, and I thought how much I could have hated him if I hadn't decided to love him for the rest of my life.

And I never did find out who I really reminded him of, because from his other side Jane Gorman claimed his attention, and he turned away from me as if she'd pulled his head round on a string.

The arrival of the pineapple meringue chantilly coincided with the start of the first race, and just guess who won?

Old Night of Joy, of course, and Black Sorrow cantered along miles behind the rest of the field, as if he hadn't even tried.

'Want me to go and collect your winnings?' Bruce, all gallant and obliging, asked Jane Gorman and she said if he would be such a darling and had he any ideas about the two-thirty?

And of course he had and, although that was the horse I would have backed, I chose a rank outsider by the name of Frustration the Third and sweetly asked Bruce if he would mind placing my bet at the same time.

Over the continental cheeseboard, I made an effort for the firm's sake and asked Jane Gorman what she did, and she said nothing actually, but most days she went down to her father's office and *imbibed.*

'I did a secretarial course,' she said, as she smoked a black cigarette in a long holder. 'But shorthand is definitely not my *thing.* All those squiggles, I ask you!' She giggled, and when Bruce came back, she giggled some more and told him she was sure it was her lucky day, and he bent his dark head close to her pale ash hair and said something I was sure was absolutely sick-making, because she blew a cloud of smoke up to the ceiling and wrinkled her nose at him.

Her horse won again, of course, and mine came in fourth and, before three o'clock, Mr Swales suggested that we all adjourn to the paddock to watch the horses being paraded.

One of the jockeys looked like Frank Sinatra must have done in his youth, and his colours were the most heavenly emerald green and royal blue, halved horizontally, worn with a quartered cap, and Jane Gorman insisted that she must put her money on him.

I had decided to sit that race out, and I watched them tear up the steps to place her bet, and saw the race with the rest of our party from the rails by the winning post.

Needless to say, old emerald green and royal blue came in second and, back in our box, I sulked away in a corner, and didn't care less that Mr Swales was giving me looks that would have killed a lesser woman stone-dead.

There was a horse running next called Love Me Not, and I

put the rest of my money on that.

It threw its rider in the first furlong and Jane's horse, Meet Me Tonight, won by a photo finish.

She was almost hysterical with excitement and Bruce wasn't exactly unconcerned. He kept smiling at her, and quite dispassionately I wished that I were dead.

'Your luck's in, Miss Gorman,' my boss told her.

She giggled and said would we all think she was absolutely mad if she put all her winnings on the last race?

'You'd be a fool not to,' said Mr Iveson, Light Engineering, and Mr Jameson, Plastics, said what fun, and everyone went with her to put her entire winnings on a horse called Happy Day.

When the race started we all crowded down the steps on to our balcony, and Jane Gorman kept saying, 'I can't look. I simply can't bear to look.'

Then Bruce spoke to me.

'You haven't had much luck today, Anne,' he said in his deep voice, and thinking that was surely the understatement of the year, I smiled bravely.

'What is money, anyway?' I asked him, and he said, 'What indeed?' and gripped my arm for a moment.

I really loved him, I thought in wonder. I loved him, and he hardly knew that I existed. To him I was merely a secretary from the office.

Sadly, I sipped my champagne, and it tickled my nose and made me sneeze the way it always does, and my eyes stung with tears.

Below me, Bruce had his arm round Jane Gorman's shoulders to steady the binoculars and suddenly everyone shouted, 'They're off!'

Happy Days was number three and, without any surprise at all, I heard the excited voice of the commentator telling us that Happy Day was coming up fast on the rails.

Jane Gorman was actualy jumping up and down and all our

little party shouted 'Come on, Happy Day! *Come on*, Happy Day!'

All except me.

I was the world's worst sport, I knew, but nothing could have induced me to cheer that horse on. I closed my eyes and found myself saying a silent prayer. An uncharitable prayer that didn't deserve to be answered.

But it was. . .

With only yards to the finish, Happy Day fell behind, and came in fifth, and there was the sudden small silence that falls at the end of a race.

I saw Bruce pat Jane Gorman's shoulder in a sympathetic gesture and I saw her knock his hand away.

I couldn't hear what she was saying, but she was angry, that much was obvious, more than angry – she had lost her temper completely and, as I watched, mesmerized, she stamped her foot in childish disgust.

Everyone else had seen it too and, embarrassed, they climbed the steep steps back into the box, and Mr Swales made a heavy joke about not letting good champagne go to waste.

But Mr Jameson in Plastics said they must be getting back to town as they had a dinner engagement, and Mr Iveson, Light Engineering, said something about the children.

There were handshakes offered all round, and although Jane Gorman thanked Mr Swales prettily for his hospitality, I could see that she was still furious, because two spots of colour showed through her make-up.

Rather subdued, we all went down in the lift, and as we neared the parking ground, Bruce appeared.

'I have to run Miss Gorman home,' he whispered, 'but are you doing anything special this evening? I mean, it's been such a marvellous afternoon, hasn't it, and it would be a pity not to end it properly?'

I stared at him. My mouth had suddenly grown dry and I

couldn't have answered him if I'd tried.

'Just dinner somewhere to commiserate with you on being such a good sport about losing all afternoon,' he said.

I found my voice. There was something that had to be said. 'It was Mr Swales's money I was losing, and I'm not a good sport at all. During that last race, my mind was seething with ignoble thoughts.'

'Was it now?' he grinned. 'We won't go into that, but I'll pick you up around eight. All right?'

'All right,' I said, and he chased off across the grass to where Jane Gorman waited impatiently.

'Sorry you didn't have better luck, Anne,' Mr Swales said. 'Perhaps it was the hat that put the horses off.'

Seriously, I said to him, 'I will always remember today as one of the luckiest in my life,' and he gave me a puzzled glance, then shrugged his shoulders and said we'd have to work late the next day.

Then we walked towards our respective cars – my boss's Bentley, and my little third-hand Mini.

To all intents and purposes, I had been on the losing side all day, but remembering the look in Bruce's dark eyes, I knew differently.

Snatching off *the* hat, I tossed it on to the seat behind and, as I drove back along the leafy lanes, all the birds in Buckinghamshire seemed to be bursting into full-throated song. . .

Telling me I'd won.

THE PIANIST

THE beautiful theme song from the film *Love Story* was their
tune and she would play it over and over again on the upright
piano in the sitting-room, so that her long-suffering parents
would look despairingly at each other and sigh.

'Oh no, not again!' their glances would say. She walked
about in a dream, a tall girl with thick and shining dark hair,
pale skin, freckles on her nose and eyes of a surprising dark
blue.

Loving him was painful; an agony of waiting for the
telephone to ring, of turning up for meetings far too early, her
heart doing strange things until he came in sight. A time of
utter selfishness, when family ties, loyalties to friends, stood
for nothing. When all that mattered was that he should love
her, as she worshipped him.

'The fiercer the flame, the sooner it burns itself out,' her
mother told her father hopefully, watching her only daughter
grow pale and thin, the intensity of her feelings changing her
from a lively seventeen-year-old into a woman with haunted
eyes who would, her mother was sure, have run to the ends of
the earth if he had beckoned.

'Why can't she see that he's no good?' she asked her
husband, and he could only answer that life was like that; that
after all, love was proverbially blind.

'He's too old for her, too much of a nothing, not even
good-looking,' they told each other, and then exasperated,
they said it to her. That was a mistake.

'You don't know him as I do,' she told them, her voice
becoming soft with longing even as she spoke his name. 'He's
. . . oh, he's everything. It's no good trying to make you
understand.'

And standing by the window, hardly concealed by the net curtains, they watched her run down the path, hair flying free. Watched her get into his car and saw the way her young face lifted eagerly for the longed-for kiss.

'Where are they going?' they asked each other, her mother and father. Then they switched on the television and watched with unseeing eyes, each of them filled with ghastly imaginings. Of furtive fumblings in lay-bys, of evenings spent together in his flat, while his friend with whom he shared was obligingly out for hours.

'She is only seventeen,' they would tell each other, then shake their heads. For to be seventeen in this day and age is to be fully grown-up, only a year away from the vote. Old enough to marry. They prayed that it would end. Then, perversely, when it did, and they saw her subdued face, stiff with hurt, white and closed against them, refusing to talk, even to speak his name – they wished him back.

And in spite of the fact that his familiar shabby car no longer waited at the kerb, she still played their tune on the upright piano: the theme from *Love Story*. Over and over again she played it, sometimes with the tears rolling down her cheeks.

'To think,' her mother said, 'that we paid for her to have lessons when she was a little girl and had almost to manhandle her on to the stool to do her practice . . . now she sits on it for hours at a time, as if she was growing from it, just playing that one tune.'

'I even found myself humming it at the office today,' her father said. 'I got some funny looks from the girl I was dictating letters to, I can tell you.'

'I was humming it in the Post Office queue and the clerk joined in,' her mother admitted. Then she smiled. 'But she does play it rather well; you have to say that.'

'No wonder, when she practises so much,' her father said. 'One thing is sure; the day that she stops playing it, we'll know she's cured.'

And then one day, it happened. She came home from her commercial college and instead of making straight for the piano, walked into the kitchen and for no reason that her mother could fathom, hugged her and announced that she was hungry.

She sat on the kitchen table, drinking milk, swinging her long legs and talking as if she'd just discovered the art of conversation. She chatted away, making her bewildered mother laugh even as she sent up a silent prayer of thanks.

But being a wise parent, she said nothing, nothing at all, until she was alone with her husband that evening.

'It's over,' she said.

'Thank God,' he said, and not being a blaspheming man, he meant what he said. 'Where has she gone tonight?'

'To a party,' her mother told him. 'Given by one of the girls in her class. I wish you'd been home early enough to see her go.'

She put down her knitting and visibly glowed with pride. 'It's as though she's come back to life again.' She dropped a stitch and didn't even sigh.

'She looked so pretty. She was wearing that blue dress she wouldn't wear when she was going out with *him* because she said *he* didn't like it. And she'd curled her hair. "Don't wait up for me," she said, and I promised we wouldn't.'

She rolled up the knitting and thrust it behind a cushion. 'How about a drink? I feel as if we ought to celebrate.'

So happy were they that one drink turned into three and then, very slightly sloshed, they climbed into bed, falling asleep almost immediately.

It must have been around midnight when they were jerked awake out of their first deep sleep.

Downstairs, soft-pedalling but loud enough for them to hear, someone was playing the piano.

Sitting upright and straining their ears, they recognized the tune at once: the beautiful theme music from *Doctor Zhivago*. Played uncertainly, as if the fingers were hesitating over the keys, but all the same played with obvious emotion.

'I'll go down,' her father said, getting out of bed – but her mother stopped him.

'No, I'll go. You're bound to say the wrong thing,' she said, reaching for her dressing-gown.

And there was their lovely daughter, sitting at the piano with an all-too-familiar expression on her face, picking out the tune with such tender concentration that at first she didn't see her mother standing hesitantly in the doorway.

Then she smiled, her eyes blazing blue with excitement.

'Oh, Mummy,' she said. 'It was the most fabulous party. And I met this boy. They were playing this record when he asked me to dance with him.' She played a few more bars, then closed the piano lid with reluctance. 'I know it sounds silly when you've just met someone, but we both decided this is going to be our tune. It seems to say, oh, just everything. I know you can't possibly understand, but it does.'

Then, leaving her coat where she had dropped it on the floor, she switched off the table lamp and glided towards the door, walking dreamily as if she were fast asleep already.

'Good night, Mummy,' she said, speaking as if from some far-away place.

RUNAWAY DAUGHTER

ONE Sunday morning, when the sun shone and the air was as warm and soft as brushed nylon, Bill's youngest daughter Belinda ran away from hearth and home, carrying two heavy suitcases and swearing never to return. Bill didn't worry overmuch. Over the years, his entire family had left home for good with monotonous regularity, usually getting no farther than the low bench on the other side of the garden wall, returning silently after a period of contemplation, their reappearance unremarked and their dramatic exit never referred to again by the family.

His wife, Eloise, still slim and dark with a curly fringe, had been an actress in ENSA when he met her at the beginning of the war, and although the birth of their eldest daughter had put an end to her career as far as the stage was concerned, she had never really stopped acting since.

All their four children had inherited her dramatic tendencies, and it seemed to Bill that his entire life had been spent in the wings as it were, watching them squeeze every ounce of unbridled passion out of the most trivial of daily occurrences.

Belinda, he remembered, had made quite a habit of packing her teddy bear in a carrier-bag, and Hugh, his only son – especially now that A-levels were pending – had left temporarily only the week before in a flurry of rage, banging the front door behind him. Even Eloise, who should have grown out of the habit by now, had recently disappeared for a good half hour on a difficult Sunday when their two married daughters and their families had turned up unexpectedly for lunch and the joint that week was no bigger than a man's fist.

'I'm nothing but a skivvy,' she'd pronounced, 'and a taken-for-granted one at that,' and he'd winked at his daughters, organizing them on the peeling of extra potatoes in confident anticipation of her swift return.

He reminded himself of all this, but it was no good. This time was different, he could feel it in his large bones. Belinda was seventeen, and in love for the first time. Really in love, or so she thought, with a long-haired boy called Jamus, a boy Bill had referred to in her hearing as 'The Great Hairy'. A mistake, and a bad one.

He should have known better; he should have known from long experience that when one of his family's big scenes was pending their sense of humour was completely non-existent, and he should have remembered that for a long time now, Belinda had stopped laughing at his jokes.

She had stood there, her long, dark hair framing her small pointed face, her eyes flashing fire, looking for all the world like a naughty twelve-year-old in her ridiculous black velvet smock.

'I have only to telephone Jamus, and he'll be round like a flash to fetch me,' she announced. 'He knows what it's like for me living at home with a lot of . . . a lot of bourgeois sentimentalists!'

'The telephone is there,' Eloise had said, with a wide sweep of an arm, and Belinda had gone all dignified and said that what she had to say to Jamus was private and confidential, and she would phone him from the call-box down the lane.

'After I've packed,' she told them as she rushed upstairs.

They followed automatically, big scenes always being played to full audience capacity as a matter of course, and Hugh came out of his room to lean, arms folded, against the door post and to support – Bill had no doubt – his sister.

Eloise by now was crying pathetically into the lace-edged handkerchief he swore she kept for such occasions.

'But you *can't* be going to marry Jamus? He hasn't even got a job. All he does, as far as I can see, is sit around on his bottom and worry about Africa!'

'Africa's problems are our problems, or should be,' Belinda told her coldly, quoting Jamus, her father knew. 'And who said anything about *marrying* him?'

Eloise, who by now was Greta Garbo to the life, in one of her old films, started walking the carpet wringing her hands. She was the only woman Bill knew who actually wrung her hands, and it never failed to fascinate him.

'You mean you're going to live in sin?' she wailed, and that was when Belinda took down the two cases from the top of the wardrobe and started to fold things into them.

Bill began to get worried. Usually when his family packed to run away from home, they packed as people do in films, in two minutes flat. A frilly nightie whisked from a drawer, a framed photograph from the bedside-table and a couple of dresses snatched from their hangers in the wardrobe. But Belinda was packing in earnest as if, knowing that she would never return, she was making sure she had everything she needed.

She laid a row of shoes neatly in the bottom of the first case.

'This is 1971, not the Victorian era, and you know there are men who literally *thrive* on the uncertainty of not being married, and Jamus is one of them.'

Greta Garbo's voice rose two octaves as she said something about Belinda never darkening her door again if she took such a step, and from the doorway Hugh stroked the revolting moustache he was in the process of growing, and said 'pshaw!'

Bill turned and looked at him, and marvelled, not for the first time, at a school system which allowed its pupils to sit at their desks sprouting drooping moustaches. The generation gap seemed to stretch like an ever-widening gulf between him and his two youngest children.

'And what will you do when the babies come?' demanded

his wife, and Belinda flounced over to the wardrobe, her little bottom twitching indignantly in the swaying smock. She took a long, frilled nightie which Bill suspected could equally have been a dress, from its hanger, and started to fold it.

'There won't be any babies, not until our relationship is thoroughly stabilized. We've discussed it.'

Bill ordered his son back to his room and, because he spoke in his normal voice, his son ignored him, curling his lip at his father from underneath the fungus.

'Go back to your room,' thundered Bill in his best imitation of Mr Barrett of Wimpole Street, and Hugh immediately responded with over-played obedience.

Eloise flopped down on the only bit of the bed not covered by the suitcases, her face more crumpled than the handkerchief in her hand. Belinda was staring at her quilted dressing-gown hanging behind the door and wondering, her father knew, if it would take up too much room in one of the cases.

He began to feel very worried.

'As a member of the affluent society,' she was telling her mother gently, 'you can't begin to understand. Admit it now. Your horizons are set no farther than the garden gate. You don't care about the terrible things happening in the world today. You and Daddy own this house, you have your own car for shopping, you play bridge and go to your Women's Institute meetings, dozing while someone stands there on the platform telling you about babies starving in a far-off land.

'You go abroad every summer, seeing nothing more of the country than the strip of beach in front of your hotel. You knit as you watch scenes of violence on television, and if someone gets killed, you don't even drop a stitch. That's what's wrong with the world. People just don't *care*.'

Bill closed his eyes. Oh, that long-haired Jamus had done his job thoroughly. He could see him, talking, always talking, dressed like a pantomime robber the last time he'd been round to the house.

'And Jamus *does* care, I suppose?' Eloise was saying bitterly as, frowning with concentration, Belinda sorted out hair rollers.

'Of course,' she said haughtily.

Before her husband's eyes, Eloise bridled beautifully. 'Well then, tell me what he *does* about it all, apart from talking?'

Her face was flushed with righteous anger and he knew she was working up to her big scene. Her enunciation was perfect: 'So you and Jamus think that your father and I are selfish and uncaring? Let me tell you something. When your father was the same age as Jamus, he was flying a bomber over Germany. When we were married, I lived in one room, going down to the shelters every night with my baby in my arms – that was your sister, Annabel.

'When the war was over, your father worked sixteen hours a day, then studied half-way through the night in order to pass his engineering examinations. I made every stitch we wore, even soled and heeled shoes, and now that we're coming up to retirement age, would you and your Jamus begrudge us the modest pleasures we've waited so long to enjoy? Don't talk to *me* about the world and its problems. At least I and my generation *did* something about them!'

It was a long speech, even for Eloise, and it seemed to Bill that before she swept from the room, pressing the handkerchief to her mouth, she hesitated as if expecting a round of applause.

'Wars solve nothing you know, Daddy,' Belinda said gently, and Bill closed his eyes again and said a silent prayer. His youngest daughter had always been the child of his heart, although he would never have admitted it, not even to himself. There was an affinity, an unspoken love that sometimes shimmered between them. He felt it now.

What he was going to say was important, so important that it could decide the whole future of his beloved daughter's life.

Going over to her he laid a hand in a kind of blessing on her shoulder. 'You know, love, I always did think that Jamus had his hairy head screwed on properly. He isn't too proud to be kept by you for one thing. You'll be keeping on your job at the library of course?'

He squeezed her shoulder. 'You young people are right to sweep away the hypocrisy my generation was hemmed around with. After all, if he isn't married to you he can just walk out if things get too much for him. Far better than being tied for life to someone he might grow tired of.'

Belinda's eyes widened as she stared for a long moment at her father. Then she closed the cases and clicked the locks into place.

'Jamus loves me,' she said simply, and Bill knew how Judas must have felt in the moment of his betrayal of Christ.

But, praying he'd said the right thing, he let her go, hearing the all-too-familiar slam of the big door, watching through the window as she walked down the long garden path, the two cases weighing her down and banging against her long slim legs with every step.

Now that the battle was over and the scene played to its close, Eloise's tears had disappeared and she was actually humming as she laid the table. Four knives and four forks, Bill saw without surprise.

He wished with all his heart that he could share her confidence, and as he hung about the kitchen, getting in her way, he felt the muscles of his stomach tighten into a hard knot of fear. 'I'll pick some sweet peas for the table,' he told her, and carrying the garden scissors went outside to stare down the long path at the garden wall.

Was Belinda sitting there on the other side, brooding on what he'd said, or was she even now ringing Jamus from the call-box?

Eloise came out and told him she was starting to make the gravy, a normal Sunday ritual because she claimed he always disappeared just as she was about to dish up. Her face was flushed pink from the heat of the oven, and he begged her silent forgiveness if things didn't work out as he'd planned.

Standing on tiptoe, she kissed his chin and in spite of his terrible anxiety, there was a question he felt he must ask her. 'Did you *really* sole and heel the children's shoes when they were young? I have no picture of you in my mind sitting on a low stool with a last clasped between your knees.'

She giggled. 'Poetic licence.'

'Belinda wasn't play-acting, you know,' he said quietly, and his wife's eyes widened into overdone reproach.

'And neither was I,' she said, and turned to go back into the house, her mind quite obviously on nothing more important than the stirring of the gravy for lunch.

Bill sighed. If *he* couldn't differentiate between what was real and what was sham, then how could he expect his seventeen-year-old daughter to know the difference? Sitting out there all alone – his mind refused to consider the alternative – wrestling with a problem that could affect her whole life.

He buried his nose in the bunch of sweet peas he had picked, not knowing why he was picking them, and the sweetness of their scent made him feel physically sick.

With an effort of will he didn't think he possessed, he stopped himself from walking down the garden to reassure himself that Belinda was still there. Instead he went slowly inside, keeping to the unspoken family rule that the runner-away must return of his or her own volition.

Sitting at the table with Belinda's empty chair reproaching him, he watched with disbelief as Hugh, quite oblivious to the drama, started to demolish a plate piled high with meat and vegetables.

'I'm not all that hungry,' he was starting to say, when the sound of the front door opening and closing quietly made him turn weak from relief.

And in true family tradition, Belinda's reappearance was not referred to, and only her pale face and red-rimmed eyes gave any indication of the silent inner struggle that had gone on behind the garden wall.

It was later, much later in the afternoon when he found himself alone with her and, his heart brimming over with tenderness and pity, he put out an arm and drew her to him. He knew she would never tell him if, in letting her go, in giving her 'permission' to go, he had been the instigator of her return. It was enough that she had changed her mind.

'Try not to worry about it, love,' he said.

And his daughter, true child of her mother, raised a pair of expressive dark eyes to his. 'Worry about what, Daddy?' she asked, with an air of innocence that would have won her an Oscar in any film.

Bill sighed. Well, all right then, he'd play it their way. After all, he had married into the profession, so to speak. 'Africa,' he said gravely. 'I feel sure that her problems, vast as they are, will sort themselves out, given a little time. . .'

PASSING STRANGERS

THERE was fog and thick low cloud blanketing out the airport. That meant delays for the planes taking off and delays for the planes coming in. They were hampered with hand luggage, the man and the girl, with coats looped over their arms; and they each carried a cup of coffee, balancing it precariously, looking round for an empty table and finding one together.

'Do you mind?' he said, and she smiled her agreement, so they sat down opposite each other – complete strangers, occupied by their own thoughts, irritated by the delay, but prepared to wait with typical British resignation.

He was a dark man of less than average height, and he wore the clerical grey suit and white shirt of the travelling executive. Not good-looking, not in the accepted sense, but with a gentle sensitivity in the quite deep lines on his thin face, giving him an expression of perplexed anxiety.

A married man, she guessed, playing her game of making up backgrounds for people she met in a crowd. Going off to a conference, leaving behind a wife who wore jeans all day and drove the kids to school in her own little car. A wife who probably believed in Women's Lib in principle, but wanted no part of it in reality.

She was a small thin girl with gleaming hair the colour of a burnished chestnut, a crazy yellow peaked cap perched on top of it, and a soft and mobile mouth with a dimple at the corners.

About twenty, he guessed inexpertly, and not beautiful, not in the accepted sense, but with an appealing kind of cameo prettiness. A girl of today, not married – at least judging by the ringless hands – but no doubt believing in what she would call deep and lasting relationships.

She took out a cigarette, hesitated for a moment – then, in a voice that was lower than he expected it would be, asked him did he mind?

Smiling, he shook his head and before she could find her lighter, lurking somewhere in the depths of her brown leather handbag, reached across with his own and flicked it into action.

'I gave it up a year ago, but I keep this handy,' he smiled; and she smiled, a teasing smile in which the dimples came and went.

'I give it up every day,' she said. 'Every cigarette is going to be my last. You know?'

He nodded. 'I confess to being the world's original hypochondriac. A programme on television coupled with a bill for the rates that knocked me sideways on the same day did the trick, but I was hell to live with for at least a month.'

A massive man with a black beard and a white turban swathing his head stopped at their table, gave them a swift scrutiny from beneath wildly curling prawn-like eyebrows, then passed on. She smiled, her eyes alight.

'Have you ever noticed how airports are like fairgrounds? You know – everyone looking larger than life? You see the sort of people you'd never meet walking down a High Street. Maybe it's the fact that they're flying off to far-away places gives them an extra touch of glamour.

'Just look at that family over there. The wife in her cream trouser suit, the husband zipped up in brown leather. And those kids. . .'

'I know,' he said immediately, enchanting her. 'Those kids have never had runny noses, or eaten fish fingers for tea.'

'And that orange-haired old dame sitting by herself, with white powder pressed into every wrinkle on her face. What is she, do you suppose? A retired actress, or an old-style courtesan flying out to spend the winter in the sun in the villa she's bought with her ill-gotten gains?'

Her fingers were curved round her coffee cup as she talked. He found himself unable to take his eyes off her face, and wondered if she talked with such spontaneity to every stranger she met. And with the wondering came an illogical stab of jealousy if that were so.

'Which flight are you on?' he asked, hoping and yet not daring to hope.

'Geneva,' she told him, and quickly he lowered his eyes before she read the disappointment in them.

'And you?'

'Rome. It's a real flying visit, in the literal sense. I've to be back in the office with my report on Thursday. And you? Is yours business or pleasure?'

'Ministering to my sister who's just had her first baby,' she said, and they were quiet for a while, staring down at the table, each wanting to know more about the other and yet knowing there wasn't time: consciously – and yet without knowing it – holding their breaths in case their respective flights were called.

'Once a long time ago,' he told her, hurrying his words as if he knew that time was running out on them, and yet wanting her to understand, 'I thought I could have been a writer, but when I left university and told my father I was going to bum round Europe for a year, he gave me hell. Reminded me of how it had been with him, rushed off to fight a war before he'd had a chance to get his qualifications. Qualifications! To my father that's a sacred word. "You'll get nowhere without them, lad," he'd say, and so he kept me at my books. He'd have locked me in my room had he found it necessary. And now I have them, but somewhere along the line the urge to write got lost.'

Along with the wife and kids in that open-plan house in the suburbs, she thought, noticing for the first time the gold signet ring on his wedding finger. But she said nothing: just sat still as a stone, listening, loving the way, the shy way his eyes slid away from hers as he talked about lost dreams.

All at once he looked up and directly at her, and she saw the image of the boy he had been once, racing across his features like the sun coming up. With a start of pure surprise she realized that already she knew more about this man than any of the men she'd known before.

'I have a small notebook,' he was saying, 'and now and again, if I see something that interests me or moves me, I write it down. Maybe just a sentence, but it's there. It's a putting down on paper what I couldn't express in the spoken word. Perhaps some day. . .'

The sentence was left unfinished. He stared at her again, noticing the tiny hint of down on her ears, marvelling at the way her eyes changed colour even as he watched – hazel to green and back again.

'More likely never,' she said, shaking her head and frowning as if the truth was an actual pain. 'Life's a compromise. You're old enough to accept that particular home truth, surely?'

'It shouldn't be,' he said fiercely. 'It's so short – we should be able to reach out and take whatever we want, when we want it, don't you agree?'

'I'm young enough to believe that but, well, things that have happened to me have taught me that it doesn't work that way,' she said, stubbing out her cigarette. 'No, it hasn't worked that way for me at all.'

She was suddenly vulnerable, so that he reached out and closed his hand over hers in a small gesture of comfort.

'But *they* don't believe it, I bet.' He nodded towards a boy and girl: she clad in a long, flowing caftan, he in home-made poncho. 'At least they're honest with themselves. If either of them . . .' he hesitated, searching for the right word, the idiom he felt she would understand, 'if either of them fancied someone else, off they'd go, free as air. They don't miss the opportunities that could change their lives. They've dispensed with outworn values for good.'

'Could you dispense with them?' she asked him then, her

voice low, and as he hesitated she saw in her imagination a bedroom where at that moment his children lay sleeping, knowing that their little world was safe and secure.

His fingers loosened their grip, just as if the same picture had come into his own mind.

'No,' he said slowly. 'I'm the sort of bloke who always misses the train that could alter my life, the obnoxious sixth-form prefect who always played fair and stuck to the rules of the game.'

He closed his eyes in anguish as an announcement began over the loud-speaker: 'Will all passengers for the flight to Madrid please make their way to . . .' then opened them again at the reprieve.

She too began to talk quickly, urgently, as if against time. 'Tomorrow I'm going to the clinic where my sister had her baby. She told me it's called *Le Bois Gentil* – The Peaceful Wood – because it stands on a tree-lined slope leading down to the lake. Don't you think that's a lovely name?'

'I do. Like music.'

'She says the baby's wrapped up like a parcel in swaddling clothes, wearing a little hat, with only his head showing. She says his face is purple and the first thing we are going to do when we get him home is unwrap him to check that he isn't purple all over.'

'Then you like babies?'

He saw the sadness that lay on her face for a moment like a drifting shadow.

'You're young enough to have as many as you would like,' he said, then regretted it, hoping he hadn't touched on some secret sorrow; but she was smiling again so that the shadow lifted, allowing the tiny dimples at the sides of her mouth to come and go again.

'I'm twenty-five years old,' she said, explaining everything and saying nothing, and as he bent his head over his coffee cup to hide an indulgent smile she saw the faint sheen of his scalp through his thinning hair. Already his face was marked by the erosion of years, though she guessed he was no more than thirty-four or five.

What was it that had caused his face to settle so easily into lines of disillusionment? She would never know, and the thought lay like a leaden weight in her chest.

'Will all passengers for the flight to Rome please make their way to. . .'

He scraped his chair back as he got up to go. He picked up his briefcase and looped his top-coat over his arm.

For a moment she thought he was going to shake hands with her, then suddenly he reached out and touched her face, softly, briefly, trailing his fingers down the contours of her cheek.

'Goodbye, then,' she said, but still he didn't speak. Instead he sat down again opposite to her, taking from his pocket a little black-bound notebook, curving his left hand round the writing the way a child does when he prints a secret.

'Read it when I've gone,' he said. He tore out the page and handed it to her, his face at that moment unguarded, trapped in some private loneliness. Then he walked quickly from her, and was gone.

She sat there without moving, the bright fall of hair concealing the expression of her face, the slip of paper held loosely in her hand.

She knew what it would tell her. His name and address, but not his home address, and the telephone number that would reach him at his office. Well, history does repeat itself, she told herself as she stared at his empty chair.

His step had a jaunty look about it as he'd left her. She'd been wrong about him all the time. She imagined him now, getting on the plane, thinking how cleverly he'd managed it all. Telling her nothing and yet conveying everything. Making her feel sorry for him, blinding her with his not inconsiderable charm, then leaving her to think about him until she came back to London eager to reach for the telephone at the first opportunity.

And she had thought. . . At twenty-five years old – certainly not old, but experienced enough and wise enough to know better – she had thought he wasn't like that. She had thought he was different.

She had known he was different. Hell! She had known!

Holding the slip of paper over the ashtray, she started to tear it up and then, changing her mind, unfolded it and read: 'I'll never forget you.'

And no one in the bustling crowded airport took the slightest notice of the girl with gleaming hair and a crazy yellow peaked cap perched on top of it, crying hopelessly into an empty coffee cup.

A MOMENT OF WEAKNESS

FIFTY years ago, Miss Mundy supposed as she sat in her drawing-room waiting for the rain to stop, she would have fitted quite easily into the general scheme of things.

As a member of what was then known as the genteel poor, her shabby coat and well-darned gloves would have been accepted as a dignified kind of uniform.

But nowadays, with a flourishing Welfare State, there was apparently no need for anyone to be poor. No need for anyone to go wanting. . . And at eighty-one, upright and spry, Miss Mundy found herself wondering how she'd cope.

She had a little money, of course, but every day that seemed to be worth less and less. . .

She had her health, too, apart from a weak chest. And, no doubt, given luck, she could live to be a hundred. . .

Though Miss Mundy suppressed an elegant shudder at the very thought of that!

She had her house, of course, which had been left to her by her parents. But the house was big – far too big for one person to live in alone.

'Why don't you sell up and buy a flat, Alice?' her friend, Emma, said. 'Those by the station are absolutely marvellous. Completely self-contained.'

So Miss Mundy had taken her friend's advice and had gone along to see a flat. And there, always polite, she had smiled at the keen young man from the estate agent's office as he showed off all the amenities. But privately she'd been appalled.

'It would be like living in a goldfish bowl with all those windows. . . And where, tell me pray, would I put my *things*?' she'd asked Emma.

And quite contentedly, that morning in October she sat in her drawing-room, waiting for the rain to stop, staring round at her things.

There was the Queen Anne desk, the sofa with its faded cover, the display cabinet with its shelves filled with Rockingham china, and the silver pieces carefully polished over the long span of years. . .

To dispose of them would have been unthinkable. . . And when she tried to imagine them in the 'through' lounge of the small flat by the station her mind boggled. Though 'boggle' was a word Miss Mundy would never have used. . .

She was waiting for the soft drizzle to stop because her umbrella had a tear in its cover, and the brown mouse-like velvet on the brim of her hat wouldn't stand up to a shower of rain.

Of course, she could have waited until the afternoon – except for the fact that she always shopped in the mornings. . . After all, to shop in the afternoon was, in her code, definitely not on.

In her younger days, ladies paid their calls in the afternoons and the shops in the High Street were almost deserted.

Even after her father had lost all his money – that strange affair that was always referred to as 'his misfortune' – they had still kept up appearances and held their 'At Home' on Tuesdays. To admit to their friends that they were impoverished would have been to show extremely bad taste. . . For only the vulgar talked about money and now, with Mother and Father long since at rest, Miss Mundy kept up the pretence.

The rain had now stopped and a weak sun was even beginning to shine through. Thankfully Miss Mundy picked up her basket from the mahogany hall-stand, and started her slow but dignified walk to the shops. . .

In the bottom of her basket lay her leather housekeeping purse and she knew to the last decimal coin how much it contained. As she walked she did little sums in her mind, nodding graciously now and again to an acquaintance.

She didn't stop, of course, for to talk on the street was a sign of bad breeding. And besides, she preferred to live as she did, shelled in her own self-made solitude.

She could never go into the supermarket without remembering the days when it had been the grocer's shop on the corner.

She remembered going in as a child. Then it had all been marble-topped counters and brass scales, and a bacon slicer that worked with a soothing whirr. Mr Parry had been the owner then, and when she went in he would tick things off on her list, and talk about the weather, and ask about Mother's rheumatism. There would be little treats, too; like when there was a new line in biscuits, he would always give her one.

Now there was no Mr Parry ready to greet her – just wire baskets piled by the door and rows and rows of shelves of tinned goods. And – in a massive deep-freeze cabinet – were stacked ready-made pies and whole frozen dinners.

If you had the money it was quite possible, Miss Mundy marvelled, to eat strawberries.

Quickly she walked round the store; margarine, a sliver of pre-packaged cheese, a packet of tea, a carton of eggs and a pound bag of sugar. . .

She was just reaching for the sugar when she saw the packet with its transparent window. Instantly her hand was arrested and the years rolled away. . .

Coloured sugar, and Mother's Georgian silver bowl. Coffee bubbling on the stove and tiny gold inlaid cups arranged on the tray. . . People to dinner, and Agnes the maid-of-all-work to wait on them all. . .

That packet of coloured sugar seemed to epitomize all that she had forgotten – a way of life she knew would never return. Taking the packet down and caressing it in her brown-freckled hands, she feverishly went over the money in her purse again.

To buy the packet was out of the question; coloured sugar was a ridiculous luxury – and Alice Mundy was conditioned to years of doing without luxuries. . . Still, she imagined it cascading in a multi-coloured stream of pinks, blues and greens into Mother's silver bowl, and she knew she had to have it. . .

All the years of deprivation, all the pretence of genteel affluence seemed to culminate in her mind in an upsurge of glorious rebellion.

And *almost* without really meaning to, she transferred the sugar to her basket, removed the silk square from her neck and arranged it as swift coverage.

A young assistant, her hair tinted a bright yellow, totalled the goods in the wire basket, leaving Miss Mundy to pack them away on top of the silk scarf. As usual she waved away the trading stamps; she had never taken anything for nothing and prided herself that she never would. . .

Then, on legs turned to not-quite-set-jelly, she walked out of the shop. . .

She had got away with it!

She had triumphed over adversity! She had struck a blow at the government, that was what she'd done! (Not that she'd have needed to if dear Mr Churchill had still been at the helm. . .)

Miss Mundy hardly recognized herself as she unpinned her hat in front of the hall mirror. Her pale cheeks were flushed, and there was a blazing light of triumph in the faded blue of her eyes.

She went into the dining room and with trembling fingers, she took the silver bowl from the top shelf of the display cabinet. Then, lovingly, she polished it with a yellow duster.

Now the moment had come, the moment when she could

have opened the packet, tipped it sideways and watched the sugar cascade in a waterfall of beauty, pinks and blues and greens. . .

This was her moment – or it should have been.

But suddenly the enormity of what she had done stayed her hand. The knowledge that she had *stolen* almost paralysed her with horror. And the guilt was physical, too, for there was a burning pain in her chest, a pain that crept up to her throat and made her eyes ache.

But she knew she wouldn't cry; Miss Mundy was not the crying kind. Only the weak, the undisciplined, gave way to tears. . .

The words from a long-ago Sunday school lesson beat at her brain: *Thou shalt not steal!*

In her mind she saw herself being arrested, saw herself standing in a dock. Saw the family name of Mundy splashed across the headlines of the local paper. . . And saw Mother and Father turn in their graves, disturbed from their long sleep by her shame.

She would take it back; she would tell the girl with yellow hair that it had been a mistake.

She was so agitated by it all that she started to pace the kitchen floor, actually wringing her hands because she knew the girl would never believe her.

Dotty old thing, she could hear her say. *Coming in here as posh as you please and pinching things off shelves. What does she take me for?*

Miss Mundy hugged the silver bowl to her sparse bosom, telling herself that her guilty secret would have to be hers, and hers alone, for the rest of her days.

But. . .

She looked at the clock on the dresser, the Westminster chime clock that Father's employees had given him in the days when the firm was thriving, before his misfortune occurred.

If she went straight back to the shop, she could perhaps

speak to the manager. She'd seen him before in his white overall – a young man with a strange fuzzed-out hairstyle. But he had kind eyes, and Mother had always set great store by the expression in a person's eyes. . .

And so with fingers that shook, Miss Mundy buttoned herself into her coat again and skewered her hat on to her head.

She would have to tell a lie, of course, but what was a lie compared with the sin she had committed?

She rehearsed her little speech all the way down to the supermarket, and as if fate was conspiring to help her, the first person she saw was the Store Manager. As usual his hair was sticking out round his head in that strange style, and he was supervising the loading of packages into the huge deep-freeze cabinet.

Miss Mundy's heart was beating so fast and so loudly, she was sure he would hear it.

'I found this packet of coloured sugar in my basket on my return home,' she said, blushing as she hadn't blushed since she was a girl. 'It must have got there by mistake. I can't think how. . .'

Her voice tailed off as she saw the expression in the soft brown eyes of the young man staring down at her.

There *was* kindness there, but now it seemed as if, in that one swift glance, he was taking in the shiny shabbiness of her navy serge coat, perhaps even noting the darns in the fingers of her gloves as she held the package out to him. Perhaps even seeing the agitated pulse beating in her throat. . .

'And you brought it all the way back, Madam?' he was saying. 'That was good of you.' He was turning the packet over and over in his hands, as if he were searching for the right thing to say next. 'You'd be surprised what a welcome change it is to find such honesty. It restores my faith in humanity.'

Miss Mundy stared down at the polished toes of her lace-up shoes. And for someone who believed in looking the person to whom you were speaking straight in the eye, she found it impossible to lift her head.

The young man was still speaking:

'We don't have a lot of call, Madam, not these days, for this line. I'm not even sure whether I'm repeating it, so would you accept this packet with the compliments of the management, as a small thank-you for your kindness in bringing it back?'

Miss Mundy drew herself up to her full height. Now she *could* look him straight in the eye. Her voice when she spoke was firm, but pleasantly courteous.

'Thank you, young man, but no. I have never taken anything for nothing, and I don't intend to start now. . .'

And bidding him a polite good-day, she walked from the store, her back erect, her pride in her own integrity fully and completely restored.

4/11　　09:30

67, KING'S ROAD

WAITING FOR THE RIGHT MOMENT

THE trouble with our son Joe is that he doesn't think. His school report says that he is careless, does not pay attention, could if he wanted to, but would rather spend his time staring through the window daydreaming.

He does not, however, spend his time at home staring through the window daydreaming. At the moment he is in the dining-room-cum-playroom, and from the noise it sounds as if he is doing a clog-dance on top of the sideboard.

I hope he will not wake his father, who is asleep with the Sunday paper over his face. But because I have the baby on my knee I cannot get up quickly enough so, alas, am far too late.

'Do you know what Joe was doing?' his father thunders, coming back with his face as rosy as the colour supplement. 'He was jumping up and down on the table, pretending it was a trampoline. In his new shoes, the ones that cost the earth.'

'More than the table, actually,' I murmur, but I know the pleasantry is a waste of time.

'And do you know what his excuse was? He didn't think! For a six-year-old he seems to be singularly lacking in thought processes, wouldn't you say?'

I have not as yet shown Joe's father the school report. I am waiting for a suitable moment, which does not seem in any hurry to arrive.

'Why don't you take him for a walk on the heath?' I suggest. 'It isn't much fun for a small boy to be cooped up with two adults and a baby on a Sunday afternoon. He's had a rough time since the baby came.'

The strewn Sunday papers are darted a glance of pure longing, and for a moment I feel ashamed. My husband has been working all week in Glasgow, being nice to everyone so as to come back with a briefcase full of orders for his firm, and next week he is off to the Midlands to be nice to everyone in Birmingham. It does not seem fair that he cannot spend his Sunday afternoon in peace.

'It's going to rain,' he says, but he is a lovely man, Joe's father, and the next minute I watch them go – Joe with his shirt hanging out of his trousers as usual, tripping over a hair-line crack in the path, climbing over the gate, then running ahead down the avenue.

I look down at the baby's sleeping face and remind myself that, in less time than seems possible, he will be leaping and falling over all around the house, slamming doors, jumping down stairs, telling bare-faced lies and forgetting to think.

'Maybe you will be different,' I tell him as I carry him upstairs and lower him into his cot. 'Maybe you will be a model of all the virtues, with eyes riveted on your teacher as she talks, bringing home reports so full of praise that we will leave them around on the coffee table for our friends to see.'

He opens one sleepy eye and looks up at me as if to ask me who I am kidding, and I tuck him in and leave him with a sigh.

I go into the kitchen and stoke the boiler, a necessary chore because we have not as yet even managed to raise the deposit for a central-heating plan. Then I start to make Joe's tea – fish-finger sandwiches, his staple diet – and from where I stand I can see the school report tucked behind the tea-caddy on the dresser. If Joe is in one of his angelic moods, which come round perhaps twice a week, I will take out the report and show it to his father.

I will point out the 'General Remarks' at the end which say that Joe is one of the most popular boys in his class.

'Surely, it is more important to rear a son who is liked by all his friends than one who is perfect but unpopular?' I will say.

But my words have a hollow ring, and when I hurry down

the hall to let them in I feel my mouth dropping open in surprise.

And the mental picture I had had of Joe standing there, holding out a bunch of wild flowers for me, with his father glowing by his side after their lovely walk together, fades as though it has never been.

For Joe is on his father's back, clinging on for dear life, and dangling from my scowling husband's hand are the new shoes, covered in dark brown mud.

'Before I could stop him. Straight into the stream without thinking. His socks are here.' And from his pocket Joe's father takes out what look like two slimy ropes and throws them down on the kitchen table.

'Mind the sandwiches,' I say, and he says a word I hope our son doesn't hear.

And, oh, the beautiful brown leather uppers, with their thick plastic soles! Not ten years ago, a family could have been fed for a week on what they cost.

'No real harm done,' says Joe's father when the culprit has been sent upstairs to wash the grime from his feet. 'I'll dry them off while you see to the baby, then the muck will brush off. Did you know the baby is screaming his head off, by the way?'

'Oh, why?' I ask Joe as I try to clean the dirt from his toe-nails. 'Why did you have to walk into the mud in your new shoes?'

And the answer comes pat, just as I knew it would.

'I didn't think, Mum,' says Joe.

But after he has had his tea he comes back upstairs and helps me to bath his little brother, and the look on his face as he bends over the bath is compounded of such pride and such love that my heart sticks in my throat. And when he offers to feed the baby, and sits there in the low chair holding the bottle at just the right angle, I tell him that it does not matter about the shoes, that Daddy will clean them up and they will be as good as new.

I am tucking the baby up once again when I smell a very strange and pungent aroma coming from downstairs. A most peculiar smell which makes me wrinkle my nose and hurry downstairs.

Peeping into the sitting-room, I see nothing amiss there. All is peace and quiet, with Joe and his father sitting together on the sofa watching a horse galloping frantically across the black and white television screen.

'Something's burning,' I say, and rush into the kitchen, and there on top of the boiler sit a pair of brand-new expensive shoes, their plastic soles slowly but surely melting in the heat. . .

I dash to rescue them, but I am too late. Like the snows in the river, as Burns once said, they have gone for ever. I hold them out in front of me and do not know whether to laugh or cry.

Joe's father comes in, and his face is a mixture of horror and astonishment and shame, equally divided. He stretches out a finger and touches them, and the smelly concoction sticks to it. Sadly he shakes his head, his expression one of gloom.

'I'm sorry, love,' he says. 'I didn't think. I just didn't think.'

And there, tucked behind the tea-caddy standing on the dresser, is Joe's school report, and I know for certain, now, that the moment when I can show it to him has come. . .

A Selection of Arrow Bestsellers

Bestselling Fiction

☐	Hiroshmia Joe	Martin Booth	£2.95
☐	The Pianoplayers	Anthony Burgess	£2.50
☐	Queen's Play	Dorothy Dunnett	£3.95
☐	Colours Aloft	Alexander Kent	£2.95
☐	Contact	Carl Sagan	£3.50
☐	Talking to Strange Men	Ruth Rendell	£5.95
☐	Heartstones	Ruth Rendell	£2.50
☐	The Ladies of Missalonghi	Colleen McCullough	£2.50
☐	No Enemy But Time	Evelyn Anthony	£2.95
☐	The Heart of the Country	Fay Weldon	£2.50
☐	The Stationmaster's Daughter	Pamela Oldfield	£2.95
☐	Erin's Child	Sheelagh Kelly	£3.99
☐	The Lilac Bus	Maeve Binchy	£2.50

Prices and other details are liable to change

ARROW BOOKS, BOOKSERVICE BY POST, PO BOX 29, DOUGLAS, ISLE OF MAN, BRITISH ISLES

NAME. . . . .

ADDRESS. . . . .

. . . .

. . . .

Please enclose a cheque or postal order made out to Arrow Books Ltd. for the amount due and allow the following for postage and packing.

U.K. CUSTOMERS: Please allow 22p per book to a maximum of £3.00.

B.F.P.O. & EIRE: Please allow 22p per book to a maximum of £3.00

OVERSEAS CUSTOMERS: Please allow 22p per book.

Whilst every effort is made to keep prices low it is sometimes necessary to increase cover prices at short notice. Arrow Books reserve the right to show new retail prices on covers which may differ from those previously advertised in the text or elsewhere.

Bestselling Women's Fiction

☐ A Better World Than This	Marie Joseph	£2.95
☐ The Stationmaster's Daughter	Pamela Oldfield	£2.95
☐ The Lilac Bus	Maeve Binchy	£2.50
☐ The Golden Urchin	Madeleine Brent	£2.95
☐ The Temptress	Jude Deveraux	£2.95
☐ The Sisters	Pat Booth	£3.50
☐ Erin's Child	Sheelagh Kelly	£3.99
☐ The Ladies of Missalonghi	Colleen McCullough	£2.50
☐ Seven Dials	Claire Rayner	£2.50
☐ The Indiscretion	Diana Stainforth	£3.50
☐ Satisfaction	Rae Lawrence	£3.50

Prices and other details are liable to change

ARROW BOOKS, BOOKSERVICE BY POST, PO BOX 29, DOUGLAS, ISLE OF MAN, BRITISH ISLES

NAME...

ADDRESS...

....

....

Please enclose a cheque or postal order made out to Arrow Books Ltd. for the amount due and allow the following for postage and packing.

U.K. CUSTOMERS: Please allow 22p per book to a maximum of £3.00.

B.F.P.O. & EIRE: Please allow 22p per book to a maximum of £3.00

OVERSEAS CUSTOMERS: Please allow 22p per book.

Whilst every effort is made to keep prices low it is sometimes necessary to increase cover prices at short notice. Arrow Books reserve the right to show new retail prices on covers which may differ from those previously advertised in the text or elsewhere.